Evan Only Knows

Further Titles in the Constable Evan Evans Series from Severn House

EVANLY CHOIRS
EVAN CAN WAIT
EVAN ONLY KNOWS

EVAN ONLY KNOWS

Rhys Bowen

This title first published in Great Britain 2006 by
SEVERN HOUSE PUBLISHERS LTD of
9–15 High Street, Sutton, Surrey SM1 1DF.

British Library Cataloguing in Publication Data

Bowen, Rhys
Evan only knows
1. Evans, Evan (Fictitious character) - Fiction
2. Police - Wales - Fiction
3. Murder - Investigation - Wales - Fiction
4. Detective and mystery stories
I. Title
823.9'14 [F]

ISBN-13: 978-0-7278-6397-3
ISBN-10: 0-7278-6397-5

Except where actual historical events and characters are being described for the storyline of this novel, all situations in this publication are fictitious and any resemblance to living persons is purely coincidental.

All Severn House titles are printed on acid-free paper.

Printed and bound in Great Britain by
MPG Books Ltd., Bodmin, Cornwall.

This book is dedicated to Helen O'Connell and her father, Thomas Fearnall of North Wales, who appears in a cameo role at her request.

Special thanks go to Sergeant Paul Henwood of the South Wales Police in Swansea, who answered all my questions with great patience and was even brave enough to give me his home E-mail address.

And, as always, thanks to my family for their support and great suggestions.

Glossary of Welsh Words

bach — little. Used as a term of endearment, similar to English "love" (pronounced like the composer)

noswaith dda — good evening (pronounced *nos-why-th thah*)

cariad — darling. Term of endearment (pronounced *ca-ree-ad*)

Hen Diawll — old devil. Harmless cussword like damn (pronounced *he de—owl-ch*)

bara brith — speckled bread (bread with mixed fruits in it) (pronounced as it looks)

Ydych chi'n siarad cymraeg? — Do you speak Welsh? (pronounced *udich-een sharad cumrige*)

Abertawe — Welsh name for Swansea. Means mouth of Tawe River (pronounced *aber-tah-way*)

Escob Annwyl — dear Bishop. Mild exclamation of horror (pronounced *escobe an-wheel*)

Nain — grandmother in North Wales (pronounced *nine*)

eisteddfod — Welsh cultural gathering. Literally means sitting (pronounced *eye-steth-fod*)

cawl — a thick lamb soup (pronounced *cowl*)

Evan Only Knows

Chapter 1

The Land Rover pulled up abruptly at the side of the narrow road. A young man jumped out, his mouse brown hair and pasty face blending in with the beige of his raincoat. It was midsummer and the sky was cloudless, making the raincoat a strange choice of garment. Equally strange, it was coupled with a pair of large green gumboots that appeared too big for him. He paused, looking and listening in both directions up and down the pass, before grabbing something from the seat of the Land Rover and sprinting to a nearby stile. He looked around once more before starting to wrap the stile, spiderweb fashion, with bright yellow plastic tape. The tape read KEEP OUT. When the stile was effectively blocked, the young man ran back to the Land Rover and took off, tires spraying gravel. As he drove up the pass, he picked up a mobile phone and pressed the redial button.

"Sector Three now secured, sir," he said.

"Well done," came the crackling voice down the line. "Now get the hell out of there before they notice."

At that very moment an elderly Rover was driving up the Llanberis Pass at a sedate twenty-nine miles per hour, clearly infuriating the driver of a white van behind it. The van bore the inscription LEEKS—THE PROUD SYMBOL OF WALES, STOPPING LEAKS—the proud aim of Roberts-the-Plumber, Bangor. It tried unsuccessfully to pass on numerous occasions but was reduced to impotent horn honkings, which the driver of the Rover didn't seem to hear.

At last, beyond the small village of Nant Peris, the Rover finally turned off the road to a parking area outside an old churchyard. Three sheep that had been cropping grass around the lichen-covered gravestones leaped up in alarm at the sound of the car and trotted away to safety behind the old church. The Rover's doors opened and three elderly gentlemen got out, each straightening creaky joints slowly and cautiously. Although they weren't wearing clerical collars but weatherproof windcheaters and stout walking boots, they had an aura of innocent surprise and unworldliness in their faces, usually seen in choirboys or monks. These three were, in fact, Church of England vicars and knew nothing of the austere lifestyle of the monastery. They stood, breathing deeply and looking around with expectation.

"I bet these old stones could tell many a tale," one of them said, walking over to the moss-grown wall that surrounded the churchyard.

"If they could, you wouldn't understand it, because it would be in Welsh." The second, the most cherubic-looking of the three, chuckled.

"Anyway, we're not going to take time to explore now." The third, leaner and fitter looking than his companions, hoisted a rucksack onto his back. "We want to make the summit before the weather changes." He raised his eyes to the mountains that rose steeply on either side. The sky was a perfect blue, without a cloud in sight.

Then turning his back on the churchyard, he crossed the road where the sign indicated a footpath up the green slopes beyond. His companions followed him until they came to a stile, straddling a drystone wall. Behind the wall was a rising pasture, dotted with sheep, but the stile was impassible. It was tied across with yellow plastic tape.

The first clergyman stopped and waited for his companions to catch up.

"They can't do this!" he exclaimed, his face pink with anger as he pointed at the taped stile. "It's a public right of way, that's what it is. It's always been a public right of way, and if any bolshie farmer thinks he can stop us from crossing his field just by putting up a piece of tape, then he can think again."

"Easy now, Ronald," the cherubic vicar said, putting a hand on his friend's shoulder. "Maybe this path is under repair, or is waterlogged. I'm sure there are plenty of alternate routes up to the summit."

"He's right, old man," the third clergyman said in languid, aristocratic tones. "No sense in raising your blood pressure over nothing. Remember what the doctor said."

Ronald sighed and turned away. "You're right. Let's take a look at the map and see where the other paths start."

But ten minutes later they were at a similar stile farther up the pass, facing a similar strip of yellow tape and the words KEEP OUT scrawled on a piece of cardboard. This time Ronald nearly exploded.

"That's it. Back to the car. We're going to find the nearest police station and make this farmer open up his damned public right of way!"

"Sorry about this, lads, but my hands are tied." Superintendent Meredith spread his hands in a gesture of apology, seeming to refute what he had just said. He was a big man with multiple chins that quivered as he shook his head. "We've had a directive from the powers-that-be that we're to give the Min of Ag all possible cooperation in carrying out this unpleasant task."

"It's not going to be easy," a voice from the audience muttered.

"Look, I know it's not going to be easy, especially for those of us who work closely with the community, but it has to be done." The superintendent attempted an understanding smile. "I feel just as badly as you do about this. But it has to be stopped now. It should have been stopped before it got to Wales. It could have been if they hadn't sat there twiddling their thumbs until it was too late."

"Bloody English, when have they ever sent us anything but bad news?" came another growled mutter from the back of the room.

If the superintendent heard this, he pretended not to. "So we've just got to buckle down, all pull together, and make sure that there is no unpleasantness, right?" He was the only one who nodded. "The Min of Ag inspectors are already in the area. You'll be approached for assistance as needed." He looked around the audience of blank faces, then went on, "So that's about it. Let's make this go as smoothly as possible, shall we then? And if it looks as if there's going to be trouble, don't hesitate to call for backup. Got it? Right then." He stood up, brushed off his hands as if they had crumbs on them, and strode from the room.

"All in this together, my arse," one of the young policemen muttered over the scraping of chairs as they got to their feet.

Constable Meirion Morgan fell into step beside a fellow officer. "All right for him, isn't it, Evan—sitting here in his office. I bet he's never been within twenty miles of a herd of sheep in his life."

The fellow officer he had spoken to, Constable Evan Evans, smiled in agreement. He was a big chap with the build of a rugby player and a boyish face women found appealing. "You know what I'm counting on, Meirion?" he muttered confidentially. "I'm just hoping they'll take their time before they get to us up on the mountain."

Meirion Morgan returned the grin. "Oh, that's right. You're transferring to plainclothes, aren't you?"

"I'm due to start my course next week."

"Lucky bugger," Meirion said. "Still, I'm not saying that you don't deserve it."

"I've been waiting long enough for the transfer to come through," Evan said. "I applied over a year ago. I was beginning to think they'd never accept me."

"They'd have been daft if they hadn't, seeing the kind of help you've already given them."

"People don't always take kindly to outside help, do they?" Evans commented.

They joined the crowd filing from the briefing room. "You really want to do that kind of thing, do you?" Meirion asked. "Can't say it appeals to me. Too much stress and terrible hours. I dare say I lack ambition, but I like being home at a reasonable time and not being called out at three in the morning."

"I think I'll like it just fine," Evan said. "I did start a CID training course once, when I was on the force down in Swansea."

"Did you now? I never knew that. What in heaven's name were you doing in Swansea? You don't look like a South Walesian, don't sound like one either."

Evan laughed. "I was born up here, but my dad got a job with the South Wales Police, so we moved down there when I was ten."

"And you were on the force down there then? What made you decide to move back?"

"Several things." Evan left it at that. "My mum still lives down there."

"Can't say I'd want to," Meirion said as they drew level with the cafeteria door. "I've only been to a city once and I felt hemmed in, if you know what I mean. Coming for a cuppa?"

"No thanks, I'd better be getting back," Evan said. "I'm a one-man shop up in Llanfair, and something always seems to happen when I'm away."

"You've got several farms around you, haven't you?" Meirion grimaced. "So have we. I'm not looking forward to it one bit, but I suppose the super is right. It has to be done."

He gave Evan a friendly nod as he pushed open the swing door into the cafeteria. Evan got a pleasant whiff of sausage and chips before the door swung to again. He paused and looked back longingly. He'd been surviving on his own for a couple of months now, and he wasn't the world's best cook. After a lifetime of living at home and then being looked after by Mrs. Williams, he was discovering that cooking wasn't as simple as it seemed. Things that looked easy enough usually required ingredients he didn't possess and never turned out like the pictures in the cookery books. Of course he could always buy a meat pie or bangers and chips at the Red Dragon across the road, but that was defeating the whole purpose of this exercise. The whole reason he was putting himself through this was for Bronwen. She had made it very clear that she wouldn't marry him until he'd had a taste of fending for himself.

Evan came out of the Caernarfon Police Station and went to retrieve his motorbike. Another good thing about transferring to the CID, he decided, would be giving up that bloody motorbike. It had been issued to outstation officers as part of an efficiency drive, so that they could cover outlying farms more easily, but Evan had never really taken to it. Not that he minded the wind and rain in his face. He'd been brought up in the mountains, after all. He just didn't feel any affinity for motorbikes.

He kicked it to life and pulled out of the station yard. It wouldn't have been so bad if he'd been issued an impressive 1000cc model, but this bike was so underpowered that it barely made it up the hill to Llanfair. Any burglar could easily outrun him up a mountainside.

The last of the housing estates was left behind, and green uplands soared on either side. A stream danced merrily beside him. Flowers grew in profusion, spilling over the drystone walls. The high pastures were dotted with sheep. It was the perfect pastoral scene, one that he usually relished, but today he looked around with a sinking feeling in the pit of his stomach. This was the calm before the storm. Maybe nothing would ever be the same again.

The town of Llanberis was chockablock with families on holiday. The ice cream vendor and the souvenir shops were doing a roaring trade. There was a long line waiting for the next train on the little rack railway up Mt. Snowdon, and a cheerful *toot-toot* announced that it had just started its climb to the summit. Evan slowed as holidaymakers strolled across the road, trailing children and dripping ice cream. He wondered what would be happening to them. Would they all be sent home? Would the whole area be quarantined?

He negotiated the holiday crowds successfully, then let the throttle out as the road narrowed and the pass rose ahead, snaking up to the high country. He felt the exhilaration of wind in his face. Green walls rose on either side, topped with sheets of scree and the rocky crags he knew so well—Snowdon and its outcroppings on his right, and, beyond the thin finger of lake, the twin peaks of the Glydrs on his left. Evan knew every route up the mountains, every challenging climb in the area, but there hadn't been much time for climbing recently.

Nant Peris, with its old church and graveyard, passed on his right. Then there were no more houses until Llanfair. As he pulled up outside his little police substation, he saw a car parked outside it and a white-haired man standing at the station door. On hearing Evan he marched toward him.

"Are you the officer who is supposed to be on duty here?" he demanded in a well-bred English voice.

"That's right, sir. Constable Evans. How can I help you?"

"Aren't police stations supposed to be manned at all times?"

"Sorry, sir. I'm the only officer stationed up here, and I was called down to headquarters," Evan said. "There's an telephone outside, and they will always send up a squad car in an emergency. So what can I do for you?"

"What you can do is go and talk to some damned farmer," the man said. "We're here on a walking holiday, and we were just about to hike up Glydr Fach when we found the path had been blocked off." Evan glanced over at the car where two other elderly men with round cherubic faces watched from wound-down windows. "My fellow members of the clergy and I have been coming here every summer since 1956, and until now we have had no problems."

Evan was just realizing the implications of the man's complaint. "The path was blocked, you say?" he asked.

"Taped across, more like it," one of the other elderly gentlemen chimed in from the car. "Lots of yellow plastic tape. And not just one path either. We drove up to the second footpath, and it had tape across it too. And the words 'Keep Out.' "

"Some bolshie farmer trying to deny an ancient right of way," the first man said. "It happens from time to time. Some chap thinks he can ignore a public footpath across his land. But we never let them get away with it. We'd like you to go and talk to him, Constable. Let him know that it's against the law to block off a right of way."

"I'll come down and see it with you," Evan said, "but I don't think the farmer had anything to do with it this time. I don't know whether you've been reading the papers, but I'm afraid that foot-and-mouth disease has spread to this part of Wales. I was just at a briefing in Caernarfon, and it doesn't look good. It seems it's only a matter of time before the farmers here have to slaughter their flocks."

The man's bluster evaporated. "But that's terrible," he said with concern. "So you think that was why they've blocked off the footpaths?"

"I would imagine so, sir. I understand the Ministry of Agriculture's men are already in the area doing inspections, and they'll be doing everything they can to stop the disease from spreading—which would mean closing footpaths, I expect."

"Of course, I quite understand," the vicar said, nodding to his fellows. "They wouldn't want to risk having anyone carrying infected soil on his boots. Well, this is a setback, I must say."

"It will completely spoil our holiday," one of the men in the car said.

"I should think it will spoil a lot of holidays," Evan said. "The timing couldn't have been worse, right at the beginning of the school summer holidays too. It will be a disaster for all the local business people."

"Yes, I suppose it will. Never thought of that." The vicar stood staring up at the mountains with a wistful look on his face. "So what do you suggest, Constable? Do you think we should get out as soon as possible and try somewhere else?"

Evan glanced up at the hills, from which came the sporadic bleating of sheep. "You're all clergymen, you say? Then I suggest you gentlemen do some serious praying. We're going to need it."

Chapter 2

Evan watched the car drive away. He pictured the same scene being replayed all over the area, families packing up and leaving, souvenir shops and cafés with no customers. Everyone in the area would be affected somehow. But with any luck he'd be out of it—sitting in a classroom in Colwyn Bay, taking notes on the art of surveillance and the psychology of the criminal mind. He stood outside the police station, staring up at the hillside. Some of this year's lambs, now fat and fleecy, were chasing one another in a last fling of youthful exuberance. Higher on the hillside he could see the square white building of Owen's farm. As he watched, a squat, solid figure wearing a cloth cap and gumboots came striding purposefully down the track toward the village with two black-and-white sheepdogs at his heels. Farmer Owens was heading down to the village. Evan wondered if he'd heard the bad news yet. If he hadn't, it would be kinder coming from Evan himself than from some officious young chap at the Ministry of Agriculture. He hurried up the track to meet the farmer.

The two dogs ran forward to meet him, tails wagging furiously.

"Mot, Gel, get back here," the farmer commanded, and the dogs scurried back to his heels.

"I was just coming to see you, Mr. Owens," Evan said.

"And I was just on my way to see you, Constable Evans," the

farmer said. "I must have called the station ten times and all I got was the bloody answering machine."

Evan noted that the farmer had called him constable instead of by his first name. "So you've already heard, have you?" he asked. "I was on my way to warn you."

"Well, then, you're too bloody late," Farmer Owens snapped. "I've had some pale-faced young prick in a raincoat telling me I'm under quarantine until further orders. I can't move any stock; I can't sell any stock. I've got a field full of fat lambs ready for market, look you. Who do they bloody well think they are, coming up here from London and dictating to us?"

"I suppose they're only doing their job," Evan said, wincing as he said it at the triteness of the remark. "They're trying to stop the disease from spreading even farther."

"Then they're doing a pretty poor job of it, aren't they? They could have contained it in Cumberland when they had a chance."

"I agree, but they obviously didn't realize how serious it was going to be. Look how quickly it crossed the Pennines and spread to the Lake District."

"But there are no cases that I've heard in our area yet," Farmer Owens said. "What gives them the right to go around slaughtering stock willy-nilly, just in case the disease might come here?"

"I suppose they're trying to create something like a firebreak, to halt the spread southward."

"They're not using my animals as a firebreak," Farmer Owens said so aggressively that his dogs cowered. "Do you know how long it's taken me to build up that stock? I've got a couple of breeding rams that cost me a year's income, and some young idiot from Whitehall tells me to be cooperative when the army arrives to slaughter them?"

"Look, I'm really sorry," Evan said.

"Sorry isn't good enough. Well, I'm not going to take it lying down, I can tell you that, Evan *bach*. It's my land and I have a right to keep trespassers off it, haven't I?"

"Trespassers, yes, but . . ."

"Then I want you to help me enforce it. Next bloody young

squirt in a raincoat who tries to come through my gate, you arrest him for me."

Evan laughed. "You know I can't do that."

"Then I'll have to do it on my own. But I'm warning you right now—let them try and bring their army trucks up to my farm. They'll not find it easy. I'm building roadblocks across both my tracks, and I'll be waiting with my shotgun."

Evan chuckled nervously. "Come on now, Mr. Owens. How would it help if you wound up in jail?"

"Just making my stand, look you, Evan. I don't really intend to hurt anyone, but if my little skirmish makes the daily papers and I can get public sympathy on the side of us farmers, maybe I'll have done some good. I'm writing to the minister of Agriculture today. I'm telling him that I keep my rams separate from the rest of the flock, so there's no need to slaughter them if it comes to that."

Evan didn't reply. He had a feeling that hundreds of such letters had been landing on the minister's table.

"Or I was thinking of putting them in my van one night and driving them across to my cousin's place on Anglesey. Surely this stupid foot-and-mouth won't be able to jump across the water to get there, will it?"

"And what if your rams have been exposed and you're the one who brings the disease over there?" He bent to pat the sheepdog's head, so that he didn't have to look the farmer in the eye. "Look, I know this is terrible for you, but it's the same for everyone, isn't it? This is one of those times when we all have to do things we don't like for the good of the whole. I bet your dad didn't want to go off to fight in World War Two, did he? But he went just the same."

"You're talking like a sanctimonious little bugger, you know that?" Farmer Owens glared at Evan. "It's all right for you, isn't it? What have you got to lose? How would you know what it's like to work your whole life for something, then watch it taken away from you? It will break my wife's heart, you know."

"I'm really sorry—"

"You said that before, didn't you? I dare say you are, but you're not prepared to help us keep those bastards out, are you? Good day to you then, Constable. I've got work to do. I'm driving the flock up to the high pastures. They'll not be so easy to catch up there!"

He turned on his heels and strode back up the track with the dogs running at his heels. Evan watched him for a while before he turned for home. When he got back to the police station, his answering machine was blinking furiously. Probably Mr. Owens, he thought, and pressed the play button.

"Constable Evans, where have you been?" came the imperious female voice that he recognized so well. "The most extraordinary thing has happened. I went to go out of my back gate and some malicious person has taped it shut. And I think I know who it was too. I saw the Parry Davies woman out on the path this morning with her horrid little dogs. It would be just the kind of thing she would do to spite me. And one of her dogs left a nasty calling card just outside my gate too. Please go and confront her. I am just getting the scissors to remove her tape."

Evan sighed. For once Mrs. Powell-Jones, wife of the Reverend Powell-Jones, minister of Capel Beulah, was not his major problem. But he'd have to go and face her before she had a confrontation with the brainless twit from the Ministry of Agriculture who was sealing footpaths without explanation. He let the answering machine play on as he went through the mail. Among the letters was one from police headquarters in Colwyn Bay. He opened this eagerly. It would be the details of his new assignment.

Then he sat there, staring in horror and disbelief. The message was from the Chief Constable, brief and to the point.

> To all personnel in North Wales Police. Due to the current emergency situation, all training sessions will be postponed. All leave, apart from compassionate, is cancelled until further notice. I hope I can count on all of you to make this difficult process go smoothly.

Evan dropped the letter, got up, and paced the room. So there was to be no escape after all. He imagined having to restrain Bill

Owens as his prize rams were led to the execution pit, and of the same scene being played over and over with other farmers who had become his friends. Even visiting Mrs. Powell-Jones seemed preferable to sitting here brooding at this moment.

Surprisingly that encounter went remarkably smoothly. When Mrs. Powell-Jones realized why her back gate had been taped shut, she was more than cooperative.

"Anything I can do to stop this awful disease from spreading, Constable Evans—anything at all. You just have to ask. We all have to pull together at moments of crisis like this. Mummy was wonderful in the war, you know. She rallied the whole community. I will speak to my husband and arrange a meeting in the village hall. We'll need volunteers to patrol the area and keep intruders out of the fields. You can start with that monstrosity, the Everest Inn, Constable Evans. Go up there and set them straight. Just because people come there and pay exorbitant amounts, they'll think they have the right to hike and climb wherever they please."

Evan left with a full list of instructions and in need of a drink. He went home for a hurried snack of bread and cheese then headed across the road to the Red Dragon, looking forward to a Guinness and good cheering up. The bar was full as he pushed open the door and ducked under the oak beam. There was the usual hum of chatter in Welsh and figures silhouetted in the smoky fug. He stood in the doorway, feeling the tension slip away, then eased his way through the crowd up to the long oak bar with his usual cheerful, "*Noswaith dda,* everyone."

Usually this greeting was returned warmly, often with the offer to buy him a pint. Betsy the barmaid's face would light up on seeing him, and she would usually pull the neckline of her T-shirt just a little lower, leaning forward provocatively across the bar. Tonight, however, he was met with stony faces.

"Hello, Betsy *cariad,*" Evan said, more than a little surprised. "The usual, if you don't mind."

"I'm busy at the moment," Betsy said frostily. "You'll just have to wait your turn."

"Hang on a minute," Evan said. "Have I done something to upset you?"

Betsy went on calmly drawing a pint with just the right amount of froth on top. "You've upset everyone, haven't you?"

"By doing what?"

"If you don't know, we're not going to tell you." She put the pint down in front of a small wiry man. "There you are then, Charlie *bach,* get that down you and you'll feel a lot better."

Evan turned to the elderly man. "Charlie?" he said. "What's this all about then?"

Charlie only half met his gaze. "Owens-the-Sheep was in here already. He told us about you. Said you weren't even sympathetic. Told him a lot of guff about doing his duty. I thought you were one of us, Evan *bach.*"

"Of course I'm on your side," Evan said. "But there's not much I can do, is there? I can't arrest the blokes from the Ministry of Agriculture for trespassing, like Mr. Owens wants me to do. And I certainly can't stand by and watch him keep the army at bay with his shotgun."

"But it's just not right, is it?" Charlie Hopkins demanded. "He's worked all his life to build up that flock. Do you know how much he paid to buy one of those rams from a fancy breeder in the South? How's he going to start again if they slaughter the lot? He'll be ruined, that's what he'll be."

"It's not as if we've had any cases in the area, is it?" Evans-the-Milk turned to join in the conversation. "I've been talking to the dairy farmers and none of them have tested positive yet. But they've got to stop selling their milk, just the same."

"If you want my opinion," Evans-the-Meat, the large, blustering butcher, poked his head between the other men, "it's a bloody English plot to wipe out Welsh sheep. They know our lamb is better than theirs and fetches a higher price, so this is a good excuse to finish us off."

"Oh come on, Gareth *bach.*" Evan attempted a chuckle. "Look how many English flocks have already been slaughtered. It was really only a matter of time before it reached us."

"I'm with Evans-the-Meat for once," Evans-the-Milk said, draping an arm around the other man's shoulders. "They've no right to come interfering in Wales. We've got our own Assembly now, haven't we? They should be making the rules, not some idiots in London."

"I tell you one thing," Evans-the-Meat went on, fired by the support around him. "I'm going to stand by Owens-the-Sheep, no matter what."

"Me too." A well-built young man in dirty overalls edged his way into the circle. "I've already told him I'll bring the bulldozer to help build a blockade across his tracks. Let's see how keen those army blokes are if they have to slog half a mile up the mountain."

"I knew we could count on Barry-the-Bucket," the butcher said, beaming at him proudly. "One of us, that's what you are, boyo. Llanfair born and bred."

"I think it's wonderful of you, Barry," Betsy said, a smile replacing the cold stare that usually repelled his advances. "A true champion of our village, that's what you are. Not like some I could name."

"Does that mean you'll go with me to the dance at the Rhyl Pavilion on Saturday?" Barry asked.

"I might think about it," Betsy replied, smoothing down her T-shirt. "I think that bravery should be rewarded. We should stand up for ourselves, that's what I say. My old dad's been dusting off his shotgun so that he can help too."

"God help us. Your dad never could shoot straight even when he was sober," Charlie Hopkins said. "He's more likely to shoot one of us in the back."

"Or kill off one of Bill Owens's prize rams!" Evans-the-Milk added as the men began to laugh.

"Know what I heard, boys? I heard he's planning to drive his sheep up to the top of the Glydrs," Evans-the-Milk said with a smirk. "Well, that's all his land, isn't it? I can just see those army blokes scrambling over rocks and leaping around precipices trying to round them up! And Bill Owens said that if they make him bring his dogs up there, he's going to give them the wrong commands so they just run around in circles!"

The men at the bar broke into more noisy laughter. Evan smiled too, but he couldn't shake off the feeling of hollow dread in his stomach. This had become a game for the other inhabitants of Llanfair, a kind of Robin Hood quest against the English authority. And he had been instructed to give that outside authority every assistance. He was now one of the enemy.

Chapter 3

As soon as he had finished his pint, Evan slipped out of the Red Dragon. The men at the bar had become quite jovial, thinking up more and more absurd schemes to thwart the British army and the Ministry of Agriculture. He couldn't find it in his heart to warn them that they'd find themselves in serious trouble. He suspected most of the talk was bravado anyway.

He came out into pink twilight. At this time of year the sun didn't set until after nine, but it had already sunk behind Snowdon, plunging the village itself into gloom. The high slopes above were still bathed in glowing light, and the sheep on them were tinged with pink. As he watched, a buzzard soared out from the high crags and circled against a clear sky. Such a perfect evening would have lured him up onto the slopes to watch the sun sink into the distant sea, but the slopes were now off-limits. He hadn't realized until this moment how much this crisis would affect his own life too.

Instead Evan began to walk up the village street, past the row of cottages where he now lived, past the shops where Evans-the-Meat and Evans-the-Milk spent their days annoying each other, until finally he came to the low wall of the school playground. A light was shining in the schoolhouse window. Evan pushed open the gate and hurried across the playground.

"Bron," he called as he opened the front door. "It's me. I need a hug or a double brandy or both."

"Wait a second. Don't open that door yet," Bronwen's voice commanded. "I've got Prince William in here."

It had been a day of many surprises, but this one bowled him over. What on earth could Prince William be doing in a village school in Wales? Learning about his subjects for the day when he became the next Prince of Wales? Finding out firsthand about the foot-and-mouth outbreak? But weren't princes always surrounded by a security escort? So why hadn't Evan been stopped as he crossed the playground and opened the door?

After what seemed like an eternity Bronwen opened the door. She was dressed in jeans and old checked blouse. Wisps of hair had escaped from the long braid she always wore down her back. She looked a little flurried and not at all like someone who was entertaining a prince.

"It's okay, you can come in now," she said. "I've got him shut in the kitchen."

"Prince William? Shut in the kitchen?"

Bronwen looked at Evan with a mysterious smile on her face. "Yes, would you like to come and meet him?"

"Now? Well, I suppose . . . I'm not properly dressed." It began to dawn on him that she could be playing a joke. "Should I be wearing my crown, do you think?"

She took his hand. "Come along. Don't keep him waiting. In you go."

She opened the kitchen door. Evan stepped inside, looked around an apparently empty kitchen until something appeared from under the kitchen table. He found himself looking at a fat, curly lamb. "But that's a sheep!" he exclaimed.

"Allow me to introduce you. This is Prince William—Eirlys Lloyd's pet lamb." She burst out laughing. "Evan, you should have seen your face! You thought I had the real Prince William here."

"Only when you first told me. I was caught off guard."

She put her hands on his cheeks and reached up to give him a kiss. "I thought I told you about Eirlys's lamb. You know young

Eirlys from Bryn Hyfryd Farm, don't you? The poor little thing came to me quite distraught today. It seems her father has been told that his flock might have to be slaughtered and that would have included all animals on the property. Well, Prince William has been a house pet all his life, so I told her to bring him down to me and I would look after him until this scare is over."

The lamb came cautiously to check out Evan's shoes.

"Bron, are you sure that's the thing to do?" Evan asked. "I'm not sure exactly how foot-and-mouth is spread, but isn't there a chance he could be infected?"

"He's been a family pet, Evan. They're not going to go around slaughtering all the sheepdogs and farm cats, are they? Anyway, I think they're overreacting."

"Don't you start," Evan said. "I've had a bad day with Farmer Owens shouting at me and everyone at the pub telling me I'm a traitor. What am I supposed to do when I've been instructed to give the Ministry of Agriculture every assistance, eh?"

Bronwen slipped her arms around his neck. "You poor thing. It must be beastly for you. Sorry—beastly isn't exactly the right word, given the circumstances, is it."

"I'm sure you'll know a way to make me feel better." Evan pulled her toward him to give her a kiss. There was a crashing sound behind them. The lamb looked up guiltily from an overturned vegetable basket. Bronwen went over and began putting the vegetables back into it. "I can see I'm going to have to lambproof the house," she said.

"You really think you can keep him here?" Evan asked.

"Why not? He's been a house pet up at the farm."

"Yes, well, a farm, that's different. They have all the outbuildings for him to run around in. You only have three rooms. I take it he's not house-trained."

"Not exactly. I've been doing quite a bit of mopping up. I'm thinking of investing in disposable nappies, but I don't want to make him feel stupid."

"Feel stupid." Evan chuckled. "Isn't is wonderful how women go daft over baby animals?"

"Oh, and men don't make more fuss of their dogs than they do of their families? Anyway, the important thing is that Eirlys adores him, and I'm just trying to help her save him."

"You're a softie." Evan stroked her cheek. "Now you'll be paying more attention to him than to me."

"Ah, so that's why you don't want him here—you're jealous."

"Listen, Bron, I just want you to do the right thing. What sort of example would you be setting to your children if you show them how to hide farm animals from the ministry? I've already had Owens-the-Sheep today telling me that he was going to ship his prize rams off to his cousin in Anglesey under cover of darkness."

"And why not?" she asked. "If they are not infected, why slaughter them? This whole thing is ludicrous, Evan. They should test each animal, and those that are healthy should be allowed to live. But they slaughter all herds within so many miles of each outbreak."

"I suppose they must know what they are doing," Evan said hesitantly. "Look, I feel as badly as you do about this. I think it's a wretched business. I felt dreadful today telling Bill Owens that he couldn't count on me to help him. I've been instructed to offer all assistance to the ministry and to the army. I don't have any choice."

Bronwen looked at him with a half smile. "I seem to remember several occasions on which you were instructed to keep your nose out of murder inquiries and you didn't."

"Well, yes, but I didn't actually disobey. Circumstances just presented themselves. . . ."

Bronwen laughed. "Oh yes, of course."

"But this is different. It's a national emergency, isn't it? You and I aren't experts. We don't know how the disease is spread or if saving one sheep from a flock will have disastrous consequences later."

Bronwen went over and put her arm around the lamb. "So you're saying I shouldn't keep Prince William here? I should send him back to be *k-i-l-l-e-d?*" She spelled out the word. The lamb looked up at her and gave a pathetic *baa* as if it understood.

"You do what you think is right, Bron. You are a responsible person."

"My children count on me, Evan. They look up to me." She gazed at him, her eyes pleading. "I can't let one of them down, can I? Especially not now that—" She broke off. "I had a piece of bad news today, actually. You remember I had a visit from the county education office inspectors last spring. Well, I've now seen their official report."

"They can't have found anything to criticize in your teaching," Evan said angrily.

"Well, no. They thought I was doing a good job, considering. . . ."

"Considering what?"

"That I had to deal with the outdated concept of multiage-level teaching. They feel the children in the village are being deprived of the chance to become world citizens at a young age. The village school is making them grow up with no clear picture of the outside world and its problems. They are being cocooned. So what they suggest is that this school and the one in Beddgelert be closed and the kids shipped down to a new, modern primary school to be built on the outskirts of Porthmadog."

"But that will be a half-hour's journey for them. And what's wrong with growing up sheltered, I'd like to know?' Evan demanded. "The longer they can be kept away from drugs and violence, the better, if you ask me."

"Me too," Bronwen said. "And they'll be in an environment where not everybody speaks Welsh so they'll soon think it's cool to speak English to each other. I think it's a bad idea all around. It's not final yet, but this is their recommendation."

"Stupid," Evan muttered. "What would happen to you if they closed this school?"

"I dare say I'd be offered a job at the new school on the coast."

"That would mean you'd lose your house too."

"Well, I thought I might be moving in with you when we finally get married," she said, getting to her feet again with a small laugh. "That was the general idea, wasn't it? And we might find we have to move somewhere else for your work, anyway. You might be assigned to headquarters."

"And pigs might fly," Evan muttered.

"Why wouldn't you?" She looked up at him, startled.

"They've postponed all training sessions until the emergency is over. Who knows how long it will take."

Bronwen moved closer and wrapped her arms around him. "Oh, Evan, I'm sorry. What a horrible blow for you. You were so looking forward to it."

"That's not the main thing right now, is it?" Evan said. "Now I'm going to have to betray people who have become my friends. I'm the one who's going to have to restrain Farmer Owens when they shoot his sheep."

"That's just not fair, Evan."

"I know. But then I'd be petty to grumble about my situation when these poor farmers are losing their entire livelihood."

Bronwen slipped her arm through his. "Look, we were planning to go and meet each other's families when your course was over, weren't we? Why don't we do it now instead? I'm on holiday after all."

Evan made a face. "I'm not. They've cancelled all leave too."

"Oh dear. So it looks as if you're stuck with it, doesn't it?"

"It looks that way."

"In which case I'd better open a bottle of wine. We'll need to drown our sorrows."

"Good idea." Evan opened the drawer and got out the cork-screw. "Better get out the large glasses."

Bronwen lifted a bottle from the bottom of the dresser, then stopped, the bottle poised in her hand. "You know what you could do? Why don't you ask to swap with a policeman who is usually behind a desk at headquarters. Explain what a lot of harm it will do to your relationship with the community and how much better it would be to send an outsider up here in your place."

"That would be great," Evan said. "I don't think they'd go for it, but it's worth a try, isn't it?"

"Go down there and be forceful," Bronwen said, handing him the bottle.

The lamb trotted up to him and bleated again.

"Oh no. Every time he sees a bottle he's hopeful," she said, laughing.

"Well, he's not getting my Rioja." Evan turned his back on the lamb. "Oh, and Bronwen, he doesn't expect to sleep in your bedroom, does he?"

The next morning Evan drove his own car, instead of the police-issued motorbike, down the hill to headquarters. As he was getting out he heard his name called and looked up to see a familiar figure in a fawn-colored raincoat crossing the station car park.

"Hello, Sarge, what are you doing here?" he called. "Oh sorry, I meant Detective Inspector, of course. I keep forgetting."

"So do I," former Sergeant Watkins admitted. "One of the girls on the front desk just yelled 'Inspector' after me three times before I realized she was talking to me. It takes some getting used to."

"So what are you doing here? I thought you were stationed in Colwyn Bay now."

"They've sent me back here, now that DCI Hughes is one step away from God and will only take the most important of cases. Bad timing, eh? I arrive back and you're off to HQ to start your course."

"Not any longer. All courses have been postponed. I'm stuck here with instructions to help the Min of Ag."

"Bad luck. It's a bugger, isn't it?"

"Especially for those of us who live and work out in the countryside. They all think I've turned traitor, but what else can I do?"

"I know. Sometimes our job stinks. But I seem to remember you've got a lot of leave piled up, haven't you?"

"At least five weeks. I didn't take a proper holiday last year, but—"

"Well then," Watkins cut in, "why don't you make yourself scarce for a couple of weeks until the worst is over?"

Evan sighed. "I wish I could, but in case you haven't heard, they've cancelled all leave too."

"Oh right. Except for compassionate," Watkins said.

"Yes, but I don't think they're likely to be compassionate to me when I tell them it upsets me to do my job, are they?"

He expected Watkins to laugh, but the inspector was looking at him thoughtfully. "So how is your mum these days? Last time I heard she was poorly."

"Yes, she did have a nasty touch of bronchitis last spring."

"Takes a long time to get over—bronchitis, so I've heard."

"Oh no, she's up and around again now, just fine."

"I said, it takes a long time to get over bronchitis," Watkins repeated patiently. "It can easily turn into pneumonia. You never did get time to go and visit her in the spring, did you? These things can flare up again when you least expect them, you know."

"Can they?"

Watkins burst out laughing. "Sometimes you're as thick as a plank, Evans."

"Oh, I see." Evan laughed too. "But I couldn't ask for compassionate leave right now. It wouldn't be right."

"Do you want to be out of the area or don't you?"

"Of course I do."

"Well then." Watkins sucked through his teeth as he thought. "Tell you what. I'll have a word with old Bill Mathias who does the duty roster. He owes me a favor, as it happens. I'll tell him about your poor mum and let's see what he can do."

"If you can pull this one off, I'll be in your debt for life," Evan said.

Watkins slapped him on the back. "I won't forget that, boyo. When you're working for me in the plainclothes division, you'll be getting all the three A.M. stakeouts. And I'll have you writing all my reports for me."

"Worth every second, if you can spirit me out of here."

"Well, go on then. Get lost," Watkins said, giving him a gentle shove. "It won't do if you're seen hanging around here. We don't want them to think it's a conspiracy, do we?"

Evan hurried back to his car. He had scarcely arrived back in Llanfair before the phone rang.

"What did I tell you?" Watkins's voice boomed down the line. "I'm a bloody miracle worker, that's what I am. I told Bill Mathias about your old mum and how poorly she has been, and he said no problem. He'll just leave you off the roster, quiet like, so that the super doesn't notice. So there you are. Get packing."

"Bloody brilliant," Evan exclaimed. "I'll go and tell Bronwen right now, and I'd better call my mum to tell her we're coming."

"So it's 'take Bronwen to meet the old folks at home time,' is it?"

"That's right. I'm not looking forward to it, I can tell you," Evan said. "In fact restraining crazed farmers only just wins out over sitting with my mother and Bronwen in the same room."

"Bit of a tartar, your old mum, is it?"

"No, I wouldn't say that. But she's very good at stirring, if you know what I mean."

"Knowing how to make you feel guilty? I've got a wife who's an expert at the same thing. She never yells or has tantrums—she just has to give me this pained look."

Evan chuckled. "Yes, I'd say that describes my mum pretty well. She's not such a bad old thing. It's just that she's never quite forgiven me for moving so far away."

"Playing on the old guilt, like I said. Rather you than me, boyo. Oh, and Evan, you owe me a pint."

"Anywhere other than the Dragon. The atmosphere is decidedly frosty at the moment."

"It can wait till you come back," Watkins said. "Go on. Bugger off before I realize that I'm getting soft."

Chapter 4

"It was a good idea of yours to slip away without telling anyone," Bronwen said as she climbed into the passenger seat of Evan's car. "We don't want the whole village speculating that we've run away together."

Evan laughed. "It will be a bloody miracle if we do slip away unnoticed. You know what this place is like. It's round the village in ten minutes each time I come to visit you—and what time I leave again too!"

"I can't imagine that anyone is awake at this hour to watch us leave." Bronwen peered out at the starry night where just a faint glow over the eastern mountains announced that dawn was not far off.

"And a good thing too, seeing that we're carrying illegal cargo," Evan commented as he got in beside her.

Bronwen swung around to the backseat where a mournful-looking lamb peered at her from its crate. "We had to take him with us, Evan. What if they had decided to have him slaughtered while we were gone? It would have broken Eirlys's heart."

"But it's still illegal, *cariad*. You know as well as I do that any transportation of livestock is forbidden at the moment. We'll be in a hell of a jam if we're stopped."

"He's not livestock; he's a pet. That's completely different."

"He'll still look like a sheep to any road check that we might meet," Evan said.

Bronwen nestled up close to him. "You wouldn't want to see a little girl's special pet killed, would you?"

"I do things for you against my better judgment," Evan said. He started the engine. It coughed several times before roaring to life loudly enough to awaken most of the village. "If we're stopped I shall claim no knowledge of what you've stowed in my backseat. I'll tell them you're a hitchiker I picked up with dubious cargo."

Bronwen laughed. "Lucky you haven't given me a ring yet, or you'd be sunk."

"Yes, well it's not official yet, is it? That's what we're doing now. Making it official."

He let out the clutch and the car moved away from the curb. At that moment he saw a strange specter in his rearview mirror. A large figure was flapping its way after them, arms waving in distraught fashion. "Oh no." Evan stopped the car.

"What is it?"

"Someone's running after us. There must be some kind of emergency."

"Hen Diawll," Bronwen muttered. "Can't we just drive off and pretend we didn't see?"

"There speaks the wonderful Miss Price, adored by the whole village?" Evan chuckled as he wound down the window.

The flapping figure caught up and paused, holding on to the roof of the car, gasping for breath. "I thought I'd left it too late, Mr. Evans." The words came out between gasps.

"Mrs. Williams," Evan exclaimed, recognizing his former landlady. "Whatever is wrong?"

"Wrong? Nothing at all. I didn't think you'd have time to make yourselves any proper food for the journey, so I made you one of my egg and bacon pies you like so much, and a *bara brith,* and a few sandwiches, just in case you got hungry."

"That's very nice of you, Mrs. Williams, but you really didn't have to—" Evan began, but she cut him off in midsentence. "Swansea is a dreadful long way away." She poked her head in through the window. "Good morning to you, Miss Price. I hope you have a lovely trip, just." She handed Evan a large shopping bag. "There's a thermos of tea too. You're going to need some breakfast."

"Mrs. Williams, I don't know what to say." Evan gave an embarrassed laugh. "How did you know we were going to Swansea?"

"Well now, that was easy enough. Evans-the-Milk told me that you'd stopped your delivery for two weeks and so had Miss Price, and then Evans-the-Post said you'd had a letter from your mother saying how she was looking forward to seeing you and to meeting Miss Price."

"I never thought he'd have the cheek to read my mail. There's no way of keeping secrets in this village there?" Evan gave Bronwen a look of amused despair.

"And no reason why it should be a secret, either," Mrs. Williams said. "What could be more natural than taking your betrothed home to visit your mother? Go on, off you go and have a lovely time. We'll want to hear all about it when you come back."

She stood there waving as they drove away.

"So much for our secret getaway," Bronwen said. "Now the whole village will know."

"If they don't already. My, but that food smells awfully good, doesn't it. Is that egg and bacon pie still warm, do you think?"

"If anyone wanted to bribe you, all they'd have to do is know how to cook well." Bronwen opened the bag and extracted the pie.

"Well, I have been trying to survive on my own, but it hasn't been easy after Mrs. Williams's cooking."

"I must say, it does smell heavenly," Bronwen said. "And she's even provided plates and a knife. I'll cut you a slice."

"Look, I see Mrs. Powell-Jones has taken over as usual." Evan pointed at the banner, draped across the front of Capel Beulah, where the Reverend Powell-Jones was minister. "Village meeting tomorrow night. Foot-and-Mouth Contingency Plans. Let's all pull together and do our bit!"

The billboard outside the chapel had a new text on it: IT IS REQUIRED OF A STEWARD THAT HE BE FOUND FAITHFUL! Across the street, Capel Bethel's billboard text was not in sympathy. I KNOW MY

SHEEP AND MY SHEEP KNOW ME. A GOOD SHEPHERD LAYS DOWN HIS LIFE FOR HIS SHEEP.

"I don't think Mrs. Powell-Jones's village meeting is going to run very smoothly, do you?" Evan said. "I'm glad we're going to be far away."

As they drove south and the rugged mountain scenery gave way to gentle green hills and distant seascapes, the sun came up over the horizon and the whole eastern sky flamed pink.

"Rain before tonight," Evan said, glancing at it.

"You're such a pessimist sometimes." Bronwen slapped his hand.

"No, just a realist. Let's hope we get there before it starts in earnest."

Bronwen's gaze swept across the countryside, taking in the hill-sides dotted with fat lambs and wooly sheep. "It looks so beautiful and peaceful, doesn't it?" she asked. "It's hard to believe that only a few miles north of here they are already starting to slaughter whole flocks. Do you think this mass slaughtering actually does any good?"

"I'm not an expert," Evan said. "But nothing else seems to stop it. They have to try everything, don't they?"

"It seems like overkill in the true sense to me. Killing healthy animals—that's just not right."

As if in agreement, Prince William gave a plaintive *baa* from his crate.

"You wouldn't think it would take all day just to drive a hundred miles across Wales, would you?" Bronwen commented as the first road signs to Swansea in English and Abertawe in Welsh appeared.

"It would have gone quicker if we hadn't stopped so many times to let that bloody sheep stretch his legs." Evan was feeling irritable. He put it down to the egg and bacon pie, plus several of Mrs. Williams cold beef and pickle sandwiches sitting heavily on his stomach, although the thought of an imminent meeting between Bronwen and his mother could also have had something to do with it.

"It's stupid that there is no direct road from North Wales to

South Wales, isn't it?" Bronwen went on. "You'd have thought they'd have put one in by now."

"You know how most people feel—the less contact between North Walesians and South Walesians, the better."

Bronwen chuckled. "We're a funny lot, aren't we? It might actually have been quicker to have gone back to England and picked up the motorway."

"Yes, but not as pretty, eh? We've seen some lovely country today."

"Before it started raining." Bronwen peered through the streaked windscreen at the gray mist.

"Funny, this is how I always think of Swansea," Evan said. "It always seemed to rain a lot. Especially when we were playing rugby."

"Let's go and visit your old rugby club. That will be fun." Bronwen rested her hand on his shoulder. "I'm really looking forward to hearing tales of your misspent youth."

The outskirts of the city came into view—large, uniform housing estates sprawling over hillsides. Evan was beginning to have serious second thoughts about the upcoming encounter. As they drove past row after row of gray, terraced houses, past pavements slick with rain and women in macks and headscarves scurrying home from the corner fish shop, it occurred to him that this could be a very big mistake. Bronwen was, after all, from another world. He hadn't yet met her family, but she referred to her parents as Mummy and Daddy. And she had been to Cambridge. Therefore she was several rungs above him on the social ladder.

Usually such things didn't bother Evan, but suddenly he was reluctant to let Bronwen see the plain row house where he had spent his youth. If he could have come up with a credible excuse, he would have turned around and driven away. Instead he gritted his teeth and kept driving until familiar landmarks came into view: the railway station and the castle ruins, the new Quadrant shopping center, the museum, and beyond it the upscale new waterfront development where the most depressed dockland area had been. Then they could see the old prison with its prime waterfront position and great views across Swansea Bay.

"This is nice," Bronwen said as the bay itself opened up on their left, gray sea merging into gray sky in the rain, with just a hint of hills visible on the far shore. "I hadn't realized Swansea was on the seafront."

"Bristol Channel, actually, but yes, they're always comparing Swansea to the French Riviera. The resemblance is obvious, isn't it?"

Bronwen gave him a sharp look. "I think it's attractive," she said, "and I like all these old houses. They've got character, haven't they?"

"You could say that. And I'm glad you like them because my mother lives in one." The road swung inland from the seafront and started to climb. Gray mist had washed out the hilltops. Townhill Road appeared through the mist at last with its gray stone, terraced houses, all alike. A whole world of gray.

"These used to be workers' cottages once, when the steel mills were flourishing," Evan said. "One of the first housing estates."

"Great views for a housing estate."

"Actually all the housing estates are on the hills in Swansea."

"A very proletariat kind of city."

"The rich don't live in the city at all. Ah, here we are then." He came to a halt outside one of the identical gray stone cottages. He had forgotten how small it was, not much bigger than the tiny two-up two-down he now inhabited in Llanfair. Small and ordinary looking. He thought he saw the lace curtain tweaked as he pulled up. Sure enough, the front door opened while he was still helping Bronwen from the car.

"Here you are at last then." His mother stood in the doorway. She seemed to have shrunk. "I thought something had happened to you."

"It's a long drive from North Wales, Ma." Evan continued to hold Bronwen's hand as she stepped onto the pavement.

"I know that, but there are so many terrible drivers on the roads these days, aren't there, and all these dreadful big lorries coming across from the Continent and breaking the speed limit, isn't it?"

"We're here now and we're fine." Evan went up to her and enveloped her in a hug. She felt small and bony, and he couldn't feel her hugging him back. "So how are you?"

"Not so bad, considering. The doctor doesn't quite like the sound of my chest yet, but then at my age, what can you expect?"

"Your age! You're only sixty-five."

"Don't shout my age for the whole street to hear." Evan's mother looked around, then her gaze fastened on Bronwen. "Does she understand us? *Ydych chi'n siarad cymraeg,* Miss Price?"

Bronwen laughed. "Of course I do. I teach in a Welsh school."

"Oh, well, that's nice. It will be a treat to speak my own language for a change."

"What do you mean, for a change?" Evan asked.

"Nobody speaks Welsh in Abertawe any longer," she said, giving the city its Welsh name. "It's all changed. Full of outsiders.

"What about your friends at the Welsh club?" Evan asked.

"Well, they've almost all gone now, haven't they?" Mrs. Evans said angrily, as if they had left on purpose. "Gladys Jones and Mary Roberts both died last year. Dropping like flies, they are." She suddenly seemed to notice that she was getting wet. "Well, don't just stand there in the rain then. Come on, inside with you."

Bronwen looked at Evan. "Do you think Prince W. will be all right in the car a little longer?"

"There's a shed in the back garden. We can put him there until . . ." He glanced at his mother.

The older woman picked up instantly. "You haven't brought a dog with you, have you?"

"No, Ma. Not a dog. A sheep actually."

Mrs. Evans laughed and gave him a playful shove. "Go on with you! A sheep—what, to remind me of my childhood home, is it?"

At this point a plaintive *baa* was heard from the interior of the car. Mrs. Evans peered out into the rain. "*Escob Annwyl!* You haven't really got a sheep in there? You're not bringing a sheep into my house."

"It's a pet lamb, Ma. Bronwen's been looking after it for one of her schoolchildren, and we couldn't just leave him at home. It's all right. Don't look like that. We can keep him in the shed when it's raining, and he can be out in the back garden when it's not."

"And have him eating all my petunias?"

"We'll tie him up then. He's really no trouble. He's been as good as gold all the way down here in the car."

"Pet lambs! What will they think of next?" Mrs. Evan shuffled back into the house, her carpet slippers flapping on the linoleum. "I've got the kettle on. So what would you fancy for your tea, Miss Price?"

"Please call me Bronwen. And just a cup of tea would be lovely. We're a little late. We don't want to spoil our dinner, do we?"

Mrs. Evans gave her son a strange look. Bronwen also sensed she had said something wrong. Evan put a hand on Bronwen's shoulder. "My mum always has her main meal at midday and just a light meal at night. So it's dinner in the middle of the day and tea in the evening."

"Oh, oh I see." Bronwen flushed. "Well, anything you like at all, Mrs. Evans. I'm not a fussy eater. I'm sure whatever you have prepared will be lovely."

"We're just working-class people, you know," Mrs. Evans said. "Never did get into these fancy ways of lunch and dinner. Your dad was always home for dinner at one when he could make it, wasn't he, Evan? And then we'd have something simple at night."

"I'm sure it will be lovely," Bronwen insisted. "Can I help with anything?"

"No, it's all ready, apart from the eggs. I thought I'd do poached eggs on welsh rarebit if that would be acceptable."

"Lovely," Evan and Bronwen said in chorus.

Evan's mother had led them down a long narrow passage that opened into an old-fashioned kitchen. Willow-pattern plates were stacked on a Welsh dresser. A table was set with a pretty lace-edged cloth. It was piled with a cottage loaf, a large wedge of yellow cheese, and a cake stand with several kinds of cakes and biscuits on it.

"We have a proper dining room," Mrs. Evans said quickly, "but

I usually eat in here. It's less lonely somehow. Cozier."

"Of course it is." Bronwen smiled at her. "Evan and I always eat in the kitchen at my place, don't we, Evan?"

"You like to cook, do you, Miss Price?" Mrs. Evans asked as she poured boiling water into a teapot, popped a crocheted cozy over it, and set it on the table.

"I love to. I took a course in French cooking last year, and poor Evan had to sample all my mistakes."

"French cooking—well, we don't go for that around here much. Plain, simple Welsh cooking has always been good enough for my husband and my boy."

Evan came to Bronwen's defense. "You should taste the way she does leg of lamb, Ma—she puts little pieces of garlic under the skin."

"Garlic? I wouldn't want my breath smelling like a Continental myself."

Evan laughed. "I'll pour the tea then, shall I?"

Tea was poured. Eggs on cheese were produced and they sat down to eat. Evan was glad they had something to keep them all busy for the moment. He had hoped that his mother would take one look at Bronwen and embrace her as a future daughter-in-law. This obviously wasn't going to happen. And he supposed he hadn't really expected it to.

"So how is it that you have the Welsh then, Miss Price?" he heard his mother asking. "I thought only poor folks grew up speaking Welsh, but you sound like you've got the hang of it rather well."

"I spoke it as a child, Mrs. Evans. My father worked for an international bank and was posted around the world—sometimes to places that were not very safe for families. So I was left at home with my grandmother near Denbigh. My father's family were the local squires and of course he didn't speak the local language, but my mother was the schoolteacher's daughter. So my *Nain* always spoke Welsh to me. My parents were rather angry when they found out I preferred speaking what they thought was a backward language to English. That's when I was sent away rapidly to boarding school."

"A backward language, indeed." Mrs. Evan sniffed. "One of the oldest, finest languages in the world, isn't it? We had poetry when the English were still running around in goat skins."

"I agree completely," Bronwen said. "I always made sure I spent as much time as possible with my grandmother just to keep up my Welsh. Of course now I use it all the time, so it's become my first language again."

"And you're teaching at the school, Evan tells me."

"The village school, yes. I only have twenty-five pupils, all ages, so it's quite a challenge. And the building is ancient. Have you seen it?"

"No. I haven't yet been invited to visit my son."

"Oh, come on, Ma," Evan said quickly. "You know you're welcome. It's just that I only had a room, lodging in someone else's house, until recently. And what I've got at the moment isn't properly furnished yet."

"When we're married, you can come and stay with us," Bronwen said.

Evan's mother gave her a sharp look. "Oh, so it's getting married now, is it? I hadn't heard more than you were courting."

"We didn't want to tell anyone officially until we had met each other's families." Evan glanced across at Bronwen. "But yes, we're planning on getting married some time soon. We haven't set a date yet, or a place."

"And where are your folks then, Miss Price?"

Evan noticed that she was not going to abandon the formality.

"They live in Monmouthshire now. My father retired from the bank, and they bought a property in the Usk Valley. Very pretty."

"And you're going there after this?"

"That's right."

"You'll only be here a few days then, is it?" She looked wistfully at her son.

"This time, yes," Bronwen answered for Evan. "Evan's going to show me all his old haunts."

"Old haunts? Makes him sound like a ghost."

Bronwen laughed. "I meant his school and the rugby club."

"Speaking of the rugby club, you'll never guess who I saw at the market the other day." Mrs. Evans's face brightened up. "Maggie. Looking very fit and well, she was. Asked after you, Evan. She seemed very excited when I told her you were going to be here, so I asked her to drop by whenever she felt like it."

"Ma, you didn't! I wish you hadn't done that. What makes you think I want to see her again? And I'm sure Bronwen doesn't."

"A lovely girl, Maggie, even if she didn't speak Welsh properly. We always liked her. She had a lot of get-up-and-go, didn't she? She used to make your dad laugh. He always said she was a real looker."

"I doubt if Bronwen and I will be home much while we're here. There's a lot I want to show her, and I suppose I should pop down to the police station and visit my old mates."

"They've moved the police station," Mrs. Evans said. "Now they've got a spanking new one, all glass and purple tiles. Whoever heard of a purple police station? I think it's the ugliest thing on God's earth."

"So where is the new one?" Evan asked.

"Just down the street from the old one, but I doubt they'll have much time for you at the moment." Mrs. Evans shook her head. "They'll be too busy with this dreadful murder."

"A murder? In Swansea?"

"Just over a week ago, it was. I'm surprised you didn't hear about it on the news. A lovely young girl raped and murdered and her body left on the family's doorstep for them to find. Dreadful, it was. One of those posh houses along Oystermouth Road. The father is a bigwig—on the city council and owns a factory."

"What's the name?" Evan asked.

"Turnbull. Alison Turnbull was the daughter."

"Turnbull—didn't he own a steel works that closed?"

"He did, but now he's started up a new business. Something to do with computers. That kind always seem to fall on their feet, don't they?" She got up and began clearing away plates. "Swansea's not what it used to be. Full of riffraff and minorities. You remember that chapel you sang at when you were a little boy? I went past it the other day and you'll never guess what it is now—a mosque, that's what it is. You could have knocked me down with a feather when I saw that heathen writing outside. And women with scarves around their heads."

"Ma, you wear a scarf around your head. I've seen you." Evan laughed.

"Yes, but only when it's raining and not in the middle of summer. In fact if you want to know what I think—"

She broke off at the sound of knocking on the front door.

"Now who could that be?" she asked, reminding Evan of his former landlady, who always asked the same question.

"I'll go, shall I?" Evan got up from his seat. He had a sinking feeling that it might be his old girlfriend, and he'd rather face her on the doorstep.

When he opened the front door, it wasn't a girl at all. It was a uniformed policeman. He looked startled when he saw Evan, then a smile of recognition spread across his face.

"It's never young Evan? Well, this is a surprise. Bill Howells, remember me?"

Evan shook the outstretched hand. "Of course, Mr. Howells. You used to belong to the bowls club with my dad."

"Well, what a treat for your mum. She talks about you all the time. She still misses your dad terribly."

"Don't we all?" Evan opened the door wider and motioned to the man. "Well, come inside, Mr. Howells. Mum will be pleased to see you."

"I don't know about that," the officer said, giving Evan a strange look. "Not when she hears the news I'm bringing her. But I thought she had a right to know."

"To know what?"

"They've got the bastard who killed that young girl. And you'll never guess who it turned out to be. Tony Mancini—the one who shot your dad."

Chapter 5

"Well, I never." Evan's mother reached out and grasped Evan's hand as she digested the news. "I knew he was no good the moment I set eyes on him. And those psychologists were saying he was just a young boy led astray and didn't know what he was doing."

"Well, he knew was he was doing this time," Bill Howells said, sitting to accept the cup of tea that Mrs. Evans had poured him. "Dumping the body on the doorstep too, for her poor parents to find. That's an added touch of nastiness, if you ask me."

Mrs. Evans had produced a handkerchief from her pocket and was dabbing at her eyes. "This would never have happened if they'd sent him to prison like he deserved."

"We were unlucky enough to get that soft-hearted judge." Sergeant Howells accepted a Welsh Cake from the plate and took an appreciative bite. "Four years in a young offenders institute and then out on the streets again. That doesn't seem a big enough price to pay for a life, does it?"

"Especially not for a good man like my Robert." Mrs. Evans put a hand over her mouth to control her emotion. "Well, I hope that judge is regretting it now."

"This time he's not a young offender any longer," Sergeant Howells said, looking up at Evan. "This time we'll put him away for good."

Evan had been observing this interaction as if the participants were somehow remote from him—characters in a play he was watching. When he finally tried to speak, he found it hard to form the words.

"When will the trial be?"

"They haven't set a trial date yet, but he comes up before the magistrate on Monday afternoon. That's why I came to see you, Mrs. Evans. I thought you might like to be there. We want to make sure the bastard isn't allowed out on bail, pardon my language, Mrs. E. And now young Evan is here too, maybe you'd both like to let the magistrate know your feelings on the subject of bail."

"I want to be there," Mrs. Evans said. "Evan can take me. It's only right that Robert has someone to speak for him."

"When he's up before the magistrate," Sergeant Howells said. "I'll be there myself, and DCI Vaughan is going to appeal against bail being granted. I'll meet you there then, all right?" He got to his feet. "I'd better be going. We're all running around like crazy at the station. We've got the place crawling with Major Crime Support Unit blokes from Talbot. We have to make this one stick." He nodded to Evan, then to Bronwen, who had remained silent. "Nice meeting you, Miss. See you Monday then, Evan. Take care of your mum, won't you? And thank you for the sustenance, Mrs. E." He put his cap back on his head. "Don't worry. I can see myself out."

There was silence after the front door closed.

"Well, I never," Mrs. Evan said again.

Bronwen touched Evan's arm. "I take it that the suspect they've just caught is the man who killed your father, then?"

Evan was staring down at the lace pattern on the tablecloth. He didn't trust himself to look up. "That's right."

"Tony Mancini. Is he an immigrant then?"

"Well, I suppose his family were immigrants originally. A lot of Italians came over to South Wales in the 1920s. We had quite a few boys at school with Italian names."

"And why was he let out of prison so quickly?"

"He was only a kid when he shot my father. And he claimed it was accidental. My dad surprised a gang unloading a drug shipment at the docks. Mancini said he was told to shoot, and he shot. He was scared and just shot wildly. So they just sent him to a young offenders institute instead of prison."

"And back on the streets after four years," Evan's mother said bitterly. "And now some other family will be going through what we did. Another empty place at the dinner table. It's not right, is it?"

Evan went over and put his arm around her shoulders. "Don't worry, Ma. This time they'll put him away for sure. We'll help make sure they do."

During the night a strong wind swept in from the Irish Sea so that when Evan woke in the morning, the sky was blue with puffball white clouds scudding across it. When he took Bronwen a morning cup of tea he found her already up, kneeling on her bed, and looking out of the window.

"What a magnificent view." She turned to smile at him. "If I lived here, I'd never get any work done. I'd be sitting at this window every day."

Evan looked out at the expanse of Swansea Bay sparkling in the sunlight between its protective arms of green hills. From up here he couldn't really see the power station or the steel works or any of the factories. Even the houses below looked clean and freshly painted.

"I used to have my desk in this window. I liked to watch the cargo boats come in." He smiled at her.

"This was your room then?"

Evan nodded.

"Then you should have said something. I'm sure you'd rather have slept in your old room."

"My mother would never have heard of it. This is her guest room now, and you are the guest."

Bronwen looked around. "So what happened to all your things?

There's nothing to indicate that you lived here once."

"Up in the attic, in boxes, probably. My mother's always been a great one for cleaning up and clearing out. I expect she'll produce the photo albums at some stage and let you see me as a chubby baby and a skinny ten-year-old."

"Oh, I do hope so." Bronwen smiled at him. "Were you a skinny ten-year-old?"

"Very. And undersized. They used to pick on me in primary school because I was a new boy and I spoke Welsh."

"And the other boys didn't?"

"Some of them spoke it at home, but never in school. In fact one teacher told us very plainly that we'd be stupid to choose Welsh rather than French or German when we went to the grammar school, because it was a dead language and no use."

"Well, I suppose he did have a point. I'm glad I speak it, but it isn't really much use, is it?"

"Only to sing songs and recite poetry."

Bronwen took a sip of the tea he offered her. "So can we get some of those boxes out of the attic? I want to see your Cub Scout uniform and your Meccano set."

"Whatever for?"

"So that I get a picture of you as a little boy, of course. I have to know what I'm marrying."

"Evan? If you've taken Miss Price her tea, I need you down here," Evan's mother called up the stairs.

Evan grinned at Bronwen. "She doesn't want me lurking in your bedroom."

"And quite right too. I'll be down in a few minutes." She slid off the bed and gave him a quick peck on the cheek. "It's a lovely day for walking."

Evan glanced back down the hall. "It's Sunday. I rather suspect we'll have to go to chapel first," he said. "Mum's still very hot on that kind of thing. And then there will definitely be Sunday lunch with all the trimmings. But we'll get out somewhere this afternoon. I can still give you my tour of the famous historic sites of Swansea."

"Dylan Thomas's birthplace, you mean? I'd love to see it."

"I was thinking more of my primary school, my grammar school, my rugby field—they're a lot more interesting than bloody Dylan Thomas. I can't see why people make such a fuss about him."

"Oh, but he was brilliant. I love his poems. 'Do not go gentle into that good night.' You have to admit that's a wonderful poem."

Evan frowned. "Funny. I came upon it when I was going through stuff after my dad died. I couldn't read it. It made me too angry."

Bronwen reached up and stroked his cheek. "Would you like me to come with you when you go to court tomorrow? I will if you want me to, but I don't want to be in the way."

"May be better if you don't," Evan said. "It might be rather hard for my mother, you know."

"I understand."

"Evan," came the shout from downstairs. "What's taking you so long up there? Leave Miss Price in peace."

When Bronwen came downstairs a little later she found a full breakfast being cooked. Rashers of bacon were sizzling in a pan. Sausages, tomatoes, and mushrooms were under the grill, and eggs were waiting to be fried.

"Oh heavens," Bronwen exclaimed. "You didn't have to go to all this trouble for me. I'm quite happy with toast or cereal."

Mrs. Evans gave her a disapproving look. "Neither my husband nor my boy ever had to start a day's work on toast or cereal. They left the house with a good breakfast in their stomachs. Good wholesome food. That's what keeps men happy."

Evan saw Bronwen making sure she didn't make eye contact with him. Instead she went over to the toaster. "I'll do some toast for us, shall I?"

"Chapel at ten," Mrs. Evans said firmly. "But I never asked, did I—are you church or chapel, Miss Price?"

"My grandmother brought me up chapel, but my parents are more church, when they go at all," Bronwen said. "But I'm perfectly happy to come to the chapel with you, Mrs. Evans."

"Right you are. We leave here at nine-forty, sharp. Got that,

Evan? I remember how you always made us late when you were a little boy, dawdling up in your room."

"We'll be ready, Ma." Evan gave Bronwen a quick glance and she smiled back.

"You might have warned me the sermon would be in Welsh and then in English," Bronwen muttered as they finally emerged from the squat gray stone building close to noon. "I could have brought a good book to stick inside my hymn book. My, but he did go on, didn't he? And all that hell fire, too. What makes people actually want to be abused and insulted for two hours?"

"Good for the soul." Evan squeezed her hand. "But the lunch will make up for it, I expect."

When they got home they were greeted by the smell of roast leg of lamb. It came out of the oven crisp and brown. Potatoes, parsnips, and onions were dotted around it, equally crisp and brown, and to these Mrs. Evans added broad beans and marrow in a white sauce.

"And I made your favorite for pudding," she said as she cleared away empty plates. "Baked jam roll and custard."

Evan silently let a notch out of his belt as the long sponge roll, oozing with jam, emerged from the oven.

After lunch Mrs. Evans went for a rest. Evan and Bronwen took the opportunity to escape. "Although after that lunch I think I could have slept all afternoon too," Evan said. "We'd better do plenty of hill walking to burn off all those calories."

They started with a quick drive around the modern town center and past the 1930s Guildhall, then, after passing an attractive park full of Sunday sun worshippers, they pulled up outside a school.

"This used to be it," Evan said. "It was Swansea Grammar School when I was there. Now it's a comprehensive, like all the others. It used to be ever so snooty, and the kids on our street used to throw lumps of dirt at my uniform."

"It sounds like a dangerous place to grow up."

"It toughened me up," Evan said. "And as soon as I started growing and playing rugby, they stopped bothering me."

"All right." Bronwen gave a mock sigh. "Show me this historic rugby field. Have they put up a plaque to you yet?"

They zigzagged back up the hill and parked beside an expanse of playing fields. At this time of year there were no rugby posts, but the grass had been groomed in the center for a cricket pitch—a slim strip of perfect green. Figures in white were dotted around it and from the open car window they heard the satisfying thwack of bat striking ball, followed by a round of polite applause.

"This is it," Evan said.

"So this is where you scored every Saturday." Brownen's clear blue eyes were teasing.

"I didn't score very often," Evan said, pretending not to get her double meaning. "I wasn't supposed to in the position I played. I played number eight."

"Sorry. I know nothing about rugby, which I'm sure is a sacrilege in Swansea."

"Middle of the back row."

"Sounds like a chorus line."

"Of the scrum."

"I only have a vague idea what a scrum is, but I bet your friend Maggie can tell me whether you scored or not. Maggie what was her last name?"

"Pole," he said. "Maggie Pole." As he said it a picture of the vivacious brunette flashed into his head. He shook his head. "Let's not talk about her. It was all over a long time ago and not exactly happy memories."

"Did you have a stormy breakup?"

"She dumped me," Evan said. "If you want the whole sorry story, I had a bad time after my father died. I was off work. I couldn't seem to get on with my life. I really needed Maggie, and she told me she wasn't prepared to wait around for a loony. End of story."

"What a bitch," Bronwen said.

Evan looked surprised at this uncharacteristic outburst.

"Well, she was. If you love someone, you don't dump them when they go through a bad patch. When I say for better or worse, I'll mean it."

"I'm sure you will." He took her hand and squeezed it.

"So now I understand why you weren't keen on seeing her again."

"And you know why I plan to keep out and busy all the time we're in Swansea. If my mother has her way, she'll trap us and invite Maggie round for tea."

"So your mum was keen on her, I gather."

"Not at the time. Only in retrospect. In fact she thought Maggie was flighty and her skirts were too short. No one has ever been good enough for me, according to my mother."

"Which is why she is so frosty to me."

"She'll warm up. Give her time."

"I hope so. I don't want to be called Miss Price all my life."

"You'll be Mrs. Evans soon, if that suits you better." Evan smiled. "All right. You've seen the site of my rugby triumphs. On to the next stop."

"You won't forget Dylan Thomas's house, will you?"

"No, I won't forget Dylan bloody Thomas."

They continued over hilly terrain, lined with uniform streets of a council housing project. Then Evan stopped outside a gray stone chapel at the top of a hill. Without saying anything he opened the car door and got out. Bronwen followed him as he walked up the path and around the side of the chapel.

"Another scene of your boyhood triumphs?" she asked, running to keep up with him because he was walking fast.

They were facing inland now, away from the sea. Green hills and valleys rolled away as far as the eye could see.

"It used to be different when I was a boy," Evan said, pausing to let her stand beside him. "This was all coal-mining country. There were black slag tips on top of those hills and mine equipment, and a smog always hung over the valleys because of the coal dust. It's hard to believe now that things can change so quickly."

He started walking again, into the little cemetery behind the chapel. "I brought you up here because I wanted you to see my father's grave." He stopped beside a plain granite headstone.

The words were already being overtaken by lichen. "In loving memory of Robert David Evans, devoted husband and father and loyal officer of the South Wales Police Force. Killed in the line of duty . . ."

Evan ran his hand over the rough granite of the stone. "He was due for retirement, you know. He could have retired six months earlier but they were shorthanded, and they asked him if he'd stay on until the end of the year. He never liked to say no to people. He was a good man. He never raised his voice, but if he told you to do something, you knew he meant it and you did it. You could always count on him. A really good . . . man . . ."

"I'm sure he was, Evan. He managed to raise a rather nice son."

"He was a great dad. Always seemed to make time for me, even when he was busy. I wish you could have met him."

"I wish I could have."

"He enjoyed life so much. Always laughing. It just seems so wrong that . . . so unfair that . . ."

He turned away and stared out at the green hillsides. Bronwen slipped an arm through his. "It's okay to grieve, you know."

"And if that creep Mancini is finally sentenced to life in prison, maybe I'll think there is some justice in the world after all."

Bronwen took his hand. "Come on. Let's go. You still have to show me Dylan's birthplace, and we need some exercise."

Chapter 6

Evan had never been in the Swansea magistrate's court before. He remembered all too vividly the last time he had been in a Swansea courtroom—every detail of the Crown Court where Tony Mancini's trial had taken place was etched into his mind. The Crown Court had been a new building, a concrete-and-glass structure that had felt all wrong to Evan. Courtrooms were supposed to be somber, majestic places, with oak-paneled walls and dark wood benches, reeking of tradition like the Old Bailey. This courtroom had been light and ultramodern, with tip-up seats like a theater and laminate countertops like a kitchen. There had been a skylight over the judge's bench, and cold light had shone down onto the gray wig and the judge's pale flabby face. Altogether wrong—and very cold. It was the cold he remembered more than anything, although, of course, that could have been shock.

This magistrate's courtroom was less modern but still spartan. None of the historic glory of the Old Bailey here, and of course the magistrates would be ordinary people in ordinary clothes. No wigs and gowns at this level of justice.

The courtroom was surprisingly full for the arraignment hearing as Bill Howells, in police uniform, led them to seats near the front. Sitting apart on the other side, Evan noticed a well-dressed couple, still as statues, staring straight in front of them. They had to be the dead girl's parents. Evan recognized that look of stunned horror, that determination not to break down in public. He knew exactly what they were thinking at this moment—that there was no way they could get through this ordeal, and yet they had to, somehow.

Members of the South Wales Police filled the benches around Evan and his mother. They nodded to Evan's mother, but she too was staring straight ahead, clearly reliving her memories. He could feel her shaking. He reached across and rested his hand over hers.

From the back of the courtroom came a relaxed buzz of conversation. Evan turned to see a large media contingent. Of course, the death of a councilor's daughter would make this a high-profile case. The conversation ceased as a door at the front of the courtroom opened and the magistrates came in to take up their positions at the bench. There were three of them—a dapper little man with thinning gray hair neatly parted in the center wearing a red bow tie, a large horsy woman in tweeds to his left, and an equally large, slightly unkempt middle-aged man in a knitted yellow waistcoat on his right. There was a long moment of silence while they seated themselves and were handed documents by the clerk. Then a side door opened and the defendant was brought in, handcuffed and escorted on either side by uniformed policemen. He still looked ridiculously young—a skinny kid with dark hair and big dark eyes, good looking in a Latin kind of way. He looked around the room with a bewildered stare. His gaze brushed Evan, and for a moment there was a glimmer of recognition in his eyes.

"Please state your full name and address," the middle of the three magistrates said in a high, clipped voice with only the hint of a Welsh accent.

"Anthony Edward Mancini, Twenty-one Caernarfon Street, Swansea." The words were barely audible.

"Speak up, boy," the magistrate insisted.

Tony repeated the words with a defiant stare.

"Anthony Edward Mancini," the middle magistrate intoned now in a sonorous voice, "you are charged with the murder of Alison Joan Turnbull on July 17. How do you plead?"

Tony looked around the courtroom again. "I didn't do it," he said. "They're trying to pin it on me because they want to get even, but I didn't do it. Why would I want to kill Alison?"

"Do you plead guilty or not guilty?" the magistrate insisted over Tony's outburst.

"My client pleads not guilty, Your Honor." A man rose from the front row of seats. If he was Tony's solicitor he looked almost as young and skinny as his client.

"Which brings us to the question of bail." The magistrate turned to his two colleagues. "Do I understand that there is an objection to bail being granted?"

Tony's solicitor rose from his seat again quickly. "Your Honors, we suggest that there is no reason not to grant bail. My client has behaved in an exemplary manner since his release from a young offenders institute. He has not presented any danger to the community or risk of flight."

The woman magistrate on the left leaned toward Tony. "Does he have a permanent address in the community, and is he gainfully employed?"

The solicitor glanced at Tony, then back at the bench. "He lives with his mother. He is currently unemployed but actively seeking gainful employment. As you know, the unemployment rate in Swansea is particularly high."

"Has he been employed since leaving the juvenile facility?" the woman insisted.

"Yes, Your Honors. He was employed at the Unico factory."

"And Unico is?" the magistrate persisted.

"The factory owned by Mr. Turnbull, Alison's father," one of the policemen interjected before the young solicitor could say anything.

The three magistrates turned toward him. "You will please wait to be asked to address the court," the horsy woman said. "Your name is?"

A plainclothes policeman had risen to his feet. "Detective Chief Inspector Vaughan, Major Crimes Division, South Wales Police." The words came out as a belligerent challenge. He was a square, sturdily built individual with the strong jaw so prevalent in South Wales. A former rugby player, Evan assessed immediately. "I am leading the team investigating this case. Tony Mancini was employed by Unico until he was dismissed a few months ago for stealing."

The woman magistrate leaned forward again toward the solicitor. "I understood you to say that this young man had a clean record since his release."

"He does, Your Honor. No charges were ever brought, and my client feels that he was unjustly dismissed."

"If I may address the court." The DCI spoke again. "It seems to me that this young man has had more than his fair share of luck and leniency. He is now twenty-one-years-old, and this is his second murder trial. In the courtroom today are Mrs. Robert Evans and her son, Evan, next of kin to Sergeant Robert Evans of the South Wales Police. Tony Mancini spent four years in a juvenile institution for the murder of Sergeant Evans. I would like to ask permission for Mrs. Evans and her son to address the court."

The magistrates exchanged eye contact then nodded. "Very well. Mrs. Evans, and Mr. Evans, would you approach the bench?"

Evan's mother grasped at his arm like a drowning woman as they left their seats and made their way forward. "Your Honors," she said. "My husband, Sergeant Robert Evans, was a good man, a good provider . . ."

"Yes, Mrs. Evans. We are not here to dispute your husband's character. Do you have anything relevant to tell us that might help us weigh up whether bail should be denied in this case?"

Evan felt his mother nudging him. "Your Honors, my father was shot by Tony Mancini during a drug bust." He looked across to see Tony staring at him. For a moment he held that intense stare, then he turned back to the bench. "He was part of a local gang that dealt drugs and was already known to the police at age fifteen. I think I am right in saying that he was out on bail for a drug possession offense when he shot my father."

The center magistrate consulted his colleagues. "Is that so?"

"It's in his records, sir," the DCI said before Evan could answer.

"Thank you, Mr. and Mrs. Evans." The woman magistrate smiled at them. "You may return to your seats." A muttered conversation followed. Evan's mother was still clutching at him. Then the center magistrate got to his feet. "The court will adjourn while my colleagues and I discuss this matter. We will reconvene in half an hour."

When the magistrates returned to announce that bail had been denied, some of the spectators broke into applause. Evan's mother and the Turnbulls didn't flinch. After the hearing had concluded, Evan and his mother came out into the bright sunlight on the Oystermouth Road. Seagulls screeched overhead, and the air was tangy with the smell of ocean. He watched the Turnbulls come out of court and drive away in a black Mercedes.

"Well, that went about as well as we could hope," Bill Howells said, coming up to them. "Thank you both for coming along. I know your testimony made all the difference"

"I'm so glad Evan was here with me," Mrs. Evans said. "I was all of a jelly. I didn't trust myself to say any more because I wanted to tell that—that monster what I thought of him. But if I'm needed to speak at the trial, I'll do my bit, you can be sure of it. Anything to make sure he's sent away good and proper this time, eh, Evan *bach?*"

Evan nodded. He was still feeling sick and shaken. There was something about the courtroom that he had found profoundly disturbing. He couldn't quite put his finger on it at the moment, but something had not been right.

DCI Vaughan came out in the middle of a group of plainclothes officers. He came up to Evan and his mother and shook their hands. "Thank you both for coming. I know it can't have been easy for you. Don't worry, we're going to make sure he gets more than four years of holiday camp this time."

As he walked away Evan heard him say to a fellow officer, "I just hope to God we can make it stick."

Bronwen returned soon after they got home. She had been on her own pilgrimage. "I walked across to Cwmdonkin Park and sat where Dylan used to sit, looking out at the 'pretty, shitty city.' "

"Miss Price. Such language!" Mrs. Evans said disapprovingly.

"Dylan Thomas's words, not mine," Bronwen answered with a smile.

"Dylan Thomas—a drunken reprobate, if you ask me, and no credit to the city of Swansea."

"Speaking of drunken reprobates," Evan said, "I have a serious need for a pint at the local. Can I treat you ladies?"

"You want me to come to a pub?" Evan's mother sounded as if he was suggesting a strip club.

"Yes, and maybe we could get some food there too, or go on to a nice restaurant?"

"So my food's no longer good enough for you, is it?" Mrs. Evans sounded hurt.

"Of course it is, Ma. I just thought you might like to eat out for a change."

"I prefer my own cooking at home, if you really want to know. All that foreign muck and everything disguised under sauces. My Robert felt the same way. 'Nothing can equal your cooking, Ellen,' he always said."

"Then I hope you don't mind if I take Bronwen out to the pub for a while. I'd like to show her my old local. We'll pick up a pasty or something so that you don't have to cook for us tonight."

"If that's what you want." Mrs. Evans's voice was tight. "I'll be seeing you later then."

"Oh dear, I'm afraid we've offended her," Bronwen exclaimed as they shut the front door behind them.

"Don't worry, that's how she always is—always was. She's got her routine and she won't budge from it. And she's good at laying on the old guilt. Never mind, you and I will go and have a good time."

Bronwen slipped her arm through his as they made for the car. "I'm looking forward to seeing your old local, and the drink will definitely do you good. You looked as white as a sheet when I first got home. Was it a big ordeal?"

Evan nodded. "I hadn't realized how big. I suppose I should be glad because it all went well—he was denied bail for at least thirty days. So he's off the streets. But I found the whole thing very unsettling."

"Of course you would. It's a horrid thing to have to go through, when you're supposed to be on holiday too."

Evan leaned down to kiss her. "Nothing a good pint at the pub and good company won't cure."

The town was bathed in rosy evening light as they parked outside a pub called the Prince of Wales Feathers. It was a typical corner pub, a tall, uninspiring redbrick building with frosted-glass windows displaying the well-known Prince of Wales's crest and motto, on an uninspiring street of shops and faceless terraced houses. Nothing like the cozy feeling of the half-timbered Red Dragon at home in Llanfair, and on first glance, Bronwen stood there, disappointed.

"Why was this your local?" she asked. "It isn't within walking distance."

"It's where the rugby crowd used to meet," Evan said. "I don't know if that's still true. Let's go and see, shall we?" He pushed open a pair of swing doors, each with a small frosted-glass window in them, and held one open for Bronwen to pass through. Inside was dark, with a couple of slot machines in the entrance hall. A notice on a stand recommended signing up early for this year's Christmas party, now only five months away. Bronwen let Evan go ahead into the bar on the right and recoiled at the heavy fug of cigarette smoke that enveloped the crowd around the bar.

"What will you have?" Evan asked her.

Bronwen glanced around. "I better not say Perrier in a place like this or I'll be lynched, won't I?"

Evan smiled. "Probably."

"In that case, half a pint of shandy. Ginger beer shandy if they've got it."

"Right you are. Why don't you find a seat while I force my way up to the bar?"

He eased his way through the crowd. He ordered the shandy

and a pint of Guinness and was just making his way back when a voice said, "It's not Evans, is it? Stodge Evans? Well, I'll be blowed."

"Hello, Harry. Good to see you." Evan's face lit up in recognition.

Immediately he was surrounded. "What are you doing here, boyo? We heard you were working up in foreign parts, up in the primitive North."

"That's right. Up near Snowdon."

"Rather you than me, boyo. Bunch of crazies up there, aren't they? Inbred as hell."

"Been playing any rugby up there? Or don't they know how to play it?"

"They probably think it's played with sheep!"

A great roar of laughter. Hands clapped Evan on the back.

"Well, drink up then, boy. There's plenty more where that came from. Are you back for good? The scrum could use a good back row man. Davies is bloody useless."

"I'm only here for a few days," Evan said. "I've brought my . . . girlfriend"—somehow he couldn't get out the word fiancée—"to show her Swansea."

"You haven't got yourself involved with one of those wild girls from the North, have you?"

"Oh absolutely." Evan laughed. "Very wild. She's sitting over there. Come and meet her."

Several rugby players followed Evan to the corner table where Bronwen was sitting. Evan put the glass in front of her and started introductions. The first round of drinks went down quickly, and Harry offered to buy another round.

"I'll come and help you carry them," Evan volunteered and followed Harry through the crowd. He had almost reached the bar when someone grabbed his arm.

"Evan! It is you!" A dark-haired young woman in tight jeans and a tank top blocked his path. She was smiling up at him delightedly. "Your mum said you were coming for a visit. About bloody time, that's what I say. I thought you'd forgotten us."

"Hello, Maggie," Evan said quietly. "No, I hadn't forgotten."

"So did you bring Blodwin, or whatever her name is?"

"It's Bronwen and she's sitting over there. You must come and meet her."

"I met her once before, if it's the same one," Maggie said, "at that *eisteddfod*. She looked positively virginal and medieval, if I remember correctly."

"She was wearing a cloak when you met her, if that's what you mean," Evan said.

"My dear, I thought she was one of the competitors at the *eisteddfod,* the way she was dressed." Maggie laughed. "Still, I don't suppose there's much selection up in the wilds where you live."

"Oh, I don't think I could have done much better, even in the biggest city," Evan managed to say evenly. "And I must help Harry carry the drinks if you'll excuse me for a moment."

She grabbed at his arm again. "There's something I wanted to say to you," she whispered.

"I think you and I have already said pretty much all there is to say."

"Not about us. About rugby. Are you playing at all?"

Evan shook his head. "No time really."

"And no clubs worth playing for up there."

"Oh, I wouldn't say . . ."

"I would. Which is why Stew is doing something about it. You remember Stew Jenkins, do you? Used to play for Llanelli? Played for Wales a couple of times?"

"Of course I remember him. Good fullback."

"Well, he's involved in professional rugby now. You know, we've got several premier league teams down here. Not bad money either. Steve's thinking of starting a team up in your neck of the woods, in Bangor—if he can lure enough quality players up there. He thinks there's enough interest to get good crowds and make it pay."

Evan nodded. "Maybe, although they are more football fans than rugby in North Wales. Liverpool or Manchester United supporters."

Maggie had sidled even closer to him, so that he was conscious of the smell of her hair and the fact that her tank top revealed a good amount of cleavage. "I was telling Stevie about you. He thinks he may be able to use you, if you were interested?"

"Me?" To his great annoyance, Evan found himself blushing. "But I've been out of the rugby world for five years now."

"It's like riding a bicycle. You don't forget."

"Come on, Evans. What's happened to that beer?" a voice demanded from the tight clique around Bronwen.

"Call me if you're interested," Maggie said as she let him pass. "You know the number."

Evan shouldered his way through to the table and deposited the tray.

"So there you are, Stodge." Bronwen gave him a wicked grin. "You never told me you had a nickname."

"It came from school," one of the other men said before Evan could answer. "He was the only one who actually liked the food. He always used to want second helpings of spotted dick and treacle pud. Hence the name Stodge."

"And of course it did describe his girth too, didn't it?"

"He always was a hefty lad."

"You look like you've lost a little weight, old man." Another of them prodded him in the middle.

"I've been cooking for myself. Best diet I know," Evan said.

"And I'm trying to make sure he eats healthily," Bronwen added.

"So you're not playing any rugby at the moment?"

"Not at the moment. No."

"You want to come and warm up with us on Saturday? We're doing preseason conditioning."

"Thanks, but I won't be here on Saturday. Bronwen and I are going to visit her parents tomorrow."

"Visit the parents? Oooh, that sounds serious."

Evan could feel Bronwen looking at him, waiting for him to say something.

"We're planning to get married some time soon," he said and saw the appreciation in her eyes.

"Oh dear. Stodge is taking the plunge. Well, drink up, boys. That calls for another round."

It was late when they finally came out into the darkened street and stood in the halo of a street lamp while Evan located his keys.

"I hope that wasn't too much of an ordeal for you," he said, opening the door for her.

Bronwen gave him a dazzling smile as she climbed in. "Not at all. I found it very educational—Stodge."

He decided to say nothing about his talk with Maggie. There was no point.

When they got home they found Mrs. Evans sitting in the living room, watching TV.

"Had a nice evening, did you? That's good," she said mechanically. She got up. "Well, I think I'll go to bed now, then, if you don't mind. Help yourselves to cocoa."

"We shouldn't have gone out and left her, Evan," Bronwen whispered as they heard footsteps going up the stairs. "Did you notice she had been crying?"

Evan nodded. "You're right. I feel terrible. I thought taking her out might cheer her up, but I don't think she's ever going to get over my dad. I don't know what to do, Bronwen."

"There's nothing you can do," Bronwen said. "Unless you want to bring her to live with us when we have a house."

"It's noble of you to volunteer, but I don't think she'd come. As I said, she's very set in her ways—always was and it's worse now. Her routine is all she's got to hang on to." He glanced up the stairs. "I think I'll make her a cup of cocoa and take it up to her. It's no good trying to get her to talk, because she keeps very much to herself, but I should let her know that I'm there if she needs me."

A few minutes later, Evan knocked and pushed open his mother's bedroom door.

"I thought you might like a cup of hot milk to help you sleep," he said. "I've put a little brandy in it."

Mrs. Evans was still sitting, fully dressed, on the edge of her bed, staring out of the window. "Thank you. You're a good boy, Evan," she said. As he went to leave the room she turned to him. "They will get him this time, won't they? You will make sure they put him away this time."

Chapter 7

The next morning dawned amazingly warm and balmy. They had planned to drive to Bronwen's house that evening but had a whole day ahead of them. Evan wanted to do something for his mother and suggested taking a picnic to the seashore. Mrs. Evans didn't show the enthusiasm he had hoped for.

"The beach on a day like this? You must be out of your mind. All the beaches will be crawling with holidaymakers. English people, most of them."

"We can pack a picnic and go for a drive anyway," Evan said. "We'll keep going until we find a secluded spot. Come on, Ma. It will do you good to go out for a drive."

"I don't know why people like picnics," Mrs. Evans grumbled. "All ants and sand in the sandwiches." Still she insisted on making a huge pile of food for Evan to load into the car. They set off along the seafront down the Oystermouth Road in the direction of the Gower Peninsula.

"This is the wealthy part of town," Evan commented. "A lot of boys from my school used to live out here."

"Ashleigh Drive," Mrs. Evans said suddenly as they passed an area of large homes. "Wasn't that where Tony Mancini murdered that poor girl? I'm sure it was."

Evan glanced up at the big houses behind walls and hedges. "I wonder what made him come out here?" he asked himself out loud.

"Probably planning a bit of burglary, I shouldn't be surprised," his mother said. "Always up to no good, since he was a little boy."

Evan gave the road a second glance as they drove past. Why Alison Turnbull? he found himself wondering.

They stopped in the village of Oystermouth at the far end of the seafront drive. "We have to show Bronwen the old Mumbles pier," Evan said.

"Whatever for? Ugly, rusty old thing."

"Ma, it's a local landmark." Evan laughed. "And remember how Dad used to take me there fishing?"

"Not that you ever caught anything," Mrs. Evans said, chuckling. "I'll wait for you in the car then."

"Oh, come with us, Mrs. Evans," Bronwen insisted. "A little walk will do you good."

"No benches in sight and I'm not walking that far. Go on. Off you go. I'll be all right here."

"You see it's not easy," Evan said as they set off. "Come on then."

The promenade along the seafront was crowded with holidaymakers. They joined the crowd, negotiating the families pushing prams, old people trailing dogs, and children trailing candy floss.

"Did you know that the oldest passenger railway in the world used to run here," Evan said. "They closed it before I was born."

"I remember reading about it in my history books." Bronwen looked around with pleasure. "You wouldn't think this was only five miles from the city, would you? You must have come here a lot when you were young."

"Yes, but don't mention it to my mother. I was forbidden to come here, but my friends and I were always riding our bikes out here in summer for a quick swim. I was also forbidden to swim alone, so I had to dry my trunks by hanging them from the back of my bike."

"Quite a little rebel," Bronwen said.

Once past the village of Oystermouth, the path narrowed between steep sandy cliffs on one side and a stoney beach on the other. When they finally reached the pier, it had a derelict look to it and a sign out in front saying, SORRY, NO DOGS. SORRY NO BICYCLES. SORRY NO PICNICS.

"Miserable lot," Bronwen commented. "I don't think we should pay fifty pence to go on it, then, do you?" She slipped her arm through Evan's. "You're extra quiet today. Was it going to court yesterday that has upset you?"

Evan nodded. "I suppose it is. The whole thing has made me very uneasy. I can't stop thinking about it."

"It was bound to upset you," Bronwen said. "But the police sound pretty confident they'll put him away this time, don't they?"

"Yes. Yes they do." Evan blinked his eyes to shut out an image that wouldn't go away.

They turned around and headed back to the car.

"Oh look." Bronwen suddenly grabbed Evan's hand and dragged him across the street. "There's a shop that makes love spoons. We have to take a look."

"We shouldn't leave Mum alone for too long," Evan said as he allowed himself to be dragged into the shop. "Is this a hint you'd like me to buy you a love spoon? I thought an engagement ring was what you wanted. You'd find a spoon harder to put on your finger."

"Silly." Bronwen laughed. "No, I just wanted to take a look. I think this was such a romantic idea—carving a spoon in secret to show your love? That is true devotion, don't you think?"

They examined the intricately carved spoons, noting that the price on the best of them came close to that of a ring.

After that the day went downhill. The beaches around the Gower Peninsula were all so full of holidaymakers that parking was impossible.

"I warned you, didn't I?" Mrs. Evans said triumphantly. "Packed in like sardines, they are."

In the end they ate their sandwiches in a pub car park and drove home again. On the way home, again they passed the street that led to the Turnbull home. Evan tried to relax and join in the conversation that Bronwen was trying to hold with his mother, but he couldn't take his mind off Tony Mancini. When his mother indicated that she had to do some shopping and Bronwen offered to go with her, he took this as his cue and drove to the police station.

The new station was exactly as his mother had described—panels of bottle glass and purple tiles that made it look more like a swimming pool or a recreation center. He managed to park in an alley nearby. He spoke to a receptionist through a microphone in a glass wall and asked for Sergeant Howells. He was told to wait. It was stiflingly hot in that glass-fronted holding area. Obviously the designers of the new police station hadn't considered heat waves in their planning and hadn't installed air-conditioning. He had almost decided to give up and go home when Bill's head popped around the door.

"Hello, Evan. This is a surprise. I thought you were off."

"We are. We're going to Bronwen's parents later this afternoon, but I had a couple of questions, if you've got a minute."

"Well, come on in," Sergeant Howells said, waving him through the door. "I'm just about to take a break and go for a coffee. Want to come?"

"Thanks."

"So what's the problem?" Sergeant Howells asked as they left the station together and crossed the street to a café.

"It was being in court with Tony Mancini," Evan said. "I found it very unsettling. I was wondering—I know you're not on the official team for this case, but they do have enough evidence to prove that he did it, don't they?"

"Don't worry yourself about that. As luck would have it, one of our blokes picked up the kid on thc Oystcrmouth Road, only a few steps from the house, right about the time the medical examiner says she was killed. Our bloke recognized him, of course, and stopped to question him. He says the kid seemed flustered and couldn't give a good reason for being out there. I mean, what good reason would someone like Tony Mancini have for hanging around a posh area like that? He tried to say that Alison Turnbull was a mate of his, but we weren't buying it. That girl was treated like a china doll—wrapped in cotton wool all her life. Posh boarding school, riding lessons, never let out of their sight. So I don't know where Tony Mancini thought he might have met her. Then you add to that the motive—old man Turnbull sacked him because he caught him helping himself to the petty cash." He gave Evan a reassuring grin. "Don't you worry, old son. We've got him this time."

Later that afternoon Evan and Bronwen loaded up the car and got ready to leave Swansea.

"It wasn't much of a visit, was it?" Evan's mother said in a pained voice. "Here today, gone tomorrow."

"We can drop in on the way back, if you like," Evan found himself promising. "I know you don't like your routine being upset."

"Routine? Anyone would think I was an old fogie." Mrs. Evans sniffed as Evan tried to maneuver the lamb's crate onto the backseat. "And I don't know why you had to keep that poor lamb shut away all the time. It wasn't as if he was any trouble. Good as gold if you ask me, poor little thing."

"It's never easy," Evan said as they drove away. "It's always a little like walking on eggshells. I bet it will be a relief to get to your parents' house."

"Maybe," Bronwen said hesitantly.

"You don't think they'll take to me? Is that it?"

"Oh no. They'll make you feel very welcome. They are great at hospitality. They're really very nice people. Just a little—overwhelming. Best taken in small doses, I always think."

It was five o'clock when they left the motorway at Newport and drove on a smaller road toward Monmouth. They were in a green valley, dotted with peaceful farms. The fields had fat cows in them, and willows marked the banks of a meandering stream. Gentle hills rose on either side.

"Here we are," Bronwen directed. "Turn left here."

A narrow road crossed the river by a humpbacked bridge. They passed between brick gateposts and continued up a long gravel drive with spacious lawns on either side. A large house came into view, gracious but relatively modern redbrick. It had bay windows, and a conservatory had been built on one side.

"Where is everybody?" Bronwen commented as they stopped and opened the car doors.

As if in answer there was the sound of a fast-approaching vehicle. A sleek, racing green Jaguar came to a screeching halt, and a woman jumped out. She was also sleek—slim, wearing tailored slacks, an open-necked sage green shirt, and with neat, short-cropped graying blond hair.

"How terrible, darlings, you almost beat me to it," she called, running across to them. "We didn't think you'd get here until almost six. The traffic around Newport is beastly these days. So I thought I had time to pop into the village. Mrs. Todd forgot to pick up endive for the starter." She pronounced it *ahndeeve,* the French way. "And I don't know where Alan can have got to. I told him to be on the lookout for you, but you know he never listens to a thing I say. I bet he's playing with those horrible animals again. Did I tell you he's started a farm of all things? At his age, and with such poor timing too. We heard about the foot-and-mouth outbreak the day he brought home the last of his rams." She had reached them by this point and gave Bronwen a kiss on both cheeks. "But no matter, you're here now, and it's so lovely to see you. We've been positively dying for you to come. And you must be Evan. How lovely." She gave him the same treatment—a brushing kiss on both cheeks. "Well, don't stand there. Do come in. You must be dying for something to drink. It's so hot today, isn't it? I thought we'd have a bowl of Pimm's on the back lawn, unless of course you'd prefer tea; but I always think tea makes one so hot, although Alan, of course, claims that it's the reverse, and his family always drank tea in India to keep them cool, which is utter nonsense to me."

Bronwen gave Evan an I-told-you-so glance as her mother put an arm around both of them and shepherded them toward the house. Evan realized that neither of them had been allowed to say a word so far.

"We really ought not to leave Prince William in the car on a day like this," Evan dared to interrupt the monologue.

"Prince William?" Bronwen's mother looked amused. "Who have you got in there?" She peered into the backseat and saw the crate. "Oh, have you brought a pet with you?"

"It's a lamb, Mummy," Bronwen said. "I'm looking after it for one of the little girls in my school. He's awfully sweet and no trouble. I thought perhaps we could find somewhere to put him. . . ."

Bronwen's mother had already opened the rear door. "Of course we can. How absolutely adorable. Let's put him in the shade for now, and then we can think about it."

Evan extracted the crate from the car and left it in a deep pool of shade under a large tree.

"Let's have some refreshment before we get any of your luggage out," Mrs. Price suggested. "It's too hot to do anything today, isn't it? It reminds me of the time we were in Saudi. Unnaturally warm for Wales. My dears, I think the world climate is changing, don't you? I'll have to throw away my fur coats if this keeps up much longer."

They were swept in through a cool entrance hall decorated with an old oak chest, topped with a large vase of fresh flowers, then along a flagstoned hallway and out onto a back patio. A perfectly manicured lawn stretched down to the river. A large copper beech threw shade over part of it, and under the tree a white-clothed table had been set up, with lawn chairs around it.

"Go and sit down, darlings, and I'll find Daddy and drinks," Mrs. Price said.

Evan sank onto what looked like the sturdiest of the chairs. Bronwen glanced at him and gave him a reassuring grin. "Don't mind Mummy."

It was pleasant in the shade. Pigeons cooed from the branches above them. The air smelled of roses and freshly cut grass. Evan felt the tension of the past days slipping away. Then from the house came a great explosion of sound—a man's voice raised angrily. "Of all the bloody stupid ideas! Where are they? It's not staying here!"

Evan sat up hastily as a large man wearing a bush jacket, shorts, and hiking boots came storming out of the house.

"This bloody lamb, Bronwen," he bellowed as he caught sight of her. "What on earth possessed you to bring a bloody lamb with you?"

Bronwen got to her feet. "And hello to you too, Daddy," she said calmly. "I brought it because it is a pet lamb and it would have been slaughtered."

"You must have taken leave of your senses." Mr. Price's voice was still at maximum volume. "Didn't your mother tell you that I've started a farm here? You could be bringing the bloody foot-and-mouth with you, for Christ's sake."

Bronwen went over to him and put her hand gently on his arm. "Would you please calm down, Daddy. You're making Evan nervous."

Mr. Price seemed to notice him for the first time and nodded to him. "What? Oh yes. How do you do. Nice to meet you." He swung back to Bronwen. "It will have to go, you know. It can't stay here."

"If you'd listen for a moment, Daddy. It has been a house pet. It hasn't even been with the other sheep. And it's going to stay in the house while we're here. We can keep it in the laundry room, if you like."

"You'd bloody well better. Do you know what I'm attempting to do on my farm, Bronny? I'm rescuing rare breeds of sheep—the old breeds that might become extinct if someone doesn't keep them going. Two of those breeds are down to seven or eight specimens in the entire country. And your little lamb might just wipe out the whole damned lot."

"It won't, Daddy, I promise," Bronwen said.

"And what about your boots, eh?" He scowled at Bronwen and Evan's feet. "And the car tires? Have you driven through disinfectant or are you carrying bloody infected soil with you?"

"We've driven through Swansea in the rain, which I imagine is pretty much the same thing," Bronwen said. "Do stop worrying, Daddy."

Mr. Price gave a sigh. "It's bad enough knowing that this rotten disease is working its way toward us and there's not a damned thing we can do about it," he said in a quieter voice.

"Do stop blustering and serve some drinks, Alan." Bronwen's mother appeared again, carrying a big glass bowl of amber liquid, on which floated a variety of flowers. Evan's first thought was that this was the table decoration, until he saw Mr. Price dip a ladle into it and fill a tall glass. "Here you are. Get that inside you." He handed the first glass to Evan.

"I'll be back with the canapés." Mrs. Price disappeared back into the house.

Evan pushed a violet aside and sipped his drink. He had thought that the encounter with his mother would be the difficult part of the trip. Now he wasn't so sure.

"I hope you don't mind," Bronwen's mother said as she shepherded them back into the house and led them upstairs to their rooms, "but I've invited some people to dinner."

"Oh, Mummy, not one of your dinner parties," Bronwen complained.

"Only a few people, darling." Mrs. Price sounded hurt. "The Fearnalls were dying to see you again. You remember them, don't you? They've got that lovely manor house across the valley. And then we owed the Davies a dinner so this seemed a good way to take care of them."

"I'm sorry about this," Bronwen whispered to Evan as her mother disappeared down the stairs, leaving them alone. "My mother is horribly social. We're just lucky it isn't a full-scale party."

"I expect I'll survive," Evan said, stroking back a wisp of her ash blond hair. "Just as long as she doesn't start planning a big wedding."

"Oh, she's bound to," Bronwen said. "Our only escape will be to elope."

"Have you actually told them we're getting married?"

"Not outright. I might have dropped a hint, and my mother is very good at picking up clues."

Evan sighed. "So what am I supposed to wear for dinner tonight? I didn't bring my dinner jacket."

"Nothing like that, silly. I expect Daddy will wear a blazer. Your blue shirt will be just fine."

Evan put on the blue shirt as directed, but still felt uncomfortably underdressed when he saw that the other men were all wearing jackets in spite of the warm evening.

"Here they are." Bronwen's mother ran to drag Evan and Bronwen toward the company. "You know our daughter Bronwen, don't you, and this is her young man Evan."

Hands were shaken. Pleasantries were murmured. Sherry and whiskies were poured. Mrs. Price produced more canapés—bacon wrapped around kidneys, cheese straws, potted shrimp spread on toast.

"So we understand that you're a policeman up in the wilds of North Wales, young man," the distinguished-looking man with iron gray hair, who had been introduced to him as Tom Fearnall, turned to Evan. "Don't imagine there's much crime up there among all those sheep."

"You'd be surprised, actually," Evan began.

"Evan has been instrumental in solving several murders," Bronwen finished for him.

"I suppose there is a lot of inbreeding, and people go peculiar shut away among all those mountains." The scrawny woman with three rows of pearls around a chicken neck gave the others a knowing smirk. This had to be Mrs. Davies, the other man's wife.

"Actually all the murders have been of outsiders. Nothing to do with our village," Evan said.

"I suppose that makes sense. It's only the big cities that produce really horrible violence, isn't it?" Mrs. Price suggested as she handed around another tray of warm cheese straws. "You've just come from Swansea, haven't you? Is everyone talking about that nasty murder there? We've been following it on the telly. She was the daughter of a prominent family, so I gather. A woman I play golf with actually knows the mother. The poor things. What they must be going through."

"I heard on the news that they caught the blighter," Tom Fearnall said.

"Evan was at the courtroom yesterday," Bronwen spoke up before Evan could warn her to keep quiet. "The man they've arrested was the same one who shot Evan's father. They let him out because he was a young offender. Isn't that stupid?"

They were all instantly alert. "How frightfully interesting. He shot your father? Absolutely beastly for you. At least they've got him this time."

Evan forced a half smile to his face and answered all their questions, wishing himself anywhere else.

"And didn't I read that he's some kind of foreigner?" Mrs. Davies demanded.

"An immigrant, you mean? Not another one!" Mrs. Price rolled her eyes. "They are everywhere these days. You will never guess who has just bought that great big house on the other side of the river, Bronny. He's a Pakistani grocer, my dear. We nearly died when we heard, didn't we, Sybil?"

Mrs. Fearnall nodded.

"Then we wondered what he'd do when the hunt wants to cross his land." Tom Fearnall gave a hearty laugh. "I can't see him riding to hounds with the rest of us, can you?"

"Do you think he'd hunt in his turban?" Mrs. Davies shrieked with laughter.

"Those are the Sikhs, darling. Different chappies altogether," her husband corrected her.

Drinks were finished and they were ushered to the dining table, spread with white cloth, crystal, and silver. Bronwen's mother darted around like a diligent bird, putting plates before them, whisking them away again—endive salad, poached sole with shrimp and grapes, then a magnificent piece of beef with individual Yorkshire puddings, new potatoes and homegrown runner beans, marrow, and peas. The food tasted wonderful, but Evan was so completely on guard the whole time that he found it hard to eat. He had always known that Bronwen came from a background different from his. She had been to Cambridge, and her folks were at least middle class. But he had no idea that the gulf between them was so wide. The whole conversation was outside of his sphere of experience. He might as well have been seated in a yurt in Outer Mongolia.

"No seconds, Evan?" Mrs. Price asked. "Go on. Don't be shy." She put another large slice of meat onto his plate and heaped vegetables around it.

"And how is that adorable grandson of yours?" Mrs. Fearnall asked.

Bronwen's mother stopped serving and beamed. "We're going up to London to see him next week. I understand he's grown so much we'll hardly recognize him."

"Has your daughter gone back to work?"

"Yes, she has. But they've got an absolutely fabulous nanny and little Dominic adores her. Gillian hates to leave the baby, but when you have a practice like hers, you can't stay away too long. She has so many patients who only want to be seen by her. The price of being so successful, I'm afraid. And her husband has just been made a partner in his law firm. They're thinking of buying a house in the country. Goldalming, maybe."

"Stockbroker belt, eh?" Tom Fearnall commented. "That will cost them a pretty penny."

"I don't think pennies are a problem for them," Alan Price said as he reached across to pour more wine. "Rolling in dough from what we can see. You should see that child's nursery. Every gadget known to man in there."

Evan looked up and caught Bronwen's eye. She made a face, and he suddenly sensed that she was as uncomfortable as he was. As they moved away from the table to take coffee in the drawing room she drew to his side. "I knew we wouldn't get through dinner without extolling the praises of my wonderful sister, Gillian, the orthopedic surgeon, and her highly successful husband, the lawyer. I'm a great disappointment to them, as you can imagine."

"Even more so now that you're marrying me, I should imagine," Evan muttered into her ear.

"Don't say that. It proves that I've shown one morsel of good sense during my life of horribly wrong decisions."

"They should come and see you at your school." Evan put his arm around her. "They should see how much good you do."

"Ah, but it doesn't pay well, does it? That is the criterion by which things are measured."

Evan squeezed her tighter. "What do we care? We like where we live and what we do."

Bronwen beamed up at him. "You're right. To hell with the lot of them."

Chapter 8

Evan couldn't sleep. The moon shone directly onto his bed through the net curtains. Even with the windows open, it was still warm in the room. He got up and walked across to the window. From outside came a symphony of night noises—crickets, frogs, the faraway barking of a dog, the hooting of an owl. He jumped as a white shape loomed from the darkness until he realized it was the owl, gliding on silent wings from the copper beech. He felt tense and uneasy, as if something momentous was about to happen. He longed for the solid reality of Bronwen's arms around him. He wished they hadn't put him in a room at the far end of the hall.

"What's wrong with me?" he asked himself. It was obvious that he felt uncomfortable in these surroundings. Bronwen's parents had been gracious and welcoming and given no hint that they were disappointed in their daughter's choice. However, there was no denying that Bronwen's background was very different from the life he was about to offer her. Would she ever regret rejecting the pampered life of her upbringing? he wondered. It was true that she had chosen to live in a cramped old-fashioned schoolhouse and to teach twenty-five village children, but had she really planned to spend the rest of her life in humble surroundings? What if she was just playing at village schoolteacher until the novelty wore off?

Evan moved away from the window and paced the room. Why should this be bothering him so much? He had been brought up by his father to believe he was as good as the next bloke. He wasn't the sort to go around with a chip on his shoulder.

Evan paused. His father. Something about his father was troubling him. Obviously going to court had inflamed an old wound in his heart. He sat at the foot of his bed and went through that courtroom scene again in his mind. He saw that skinny, dark kid acting the innocent again. They had been unlucky with their judge last time. Tony had claimed it was all an accident, he hadn't meant to kill anybody, and the softhearted judge had believed him. The judge had told the court he was willing to believe that there was good in the boy and that he had a chance of rehabilitation. He was therefore sending him to a young offenders institute. Evan remembered the horrified intake of breath and his mother exclaiming, "Five years? Five years for my husband's life?"

The anger that he had bottled up for five years came boiling to the surface. What if Tony managed to con his way out of this one too? He had managed to persuade his employer not to press charges when he was caught stealing at the factory. He was good at knowing how to press the right buttons and play the misguided wayward child. Bill Howells had seemed confident enough, hadn't he? And yet when Evan analyzed what he had been told, it all seemed like circumstantial evidence. Tony had a grudge against Turnbull for firing him. Tony was caught running away from the scene of the crime at about the time the medical examiner said the girl had been murdered. But, as far as he knew, Tony hadn't confessed to anything.

Evan felt a sudden chill going down his spine. He had to do something to help ensure that Tony Mancini did confess. He couldn't just stay here, wasting his time having inane conversation over bowls of Pimm's while his mother was going through hell at home. He needed to be occupied, working on the case. He should go back to Swansea right away.

"It's none of your business," he told himself. "The South Wales Police know what they are doing. They won't want you interfering, so go back to bed and get some sleep." He climbed into bed, but sleep wouldn't come. He lay there until the night noises were replaced by the first crow of a rooster, the dawn chorus in the woods beyond the river, then by a cold light coming in through the window. Then he got up again and pulled on his robe against the early morning chill. One thing had become perfectly clear to him. He would never find peace until he confronted Tony Mancini. He had to face him and tell him what a mess he had made of other peoples' lives. Surely the local police would grant him that request, and perhaps talking to Tony might help with this case. It was too much to hope that it might result in a real confession, but it might help to break him down a little. He left his room and tiptoed down the hall to Bronwen's door.

For a long moment he stood there, watching her sleep. Her fair hair was spread across the pillow like a princess in a fairy tale. She looked so peaceful and beautiful that it almost took his breath away. He couldn't believe that she had chosen him. Then he reached out and touched her bare shoulder gently. "Bron," he whispered.

She woke with a start, sitting up and staring up at him in alarm. "What is it?" Then a smile spread across her face. "Oh, it's you. I don't think you're supposed to come creeping into your fiancée's bedroom, you know. It's not done in the best of circles."

He sat on the bed beside her and caressed her shoulder. "My intentions are quite honorable."

"Pity."

"Look, Bron, I've been up all night thinking. And I've decided I have to go back to Swansea right away."

The smile faded from her face. "Why—what's happened? You haven't decided not to marry me because of my ghastly family, have you?"

"Of course not. And on levels of ghastliness, I think my mum is still one step above your folks. They've been very nice to me, which is more than I can say for my mother."

"But you're still escaping. I know you don't feel very comfortable here. I don't either. I can't stand the thought of a week of sherry parties and croquet on the lawn."

"I can't say I was looking forward to it too much, but I would have stuck it out for your sake. Who knows, I might have learned to like sherry." He took both her shoulders and turned her toward him. "Look, I've decided I can't just sit here doing nothing. I'm worried Tony Mancini will be let off again. From what I've heard they only have circumstantial evidence, Bron. Any good lawyer could get him off. I can't let that happen."

"Oh, and what do you think you can do about it? Evan the great detective finds the missing evidence that has eluded the local police? That won't make you very popular."

"Nothing like that." Evan gave a nervous chuckle. "I just want to be involved in some way. I need to feel I'm doing something for my dad. I was useless last time I know. I was so shocked and stunned that I was no use to anybody, especially not to my mum when she needed me. I'm ashamed of myself, Bron. I want to make it up to everyone."

"Of course you were upset last time. You were grieving for your dad, Evan."

"But now I get the chance to do my part. I want them to let me talk to Tony Mancini. If I could make him see how his actions have wrecked lives, maybe I could do some good."

"You think he's going to take one look at you, then break down and repent? Isn't that rather naïve, Evan?"

"No, I don't think that," Evan snapped. "Look, maybe I need to do it for me then. I've been carrying around all this anger for five years. Maybe it will help me get some peace of mind at last."

"If it helps you find peace, that's different," she said. "But I'm not sure you'll get the result you want. This is a kid who has been in trouble with the law all his life. You may find yourself coming away angrier than you started."

"That's a risk I have to take. I have to do it, Bron."

Bronwen shifted away from him. "I still think it's an excuse to go running out of here, leaving me alone."

"I'll be back as soon as I can. I promise. And you'll have fun. I expect your mother will hastily arrange tennis parties to try and match you up with someone more suitable before it's too late."

Bronwen threw herself into his arms. "You are silly. And infuriating. Why do you always have to do your duty like some bloody Lord Nelson!"

A discreet cough behind them made them turn around. Mrs. Price stood there with two cups of tea in her hands. "I had a feeling I might just find you both in here," she said with a knowing grin on her face. "I should have been a little more thoughtful and modern, shouldn't I. I'll have Mrs. Todd make up the double bed in the blue guest room tonight—only don't tell Daddy. He's still rather old-fashioned about such things."

She put down the cups of tea and tiptoed out again, closing the door carefully behind her.

"There you are," Bronwen said. She had gone rather pink. "You have Mummy's blessing."

"Damn," Evan muttered. "I spent a whole night trying to sleep alone, not wanting to risk your reputation. And now I'm off to Swansea to that lumpy mattress at my mother's house."

Bronwen glanced at the door. "It's very early still, and she did close the door behind her."

"It's your parents' house, Bronwen. And your father is old-fashioned about such things, remember."

"My father also goes out walking with the dogs at the crack of dawn." She turned back the sheet and patted the bed beside her. "And I'm feeling very cold."

Evan didn't need inviting twice.

Chapter 9

There were a dozen times during the two-hour drive that Evan decided to turn back. His hasty departure had been well received by Bronwen's parents, who obviously thought he was escaping from their carefully planned social schedule. When he finally found a parking spot in a back street behind Kingsway and cut through an alley to the police station, his feet felt as heavy as lead. What did he think he was doing here? Bronwen was right. It was none of his business. The DCI would probably think he was poking his nose in and not take kindly to any offer to help. But it was too late to turn back now.

He asked for DCI Vaughan and was told he was out on a case. Evan could wait if he liked. He joined the ranks of those in the aquariumlike waiting area. From time to time the door opened and various people from the benches were summoned into the inner sanctum. Some went willingly, others glanced around uncertainly before they stepped through that doorway. That was the interesting thing about police stations, Evan thought. You never knew which side of the law anyone was on. He took out his handkerchief and mopped his forehead. It really was extremely hot in there.

After a while Bill Howells came through the door.

"Well, look who's here. I thought you were off yesterday. We can't get rid of you, can we?"

"I decided to come back. I'm here for a word with DCI Vaughan," Evan said.

"Oh yes?" Bill Howells held the door open for Evan to go through.

Evan waited to speak until they were alone in the hallway beyond. "Actually what I'd like to do is talk to Tony Mancini. Do you think they'd let me see him? I never got that chance before."

"I don't see why not," Bill said. "I can ask the DCI for you, if you'd like. The kid's not going anywhere. Just cooling his heels in the jail. Of course you'd like to talk to him"—he nudged Evan in the side—"and if you delivered a little justice of your own—a quick knee where it would make him sing boy soprano—I don't think anyone would mind too much. We all felt pretty bad about your dad, you know. And that little fart walking out free and cocky after a couple of years playing Ping-Pong and weaving baskets. It's about time he got what was coming to him."

"I just want to talk to him, Bill," Evan said. "Five years ago I'd have given anything for the chance to beat him up, but not now. I'm over that stage."

Bill Howells glanced around. "Not everyone around here is over it, I can tell you. The DCI had to take certain members of the force off the case because he couldn't trust what they might do if they found themselves alone with Tony. He wants to make sure it's all done strictly by the book. He doesn't want any loopholes for that little weasel to wriggle through."

"That's another thing that's got me worried," Evan said. "The evidence you've given me doesn't seem too strong so far. Are they holding back their trump cards, do you think?"

"Don't ask me. I'm not part of Vaughan's Major Crimes team, but I tell you one thing, boyo, he's a good bloke, Vaughan. He knows his stuff."

As if on cue, the door behind them swung open and DCI Vaughan himself strode through, with several members of his team in his wake, like ducklings hurrying to keep up with the mother duck. As they turned the other way, Bill Howells called out to him and introduced Evan. The frown lines softened on the older man's face as he shook Evan's hand.

"Robert Evans's son? That's right. You spoke up in court. Good of you to come. It couldn't have been easy for you. You used to be on the force here, didn't you?"

"Yes, sir."

"But you'd had enough after what happened to your father. I can understand that."

"I'm with the North Wales Police now," Evan said. "Just about to start training with the plainclothes division."

"North Wales Police? Good God. What on earth took you up there?"

"It's a long way from down here."

"So you're up among the sheep?" The older man smiled.

"Yes, sir."

"Well, I suppose you don't have to put up with the rubbish we get down here. Your father was a good man. I started out under him in this very manor. But don't you worry. We're doing everything we can to nail the little bastard this time."

"I was wondering, sir." Evan paused and took a deep breath. "Would it be possible for me to speak to Mancini? I never got that chance before, and it's something I feel I need to do."

"Yes, I can understand that," DCI Vaughan said. He paused, staring long and hard at Evan. "It will all have to be done through the proper channels and with his solicitor's permission, but I don't see any problem there. They've appointed him a little squirt still wet behind the ears. Doesn't know his arse from his elbow if you ask me. So you go and tell him you're there with my permission. Only, Evan—keep your hands to yourself, won't you. At least if anyone is watching."

"Don't worry, sir. I'll behave myself. Oh, and sir? I know this investigation is none of my business, but if there's anything I could do to help . . . I need to feel I'm doing something, if you can understand that."

"Of course you do. We all do. Believe me, everyone in the South

Wales Police wants to nail the little bastard this time. So go and talk to him, and Evans, you're welcome to ride along if you like."

Evan's face lit up in a big smile. "Thanks very much, sir."

He felt energized and hopeful as he made his way to the solicitor's office in one of the few older buildings left on Kingsway. Swansea had been badly bombed in the war, and there weren't many old buildings in the city center. The young solicitor wasn't listed as a partner and had a small office off a dark upstairs hallway. He glanced up from a crowded desk when Evan came in and in the subdued light looked little older than a schoolboy. "Richard Brooks. Do sit down. You're Robert Evans's son?" He made a face. "Funny, but Tony asked to see you. Maybe it's been playing on his conscience all this time and he wants to make amends. I hope so. It's something we can bring up for the jury if he does apologize to you."

"They have a strong case against him, do they?" Evan asked.

The young solicitor made a face again, the sort of face fifth-formers make when asked a particularly tough question they don't know how to answer. "I am not privy to what evidence they have against Tony, but I do understand that they are sure they've got their man. Tony, of course, maintains his innocence."

"And you believe him?"

"I'm his solicitor. I have to believe him."

"And if you weren't his solicitor?"

The young man shrugged. "He's not the easiest of clients. It's hard to know when he's telling the truth. Of course, I'll do my best for him. I'm currently trying to get a top-notch barrister to represent him, but of course we can't pay the fees they expect." He got to his feet. "So, when do you want to visit Tony? I will naturally have to come with you."

"Whenever you are free," Evan said. "But will it be possible to speak to him alone? I'll report to you if he says anything that could help his case."

"I suppose that will be all right." He looked hard at Evan, assessing him, then nodded again. "Yes, I think it will be all right. Later this afternoon then."

Evan got to his feet. "Thank you. It's very kind of you."

The solicitor managed a weak smile. "Let's hope it may be a turning point for Tony, because frankly I don't see much hope for him."

Evan stopped off at his mother's house and had to endure a long interrogation session as to why he had come back alone, without Bronwen.

"Are you sure she hasn't thrown you over?" she asked more than once. "She's a high-class girl. Anyone can see that. Although she speaks a lovely Welsh."

"No, Ma, she hasn't thrown me over. I've just got some things I have to do here. I'll be going back to her parents' house tomorrow, probably."

"I've already washed the sheets from your bed," his mother said accusingly. "Now I suppose you're going to make them dirty again."

"I'll sleep on the sofa."

"Indeed you will not. You think I can't provide a warm welcome for my own son?"

Evan sighed and went upstairs to make up his bed.

A clock somewhere on the hill was chiming four as Evan and Richard Brooks walked together down to the waterfront and approached the impressive wall that surrounded the prison. Once inside the main gate, they were searched then led across a narrow yard. Beside the original gray stone rectangle, there was a newer octagonal unit that looked like an overgrown chapel. It was to this unit that they were led. They were shown into a windowless interview room equipped with a table and two chairs. After a few minutes the door opened and Tony Mancini was brought in. When he saw Evan he reacted nervously.

"What's he doing here?"

"He wanted to speak to you," the solicitor said.

"Sit." The guard pointed at a chair on one side of the table.

"You can't make me." Tony struck a defiant pose. "I haven't even been tried yet, and I'm innocent until proved guilty. I know the law."

"You will be. Sit." The guard put a big hand on his shoulder. Tony's eyes darted around the room as he perched on the edge of the chair.

"I don't have to speak to him if I don't want to. I don't have to talk to no one."

"You wanted to the other day," the solicitor said.

"Yeah, well, I changed my mind." He eyed Evan defiantly.

"Can you leave us alone for a while?" Evan asked. The solicitor nodded and indicated for the guard to leave.

"Hey, I said I didn't want to talk to him. Are you fucking deaf?"

The door shut behind them. The place smelled of disinfectant with just a hint of latrines; it brought back memories of the boys' bathroom at Evan's primary school, a place where bigger boys had waited to bully skinny undersized kids like himself.

Tony's posture indicated he expected to be picked on in the same way. "You better not touch me," he said. "You lay a hand on me and you'll be sorry."

"Not as sorry as you'd be. I'm a lot bigger than you." Evan's gaze challenged him.

"You'd be laughing on the other side of your face if I was carrying my knife."

Evan pulled up a chair to the other side of the table. "Look, Tony, I'm not here to attack you, so just relax."

"Then what are you here for?"

"Why did you want to see me?" Evan countered.

"Because—Forget it."

"I'm here because I never got a chance to talk to you earlier," Evan said. "I just needed to tell you that you messed up my mom's life and my life too."

"Look, mate, I told you. I never meant to kill nobody."

"You fired the gun."

"I was lookout man, see. Jingo gave me the gun and yelled for me to shoot. I pulled the trigger. I didn't expect to hit no one."

"Who's Jingo?"

"A bloke I used to know."

"I didn't think he was prime minister. In a gang together, were you?"

"Something like that."

"So where was this gang?"

"Up in Penlan. You're not nobody up in Penlan if you don't belong to a gang." Penlan, Evan remembered, was the toughest of the council estates, sprawling in ugly rows across the hills at the back of the city. "And what happened to Jingo?"

"Nothing. He's still around. Why?"

"Are you still with the gang?"

"Nah. Been going straight, haven't I? Good little boy, and all that."

"You still live up in Penlan?"

"No, I bloody moved out to a mansion on the Gower. What do you think?"

Evan felt his hand curl into a fist beneath the table. He breathed deeply. "So you didn't mean to kill anyone. What about this time? Was that an accident too—an 'accidental' rape and murder?"

"This time?" Tony glared at him defiantly. "I told you, I didn't do it. They're trying to nail it on me, but I didn't do it. I liked Alison. She was all right."

"You knew her then?"

"Of course I fucking knew her."

"Watch your language, boy. You're talking to a police officer."

"You're a fu—, a copper too?"

"Yes, and I'm getting tired of putting up with your mouth. In fact I'm getting tired of you. You deserve everything you bloody well get."

He got to his feet then controlled himself and sat down again. "Tell me about Alison. How did you know her? She doesn't sound like your sort of girl."

"We met clubbing on a Friday night."

"Clubbing—where?"

"The Monkey's Uncle on Kingsway."

"Alison's parents let her go to the Monkey's Uncle?"

Tony smirked. "Of course not, stupid. They didn't let her go nowhere. She used to climb out of her window and get picked up by a friend's car. She was a nice little dancer. A nice kid. I liked her."

"What were you doing out by her house that night?"

"I went out there to give her something. Something I'd promised her."

"So what happened? Did you see her?"

"Yeah. I saw her. I met her out in her front garden, but only for a moment. Then she said she heard someone coming and I'd better beat it. She said her father set the dog on people he didn't like, so I nipped through a gap in the hedge, pretty lively, like."

"And did you see who was coming?"

"I heard her speaking to someone. I've no idea who."

"So she was alive and safe in her own front garden when you left her."

"That's right."

"What time was this?"

"Around nine-thirty, I suppose."

"And what did you do then?"

"Me—I was running to get the bus on the Oystermouth Road, when some fu—some sodding copper recognized me. He stopped me and wanted to know what I was doing out there. I told him it was a free country and to mind his own sodding business. Then he let me go. In the morning they came to get me. That's when I heard she was dead."

"And you didn't see anybody near her house?"

"Have you been out there at night? It's the middle of bloody nowhere. Only one streetlight and her house is up a long drive. I didn't see a soul."

"So if you didn't kill her, who did?"

"Search me. You're the policeman, mate."

"Any idea who might have wanted her dead? Did she ever talk to you about being afraid of anybody—a boyfriend she had dumped, maybe?"

"We never talked much. It's too loud to talk in the club."

"What about her friends? What do you know about them?"

"Oh yeah, of course I knew her friends. We hobnobbed together at the bleedin' country club every Saturday night, didn't we? What do you think? I had no idea who she was until she told me where she lived. That's when I found out that old man Turnbull was her father."

"The one who sacked you from his factory for stealing?"

"I didn't take nothing."

"Then why were you sacked?"

"The foreman sent me up to Turnbull's office. He wasn't there. I was just taking a little look around for myself, curious like, when he came in, and he blew his stack. Sacked me on the spot. Never gave me a chance to explain—just like the rest of them. Well, I tell you this. I'm sorry Alison's dead, but I'm glad that bastard got what was coming to him. Let's see how happy he is with all that money now he doesn't have his precious little darling daughter."

He glared at Evan defiantly. When Evan said nothing, he went on. "She hated their guts, you know. Her parents. She couldn't stand them. She said they treated her like a little kid, and they wouldn't let her out of their sight. As soon as she turned eighteen, she was going to move to London and never come back."

They sat there in silence.

"She was nice," Tony said. "Easy to talk to. Not at all snooty like some of them posh birds you meet. I hope they catch the bastard that did it. Of course, they won't even bother to look, will they?"

Evan stared at him long and hard. "So you want me to believe that Alison was alive when you left her that night."

"Believe what you like, mate. It don't matter to me. Nothing you say is going to make them change their minds. They're out to get me."

"Why should I say anything?"

"Of course you wouldn't, would you? I bet you're really happy about this."

Evan got to his feet. "I'd better be going."

"Yeah. Go on. Bugger off."

"If you take my advice, you'll act politely when anyone comes to question you. The way you act has guilty written all over you."

"Oh, piss off," Tony said.

Evan sighed and left the room.

Chapter 10

Evan came out of the prison to find that the hot weather had broken and dark clouds were rolling in from the west. About the average length for a usual Welsh summer, he thought, Two days of sunshine and then more bloody rain. He felt the pressure of the approaching storm echoing the tension in his head. Why on earth did he have to go and visit Tony Mancini? Bronwen was right. The encounter hadn't brought him any closure—instead it had opened a whole new can of worms. Not that he believed Tony was telling the truth. He was known as a convincing liar. He'd conned the judge at his last trial easily enough. But now a seed of doubt was planted and wouldn't go away.

He drove straight home and called Bronwen.

"You've got a lot to answer for," she exploded before he could say anything. "I had to endure one of Mummy's lunch parties today. They'd all come to meet you, so I had to face them alone. Not something I'd have chosen to do. I had to listen to what a delightful chap Edward had been and how they couldn't understand why we broke up."

"So you never told them the real reason?"

"Would you have told my mother that my husband ran off with another man? It would have been poor naïve Bronwen. We'd better find a more suitable chap for her next time."

"So I gather I didn't measure up."

"I wouldn't say that. They think you must be delightfully quaint. A village copper. Mr. Plod. They were devastated that you weren't there. I told them you were called away on an important case you were solving and you'd be back soon. I hope that's true."

"I don't know, Bron. I went to see Tony this afternoon."

"And?"

"And I've never met anybody I'd like to send to prison more than him. He's an obnoxious little twit. His own worst enemy."

"So are you glad you went?"

"No. He says he didn't do it."

"Well, he would, wouldn't he?"

"Yes, but . . ."

"And you said he's a great con artist. Don't tell me you believed him, Evan?"

"No, of course I didn't." Evan attempted an easy laugh. "He's going to get what's coming to him and serve him right. It's just that—I need to find out for myself, one way or the other."

"And if it's the other?"

"I'm not sure. I'm really not sure."

"It's not up to you, Evan," Bronwen said. "Why don't you just come back here and suffer beside me? We've got sherry at the Fearnalls tomorrow. And Daddy's dying to show you his rare sheep—oh, and speaking of sheep, we've had problems with Prince William, I'm afraid."

"You mean our adopted son hasn't been behaving himself?"

Bronwen laughed. "Daddy is paranoid that Prince William will get out and infect his precious darlings. And we forgot to warn Mrs. Todd that he was shut up in the laundry. She went in with a load of washing, dropped it on top of him without looking, then thought the place was haunted. She had to be calmed down with a large brandy."

Evan chuckled.

"I miss you," she said simply. "I wish you'd give this up and come back."

After he had hung up, Evan felt uneasy, unsettled. He drifted from room to room until his mother summoned him to supper.

"I had a chance to pop out and get your favorite, liver and bacon," she said, putting in front of him a plate piled with three slices of lamb liver swimming in rich brown gravy, adorned with fried onions and rashers of bacon. This was completed by mashed potatoes, peas, cauliflower, and marrow. He was reminded of Mrs. Williams, his former landlady, and found himself wishing he was back in Llanfair, before any of this painful business had started.

"But you don't usually have a big meal in the evening," he said.

"I knew you'd be hungry and needing a good meal." She smiled, pleased to have done something right.

Evan tucked into the food, feeling comforted by his mother's cooking.

"This is very good," he said. "You always were a good cook."

"No one to cook for these days, so I don't bother much," she said, deliberately looking away from him.

"I went to see Tony Mancini today." The words came out before he had a chance to decide if he should have told her or not.

"That devil—you went to see him? Why in God's name?"

"I just felt that I needed to talk to him. I never had the chance before."

"I hope you told him just what you thought of him and how he wrecked so many lives and how he's going straight to hell if he doesn't shape up and repent."

Evan smiled. "I didn't exactly say that."

"So that's why you came back here? To see him?"

"I want to see if they'll let me work on the case," he said.

His mother actually smiled. "Your father would have been proud of you. You make sure he didn't die in vain, Evan."

He felt uncomfortably full when he got up from the table. "I think I might just pop down to the pub," he said.

He could detect the instant frost in the air. "No wonder you're not able to save up for a new car if you spend all your money drinking at the pub," his mother said. "You'll not be popping out to the pub every night when you're married, I can tell you that. She'll make sure you stay home."

"I won't be long."

Evan went out into the moist evening air. A fine rain was falling, hardly more than a mist. Clouds clung to the hilltops and blotted out the far side of the bay. He started down the hill toward the pub. When he got close he heard the sound of loud voices and laughter and pulled up short. He didn't feel in the mood to be jolly. And Maggie might be there. He really didn't want to face her again. He crossed the street and walked by on the other side. As he walked, he remembered his conversation with Maggie. So much had happened that he had pushed it from his mind until now. Could she really think that he might play professional rugby for the new team in Bangor? He'd been a pretty handy rugby player in his day, but he hadn't played seriously for five years now. He was over thirty. Ridiculous. And yet the thought gnawed at him. Professional rugby players made good money—much better than police constables. If he was about to embark on a new life with a wife and a family, shouldn't he at least consider it?

He broke into a jog. He'd need to get in shape, and that wouldn't be easy. He pumped his legs faster but only managed to go one more block before he was out of breath. Obviously some serious training would be needed before he tried out for the team. He walked back up the hill, making a mental training schedule in his head.

"That was quick," his mother commented when he got home.

"You were right. I am drinking too much beer," he said. He went through the house and out to the shed at the bottom of the garden. With any luck his old weight set would still be there and he could pump a little iron before he went to bed. His upper body muscles would need toning if he wanted to be of any use in a scrum again. In the orange light of a nearby street lamp he found the weights exactly as he had left them. A bar with weights on it rested on the stand. When he tried to pick it up, he found he couldn't even move it. To his shame he had to exchange the weights several times before he could get the wretched thing off the stand.

"Who am I fooling?" he asked himself. He'd never manage to get back into rugby playing shape again. It was all downhill after you turned thirty. There were plenty of fitter chaps. They wouldn't want him.

Then he chided himself for such negative thoughts. If he'd been able to lift those weights before, there was no reason why he couldn't do so again. He'd take them back in the car with him and work on them every morning. And he'd start running faithfully too. It would be a good challenge. He'd been getting soft for too long.

As he stood there thinking in the darkness, he became aware of where he was. The old familiar smells reached his nostrils—the sawdust from his father's workbench, the rich aroma of potting soil, fertilizer, and long-ago mown grass, together with his father's brand of tobacco. They all lingered, almost too faint to notice. He breathed deeply and stood staring at the workbench, willing his father to appear there before his eyes. "I wish you were here," he whispered. "I still need you."

All his father's tools still hung in their places as if he'd never been gone. A big box of pieces of wood stood beside the bench. His father was a thrifty man who refused to throw anything away. The wood gave Evan an idea. He rummaged around and came up with a nice smooth piece of darkish wood. Bronwen had hinted that she'd like a lovespoon. Women appreciated sentimental gestures like that, didn't they? What better time to try his hand at one. He took down a chisel and some sandpaper and went back into the house to draw a design. It took him about fifteen minutes to remember that he had failed woodworking at school.

At last he gave up and went to bed. It felt strange lying in his old bed, in his old room. He remembered lying there as a child, listening for his father's key in the door, the gentle hum of conversation downstairs, his father whistling "Men of Harlech," his favorite song, as he took out the rubbish—all those comforting signs that everything was right with the world.

What was he going to do about Tony Mancini? He could take up the DCI's offer and ride along in one of his squad cars. He could see exactly what evidence they had collected and then make up his own mind. That was, after all, what the jury would have to do. Comforted, he fell asleep.

He woke in the middle of the night to the wind battering his window frame and to the peppering of rain on the roof tiles. When he was a little kid he had been afraid of storms and run into his parents' bedroom. He'd been afraid of a lot of things when his family first moved here. His dad was the rock he had clung to. His thoughts moved to that night, five years ago. That had been a blustery night too, with squawls of rain. He remembered the telephone call that had woken them, the squad car that had rushed them to the hospital, his dad lying there, hovering between life and death for a while. Evan had watched him slip away, knowing he was powerless to do anything about it.

Then he was in that courtroom, that cold and sterile place. He remembered Tony, looking ridiculously young and vulnerable, sitting sprawled in his seat in his black leather jacket as if he was oblivious to the significance of the occasion. When he heard the charges against him read, he had looked up with an almost cocky grin.

"Did you pull the trigger that killed Sergeant Evans?" the prosecuting barrister had asked.

"I s'pose I must've," Tony had answered. Cocky—yes, that had summed it up. Almost pleased with himself, as if shooting a police officer was a pretty cool thing to have done. Suddenly Evan realized what had made him feel so uneasy when he had seen Tony in court this time. Evan had been to court enough times to have seen innocent men in the dock. The bewildered panic in their eyes; the incredulity that nobody believed them. He realized with a cold, sickening feeling of certainty that Tony Mancini was probably telling the truth. He hadn't killed Alison Turnbull.

So what should he do? He got up and paced the room, slapping his fist into his palm as if the solid sound would crystallize his racing thoughts. This is not my problem. If he's innocent, then he'll be proven innocent in court. British courts are fair. They won't convict without sufficient evidence. He tried repeating these lines over and over, but he couldn't shake off the feeling that Tony was going to spend his life in prison for a crime he hadn't committed.

And if Mancini did go to prison, Evan reasoned, it was only fair.

Justice would be served at last. His mother and the South Wales Police would be happy. Presumably he should be happy too. It would be so easy to get in his car, drive back to Bronwen, and put the whole thing out of his mind.

"I don't want to do this," he muttered. As if in answer he saw himself on a hillside, talking to Bill Owens. "Sometimes we have to do things we don't like for the greater good of the whole." That's what he had said, and Owens had called him a sanctimonious little bugger. He'd been right, of course. His own words were coming back to haunt him.

Chapter 11

The next morning Evan set out for the police station. If DCI Vaughan would really let him tag along with his team, then he'd be able to check out Tony's story for himself. He didn't have to mention to anyone else that he had a sneaking suspicion that Tony might be innocent this time. As he drove down the hill into the town, he decided that he wanted to take a look at the scene of the crime for himself first and swung right, into the Oystermouth Road. City streets gave way to green lawns and playing fields until finally there was the bay on one side and landscaped front gardens on the other. This was where Swansea's elite lived, behind high hedges or stone walls. He turned into Ashleigh Road and followed it as it began to climb away from the waterfront.

The Turnbull's house was called The Larches. It was on a small cul-de-sac, almost invisible behind a high yew hedge. Somber laurel bushes and rhododendrons lined the drive, while a couple of the trees for which the house was named shielded parts of it from view. Evan parked at the end of the cul-de-sac and got out of the car. He had gone jogging again that morning and his muscles protested as he started to walk back to the Turnbull's gateway. As Tony had said, the street had the feeling of being remote and cut off from the world. He could only see a couple of other gateways, and the houses were invisible behind high hedges and tree-filled front gardens. A gloomy place, Evan thought and shivered. It was no longer raining, but the air was moist and water dripped onto him from the trees. He stood outside the Turnbulls' house, taking in the brick gateposts and the glimpses of Victorian opulence beyond. It was a tall, ugly brick house with bay windows and a turret on one side. Ivy grew up the walls, and curtains were drawn across the windows.

At the end of the drive Evan hesitated, conscious that he shouldn't be doing this and had no right to be here. He glanced up at the house again. Nothing stirred, no lights glowed behind those closed curtains. It gave the impression of having been abandoned long ago. Maybe the family had gone away for a while, finding it too painful to live so close to their grief. No harm then in taking a quick look at the crime scene. There was no longer any incident tape or any other sign that police had been here. Emboldened, Evan continued down the drive. Flowers were blooming in neatly tended herbaceous borders. The lawn was manicured like a bowling green. To the left of the house was a large garage, and behind a conservatory he caught a glimpse of what must be a swimming pool. No expense spared here, a little paradise behind high hedges.

He reached the front porch and stood staring down at the spot where the crazy paving of the front path met the flight of three stone steps. The steps led up to a massive front door with a stained-glass panel in it. An impressive entry, probably built by a Victorian Turnbull ancestor to let the world know that there was prosperity inside.

There was, of course, nothing to be seen on the grounds. Evan hadn't heard how Alison Turnbull died, but he knew her body had been dumped on the doorstep for her parents to find. A particularly nasty twist—the kind of act committed by someone who wanted to get even. He reminded himself that Tony Mancini had a reason to get even with Mr. Turnbull. He had been fired from his factory. But that was six months ago, and Evan knew from experience that the desire for revenge cools with time.

Evan tried to sum up what he knew about Tony. Obviously he was capable of killing. When you have done it once, they say the second time is easy. But would someone like Tony rape and murder the boss's daughter to get even? A girl he said he enjoyed dancing with, a girl who was easy to talk to and not snobby like the other posh birds? Evan could picture Tony hurling a brick through a window, helping himself to the family jewels, even stabbing Mr. Turnbull, but not dumping Alison's body on the doorstep. That demanded a particular brand of sadism, and for all of his unpleasant traits, he didn't think Tony was sadistic.

Evan glanced around. If her body had been dumped on the doorstep, where, then, had she been killed? In the garden or somewhere else and her body brought here in a vehicle? There were certainly plenty of shrubs and bushes in the garden for a lurker to have taken her unawares. And if she had been brought in a vehicle, then had someone risked carrying her the whole length of the driveway to dump her? Dead bodies, even those of young girls, are not easy things to carry. And this also brought up the question of timing. If Tony had been telling the truth, he had left Alison alive, in her own front garden, around 9:30 P.M. that night. She had sent him away when she heard someone coming—though whether that was the sound of an approaching vehicle or footsteps, Tony hadn't made clear. Could it have been someone in a vehicle who whisked her away, killed her, and then returned to dump her body? A little hard to believe, he decided, but he had to check all the angles. He'd get the police to tell him if they had found the actual spot where she was killed.

He was about to leave the path and investigate the front garden when a great volley of deep barks echoed from the house. Tony had mentioned the dog. Alison had told him that her father set it on people he didn't like. Evan was about to beat a cautious retreat when the front door opened and a dog the size of a young pony came flying down the steps. Before he had to defend himself, however, a voice commanded, "Brutus, come! Come here at once!" The dog stopped in its tracks, sniffing suspiciously at Evan.

A woman stood at the top of the steps, staring coldly at Evan. "If you are another reporter, you'd better go away quickly before I set the dog on you," she said in a cultured voice with no trace of a Welsh lilt.

At first glance she appeared quite young, but Evan saw that this must be the result of a face-lift. Indeed, she had that surprised baby-doll look that is often the product of surgery. The rest of her was superbly groomed. Her blond hair and makeup looked as if she had just left a beauty salon. She was wearing a silk dress, high-heeled shoes, and pearls. Evan didn't think that anyone apart from the royal family wore pearls these days.

"I'm sorry to disturb you," he said quickly, as the dog was inching closer. "I'm not a reporter. Are you Mrs. Turnbull?"

"Yes, I am. And you are?"

"I'm Constable Evan Evans of the North Wales Police."

Her perfect face registered surprise. "North Wales Police? What have they got to do with this?"

"I'm not here in an official capacity, madam. My father was the policeman who was shot by Tony Mancini. I wanted to express my condolences and to see if there was anything I could do to help."

"Oh. The policeman's son. Of course. I saw you in court. How kind of you to come. Please do come in. Brutus, leave him alone. Go to your bed." This last was addressed to the dog, who gave Evan a questioning look before slinking ahead of them into the house. Evan came up the steps and followed Mrs. Turnbull into a drawing room on the left of the front door. The heavy velvet curtains were drawn, and she flicked a switch, lighting a large chandelier in the high ceiling. The room was mixture of Victorian opulence—Chippendale chairs, marble-topped end tables, a large brocade sofa, a good oil painting of the Scottish Highlands, and some more recent acquisitions. There was a very bright oil painting of a Spanish bullfighter on one wall, a portrait of a pretty young woman whom Evan recognized as a younger Mrs. Turnbull, and a drinks cabinet decorated with mother of pearl. Old money meets new, he decided.

"Please sit down, won't you?" Mrs. Turnbull led him to one of the Chippendale chairs beside a marquetry card table, then pulled out another one for herself. "Will you take tea or coffee?"

"Nothing for me, thank you," Evan said. "I know how very distressing this must be for you."

"It's like living in a nightmare," she said frankly. "Every morning I wake up and hope I'll find it was all a bad dream, and of course it isn't. Every day I have to force myself to get out of bed."

Evan nodded. "I remember feeling exactly the same way. Trying to stay asleep as long as possible because it's preferable to waking up."

She looked at him with appreciation in her eyes. "Exactly. It's good to talk to someone else who has been through it. Other people are well meaning, but they just don't understand. I even had one stupid woman tell me I was still young enough to have another child. As if another child could replace Alison!"

"Tell me about Alison," he said.

Her face lit up for a moment. "She was a lovely girl. She was going to be a great beauty, you know. Completely unconscious of her good looks, of course—still at that shy and gawky stage. Of course being at a girls' school it does take longer to learn how to move in mixed company, doesn't it?"

"I don't know. I never went to a girls' school."

She smiled at the remark, and Evan got the impression that smiling felt strange and new for her.

"She was just going into her last year at Malvern Abbey, getting ready to apply to universities. She was quite bright, you know. Not exactly what you'd call studious, but she had a good brain when she wanted to use it—just like her father."

"This young man—Tony Mancini—" Evan began hesitantly. "He claims that he was a friend of Alison."

"A friend of Alison? How totally ridiculous! How could he possibly have known Alison? She was away at school all year. Only home for the summer holidays for a week or so before . . . before . . ." She collected herself. "He's from the slums, isn't he? One of the housing estates? How could he possibly have met my daughter? She went riding or to the country club to play tennis with her friends, and I always drove her. We took good care of Alison, Mr. Evans. She was—very precious to us—our only child, you see."

Again she fought to compose herself. "There is no possible place that Tony Mancini could have met my daughter."

Evan decided to say nothing about the club.

"Then do you have any idea why he chose to kill her?"

"Do murderers need a reason?" she asked, her voice harsh with anger. Evan noticed that she had long bony fingers, decorated with several large rings. These fingers clutched at the silk of her dress like bird's claws. "Maybe he is deranged, on drugs—I don't know. It's possible he spotted Alison through the hedge, was attracted by her beauty, and tried to rape her. She struggled and he had to kill her."

"Then surely he would have fled straight away. Why take the time to dump the body on your doorstep?"

Uncertainty flickered across her face. "I have no idea. I don't know how the criminal mind works, Mr. Evans. You're a policeman. Maybe you can tell me."

"About what time did it happen, Mrs. Turnbull?"

"We found her about quarter to ten at night. She hadn't been dead long, they tell us."

"What was Alison doing in the garden at that time of night?"

"I have no idea," she snapped. "We didn't keep our daughter a prisoner, in spite of what the newspapers say. It was a warm night. She might have gone for a stroll outside. She might have been reading on one of the garden benches until it got too dark to see. I assumed she was quite safe in our own garden. I was home at the time, after all."

"You were home? I understood her father came home and found her . . ."

"My husband returned from a council meeting," she said. "I was playing bridge with my friends, right here at this table."

"And you heard nothing?"

Did he see a flicker of indecision cross her face? "I had already drawn the curtains. As you can see, they are quite thick and muffle sound. And we do, of course, have double glazing in all the windows."

"But even so, if she had cried out, wouldn't you have heard something then?"

"I told you—I heard nothing until I heard my husband's despairing cry. I ran outside and she was lying there in a huddle on my doorstep. We had been in the dining room having refreshments so possibly that's why we heard nothing. My God, Constable, don't you think I would have rushed to my own child's aid if I'd heard her?"

"Of course you would, Mrs. Turnbull, I just wondered . . ."

"Look, I'm afraid this conversation is becoming very disagreeable. I've already been through it a hundred times with the police. Telling you again isn't going to do any good."

"I'm sorry. I was just trying to help," Evan said. "Just trying to see if there was any little point that might have been overlooked. It all comes down to a question of motive, doesn't it? Why did Tony Mancini kill your daughter?"

She glared at him fiercely. "Do criminals like that need a motive? He probably killed her for fun, the way he killed your father." She leaned closer to him. "They tell me he's a thoroughly bad lot. If that sort of person was locked away for life, the world would be a better place, don't you think?"

"If he's found to be guilty," Evan said. "That's why we have trial by jury in this country."

Her eyes flashed angrily. "Any decent jury would find him guilty. They all know us here. They know all the good work my husband has done for this city. He has dedicated himself to his council work, and I have my charities . . . They'll make sure justice is done, won't they?"

"I'm sure they will." Evan got to his feet. "I'm sorry if I've upset you coming here, Mrs. Turnbull. Maybe you should get away for a bit—take a little holiday until this is all over."

"How can we get away?" she demanded. "Frank will never leave the factory for two minutes, or his council job either. He lives for his work. That's all he lives for now."

The dog followed Evan to the front door, sniffing at his heels, as if just waiting for the opportunity to take a good bite.

Chapter 12

Evan was thoughtful as he drove from the Turnbulls' house. Was it possible for anyone to be playing bridge while a murder was taking place outside the window? Of course, she might not have been killed anywhere near the house, and her body might have been dragged to the front steps. He realized he didn't even know yet how the girl died. He hoped the Major Crimes blokes wouldn't mind answering some questions as he tagged along.

The receptionist at the police station recognized Evan this time and merely nodded when he said he had to speak to the Major Crimes Unit. He found only two junior members of the team in residence in the room they had taken over. They had obviously been reading the paper and drinking tea, because they were still scrambling into busy poses as he came in.

"Any idea where I might find the DCI?" Evan asked.

"Out and about, mate. Busy as usual," one of them answered. "Anything we can help you with?"

"He told me I was welcome to ride along, so I thought that maybe—"

"You're Evans, right?" the older of the two asked. His tie lay on the desk in front of him, and his shirt was open at the neck. Evan wondered if plainclothes boys were really allowed this degree of laxness, or whether it was just because the boss was out and about. "Robert Evans's son? I remember you. I was in training with you for a while over in Bridgend. You left to go up North, didn't you?"

"That's right. I remember you too. Huw, isn't it?"

"Huw Hopkins. Quite right. Good memory you've got there. And this is Dave Parry. Wet behind the ears still, Dave is."

The younger man grinned. "And don't they let me know it. All they let me do is make the bloody tea."

"And quite right too," Huw Hopkins said. "Can't risk any cock-ups on a case like this."

"It's going well, is it?" Evan asked. "You've got enough evidence?"

"We're still waiting for the forensics to come in," Huw said.

"So do they know how and where she died?"

"She was suffocated," Huw said. "Bloody great hand over her face while he was raping her. We don't have an exact spot where it happened, but it was somewhere in their garden. She had grass in her hair."

Evan pulled up a stool. "I went to see Tony Mancini yesterday," he said.

"What did you think? Annoying little prick, isn't he?

"He is. I had a great desire to punch him one."

"Nobody here would have minded if you had done, boyo. Between you and me there are some of us who would like to get a confession out of him, one way or another, but the DCI's shit scared that Tony would bleat to the press."

"Tony claimed he was at the house visiting because Alison was a friend of his," Evan said. "Any truth in that?"

"A friend of his, that's a good one," Dave chimed in.

"So there's no way they could have met then? No mutual friends? Nobody else with a motive?"

"What are you, his bloody lawyer?"

"Just trying to get the facts straight," Evan said.

"Did I hear you're on the force up North?" Huw Hopkins asked.

"That's right."

"I expect you've arrested a good few sheep in your time then."

Evan smiled although the joke was rapidly becoming old. "There won't be any sheep left to arrest soon."

Huw stopped grinning. "Oh. Right. So it's pretty bad up there now, is it?"

Evan nodded. "One of the reasons that I'm down here. I didn't want to have to watch that happening to friends of mine."

"I bet you're glad you turned up down here just in time, aren't you?" Dave asked. "In for the kill, so to speak. You going to stay for the trial then?"

"No, I'm due back at work next week, but I may drive down for it."

"There will be a lot of hoopla," Huw said. "What with Turnbull being such a prominent man and all."

"Tell me about the Turnbulls," Evan said. "I know nothing about them."

"Old man Turnbull," Huw began, "you must have heard of him when you lived down here. He's always been a big noise in Swansea. Of course he inherited the family steel works and that went belly up. Then he resurfaced with his current computer factory. Doing well, so I gather. That kind always fall on their feet, don't they? And he's been on the council for years now. Finally gets his chance to be lord mayor in the New Year."

"And what about as a person?"

"I don't exactly play golf with him or drink with him at the local." Huw chuckled.

"I hear he's a pain in the arse," Dave chimed in and got a frown from his senior officer.

"He likes to hear his own voice and get his own way, that's for sure. Goes in for good old shouting matches at council meetings, so I've heard. But he gives a lot to local charities too. He's a labor council member, which is a laugh, considering that he drives a Bentley and sent his kid to one of the most exclusive schools in the country. But he likes to be seen as a great champion of the workingman."

"Do his employees like him, do you know?"

Huw Hopkins shrugged. "I wouldn't know. Although, just a

minute—I can give you one employee who wasn't too happy with him. Earlier this year our blokes got called out to the Turnbull residence. Man disturbing the peace late at night. We found this chap, drunk as a coot, yelling obscenities in the Turnbull's garden. It seems he'd been sacked the previous week for being drunk on the job. But that's the only one who comes to mind."

"And what about her, Mrs. Turnbull? She looks like a classy lady."

Huw glanced at Dave and snorted. "Yes, she's worked hard enough at it. Do you know where he met her? Working as a barmaid in her daddy's public house when he was a student at the Oxford Polytechnic. Now she's conveniently forgotten that part of her life. Talks about 'Mummy' and 'Daddy' and 'the pony club.' They're both as bad as each other. He tells people he was at Oxford, when it was only the poly, not the university." He grinned. "I can just see them now as lord and lady mayor. It will suit them to a T." He leaned closer to Evan. "Rumor has it that she was nagging old Turnbull to pull strings to have Alison presented at court, as a debutante, you know. As if a girl like that had a hope in hell. She wanted him to build a hospital for crippled children or something so he'd get on the honors list." He chuckled. "Funny what's important to some people."

"Was their daughter important to them?"

"Important? From what I hear, they worshipped her. Treated her like a little goddess. Of course she was a horrible spoiled brat because she'd always had everything she wanted. But the mother just doted on her. Went everywhere with her."

"So what Mancini claimed has to be rubbish," Dave added. "There's no way that Mummy would have let her meet a member of the lower classes."

"And if she sneaked out without Mummy knowing?"

"Hardly likely." Huw got to his feet. "Tell you what. I've got some things I have to return to Mr. Turnbull. If you come with me, you can ask him yourself."

Evan got up too. "Thanks. If you're sure you don't mind?"

"I'd welcome the company. We'll leave dogsbody here to hold down the fort." He grinned at Dave as he headed for the door.

The Unico factory stood behind neatly manicured green lawns on top of a windswept hill at the back of the Penlan housing estate. It was a long, low, featureless building of concrete and glass. A sign mounted in the middle of the lawn said simply UNICO. Otherwise there was no hint as to what went on behind the wrought-iron railings. Huw parked the squad car in a space marked EMPLOYEE OF THE MONTH.

The reception area, with its vinyl chairs, large potted plants, and receptionist in a glass cubicle could also have belonged to a dentist's office or a superior government department. Evan looked around, saw no hint of what Unico actually did, and found this strange.

"Can I help you, sir?" the young receptionist asked pleasantly, her eyes traveling quickly and appreciatively over Evan's body.

Huw pulled out a warrant card. "South Wales Police. We need to see Mr. Turnbull for a few moments."

"Oh dear. He's awfully busy this morning," she said. "Is it about—you know. His daughter? Well, I suppose you'd better go through, then."

"Thanks. We know the way." Huw Hopkins was already heading for the swing doors. Evan followed him down a long hallway carpeted in soft rose. From behind closed doors he heard telephones ring and the sound of conversation, but again this hallway was deserted, like an upscale hotel. At the end of the hall Huw knocked before entering an outer office. An attractive young woman sat at a desk, chatting animatedly on the phone. She had her legs crossed, and her skirt was short enough to reveal a tantalizing length of thigh. She started when she saw the two men and hastily sat in a more decorous position, saying, "Got to go. Bye," as she put down the phone.

"I'm sorry. The front desk usually notifies me when we have a visitor coming. Are you here to see Mr. Turnbull? I don't have you down in my appointment book."

"South Wales Police," Huw repeated. "We'll only take a few minutes of his time."

The secretary's face looked hopeful. "Have you got some proof yet? He's been so worried, poor thing. He's scared that they won't come up with enough evidence to send that little punk to jail."

"I'm afraid we don't have the forensic results in yet. Any day now," Huw said. "Do you think we can ask him a couple of quick questions?"

She gave them a beaming smile. "I'll see what I can do."

She disappeared through a door and almost instantly they were invited inside the inner sanctum. This was a spacious room, thickly carpeted in pastel tones, with windows opening onto a patio where a fountain played. On the walls were photos of Mr. Turnbull in his councilor's robes, shaking hands with the prime minister, meeting the queen, and even one sharing a pint with the first minister of Wales. The man himself, seated at a vast mahogany desk, looked less impressive than his photographs—big boned, slightly bloated, with small piggy eyes and sandy hair carefully combed to hide the beginnings of a bald spot. His shirtsleeves were rolled up and a jacket hung on the back of his chair. He got up as they came in, then stared at Evan suspiciously.

"You're not one of the usual lot. I've seen you before somewhere. Not the press, are you? I've made it very clear I'm not talking to the press."

"No, sir. I'm not on the official team. I'm Constable Evan Evans. You saw me in court the other day."

The scowl left the big man's face, and he extended his right hand. "Oh. Yes. That's right. Your testimony stopped them from granting bail. I'm very grateful."

Evan shook the big meaty hand. "I came along with Sergeant Hopkins to offer my condolences and see if I could be of any assistance."

The big man nodded. "That's very charitable of you, young man. I appreciate it. It can't have been easy for you either. If I could have got at the bastard, I'd have put my hands around his throat."

"I know how you feel," Evan said.

Mr. Turnbull waved to two chairs. "Take a pew. Although I'm not sure exactly what I can do for you chaps today. I thought we'd been over everything a million times already."

Huw leaned across and handed Turnbull a package. "I'm just returning the things you gave us, sir. The photos of Alison we showed around. We've made copies. Here are your originals back. You told us not to disturb Mrs. Turnbull."

"Quite right." Turnbull nodded.

"And Constable Evans wanted to ask a couple of questions."

Turnbull glanced at his watch. "I've only got a minute because some Japs are coming to inspect the factory. That might just mean a nice, fat order."

"What exactly do you make here?" Evan asked.

"Computer housing. That's what we do," he said, and for a moment a satisfied smile replaced the lines of tension. "When I knew I'd have to close the steel works, I said to myself there're all those plants sprung up in South Wales making silicon chips and motherboards and what-have-you. But is anyone making a good solid shell to put them in? I knew quite a bit about lightweight metals. We've done quite nicely, thank you. If you'd like a tour of the factory some day, you only have to ask. Not today, of course. I'll be tied up with my Oriental chappies."

"I don't know how you can concentrate on your work right now," Evan said. "I was incapable of doing anything after my dad . . ."

"I've always lived for my work." Mr. Turnbull glanced around his office, the bleak look returning. "Now, it's all I've got. I just need to keep going so that I don't have time to think. It's poor Margaret, stuck at home with nothing to do all day, who worries me. She was always fragile emotionally, and I'm afraid this may be too much for her."

"Maybe you should both get away for a while," Evan suggested. "Take your wife on a cruise."

"You couldn't pay me to go on a cruise at the best of times, young man," Turnbull snapped. "A lot of ancient widows. Boring as hell. My wife's welcome to go away any time she wants, of course. But I'm not leaving until that bastard is safely behind bars. Besides, I can't get away at the moment, even if I wanted to. You'd be amazed how much time my council duties take up, seeing as how I'll be taking over as lord mayor at the end of the year. That will be good for Margaret. She loves having the chance to get tarted up and play at Lady Muck." He managed a brief grin, then sighed. "God knows she needs something to look forward to right now."

Evan had been glancing at the photos on the walls, then his eye fell on a framed picture on the desk. It was half turned away from him, but he could see it was of a young girl, sitting in an armchair with her arm around a big dog.

"Is that Alison?" he asked.

Mr. Turnbull picked it up and the lines on his face softened as he looked at it. "Not a recent shot, of course. She looks—looked—really grown up now. You'd never have taken her for seventeen. You know how they dress these days—tarting themselves up. Asking for trouble if you want my opinion."

Evan caught his eye. "Is that what you think happened? Alison was asking for trouble?"

The big man shrugged. "What do I know? I'm an old fuddy-duddy. But in my opinion, it's not fair the way they go around in these skimpy clothes, exposing all that bare flesh. Young boys have raging hormones, after all. Not that it excuses anything, but it makes you wonder. Maybe that scumbag Mancini caught a glimpse of her and followed her home. She was a beautiful girl. A really lovely . . ."

Huw Hopkins cleared his throat, and Evan realized that he had been monopolizing the conversation. "Sorry," he said. "I've been asking too many questions."

"I've got one small thing I wanted to mention to you, sir," Huw said. "Tony Mancini claims that he knew your daughter."

A look of scorn crossed Mr. Turnbull's face. "Knew my daughter? How could he possibly know my daughter? She went to the finest schools. We drove her everywhere. Of course he didn't know my daughter. He was a predator, a depraved animal. In fact knowing his behavior in the past, he probably came to my house to steal something and found Alison instead."

"Was he trying to steal something when you sacked him?" Huw asked.

Turnbull put the photo back on the desk top. "That's right. Caught him red-handed in my office, cheeky little bastard."

"He says he wasn't stealing anything, just snooping around a bit," Evan said.

"Everyone says the kid is a born liar. Changes his story every two seconds. I know what I saw. I came into this office, and he had my desk drawer open and was rummaging in it. I called security and had him searched, and he had two twenty-pound notes in his pocket. I keep my petty cash box in this drawer. Riffraff like him don't walk around with forty pounds in their pocket. I had him dismissed on the spot."

"Do you think revenge might have been a motive, then?" Huw asked.

A great shudder ran through Turnbull. "If it was, then he couldn't have done anything worse than getting at me through my daughter. When I came across her, lying there in a huddle at the bottom of the steps—she looked so peaceful, I thought she was asleep, you know. I bent down to try to wake her up. . . ." His voice cracked and he shook his head violently as if trying to shake out too painful thoughts.

"You'd been out, had you, sir?" Evan asked gently.

"What?" Turnbull seemed unaware that he had been in the middle of a conversation. "Of course I'd been out. I'd had a council meeting all evening. I was just coming home. Some homecoming."

"What time was this, sir?"

"We've been through all this before," Turnbull said angrily, then mastered himself. "I shouldn't be snapping your heads off. I'm sorry. I know you're trying to do the best you can. I came back between nine-thirty and ten. I didn't exactly stop to check my watch when I found her. She couldn't have been dead long. She was still warm. Still warm, you understand." He closed his eyes as if closing them would eradicate the picture he could see.

Evan nodded. "I can't imagine anything more terrible for you, sir."

"And apparently they picked up Mancini running away, a mere stone's throw from us. That was a stroke of luck, wasn't it? The only stroke of luck we've had so far."

Evan glanced at Huw and nodded.

"I understand he's been a bad lot since he was born," Turnbull went on. "They say nowadays that the chemistry gets scrambled in the brain and that produces the criminal mind. The only solution is to keep that kind of person locked away from society. I want you blokes to promise me he won't get off lightly this time."

"He won't, sir. I guarantee he'll be put away for life," Huw said.

"Tell me about Alison, sir," Evan said. "What was she like?"

"Very pretty. Always was. When she was a toddler people used to stop the pram to make a fuss of her. She was such a delicate little thing; she used to flit around like a little butterfly, always dancing and showing off for us and pretending to be a princess or a fairy or something."

"And when she grew up, what then? How did she get on with you and your wife?"

"Get on with us? She was a good girl, if that's what you are insinuating. No trouble at all. Obedient. Of course she and the wife had the occasional spat over what she was allowed to wear and what films she was allowed to see—like any typical teenager. But she'd soon calm down and then be her sweet self again." He leaned across his desk, closer to them. "And you know the irony of it all—we made sure we took good care of her, because she was our only one. Never let her out on the streets or to the public swimming pool like the other kids. My wife always drove her everywhere. Never let her out of her sight. We vetted her friends carefully and sent her to the best schools—and what good did it bloody well do?" He fought to master himself again.

"Did she have a boyfriend?" Evan asked.

"She was too young for that kind of thing," Turnbull said quickly. "There were a couple of young chaps—sons of our friends—who used to escort her when there was a country club dance or a Masonic lady's night, but she wasn't too keen on either of them. If she had been, I don't think we'd have minded her going to the pictures with one of them. Both nice lads. Well brought up. Away at public schools most of the year. But she didn't take to them. I think she was waiting for Prince Charming to come along. She had grand ideas, like her dad." A wistful smile crossed his face.

He took the photo in his hands again, examined it again, then opened a drawer and put it away. "So now all that's left is my work," he said.

As if on cue there was a tap on the door and the short-skirted secretary came in. "The receptionist says that Mr. Yashimoto and his party have arrived in the building, sir. Would you like me to bring them to your office, or do you think you should go and greet them personally?"

"I think I'd better go, thanks, Miss Jones. They're hot on protocol over in the East, aren't they? All that bowing and stuff." He got up and extended a hand to Evan then Huw. "Thanks so much for stopping by. I appreciate your help. Maybe I'll see you at the trial, if the wife and I can find the courage to face it."

Evan shook the hand, noticing the big man's strong grip. A powerful man, used to getting what he wanted all his life. He followed Mr. Turnbull from the office.

"Better have the kettle on to make them some tea, Miss Jones," Turnbull said.

"Very well, sir." She smiled at him for a fraction of a second then turned to the two policemen. "Can you find your own way out?"

"We'll manage, thanks." Huw Hopkins said.

"Thank you for your time, sir," Evan called after Turnbull.

"You certainly gave him a good old grilling, didn't you?" Huw Hopkins asked as they walked down the hall together. "I didn't realize the North Wales Police were so forceful."

Evan flushed. "I'm sorry. I didn't mean to take over like that. I was just trying to get all the facts for myself."

"No problem. Kept me away from the paperwork for a while. So what was your impression of him then?"

"Exactly what you'd told me. Big, blustering, likes to get his own way. Really cut up about his daughter, but who wouldn't be?"

"The secretary is easy on the eye." Huw gave Evan a nudge. "Good pair of legs."

Evan turned to glance back at Turnbull's office. Through the open door he saw Miss Jones pick up the phone and smile as she started chatting again. Evan had sensed some kind of undercurrent in the simple exchange between secretary and boss. And why had she come into the office herself, when there was a perfectly good intercom on her desk?

"I thought that was interesting about the boyfriends, or lack of them," Evan said.

"What do you mean?"

"It seems there were two young men whom Alison didn't really fancy. Has anyone checked up on them yet?"

"No. Why should they? We've already got Mancini. Case closed."

Evan said no more, but climbed into the squad car beside Huw Hopkins. As they drove down from the factory, they passed the Penlan estate, sprawling on his left, row after row of identical brown pebble-dash council houses. A visit to Tony's mum might not be such a bad idea, either. Then he stopped this train of thought abruptly. Without meaning to, he was throwing himself into a real investigation. What exactly did he hope to gain from all this? The truth, he answered himself. If he believed that Tony Mancini hadn't done it, then he'd have to find out who else might have had a motive and opportunity for murder.

. . . If he believed Toni Mancini hadn't done it. That was the crucial point, of course. Mr. Turnbull had labeled him as a liar since birth, and frankly Evan hadn't come away with any warm feelings toward the young man. It would be the ultimate twist of irony if he jeopardized his own police career for someone who had not only killed his father but turned out to be a consummate liar as well.

As they came into the police station and walked toward the incident room, they could hear animated conversation through the half-open door. Huw went in ahead of Evan. DCI Vaughan was seated at the table with a couple of detectives Evan hadn't yet met.

"Oh, there you are, Hopkins," the DCI boomed in his big voice.

"And Evans too. Did you get to see Mancini, lad?"

"Yes, sir."

"Obnoxious little bugger, isn't he?" Vaughan said, smiling affably. "I hope you didn't knock the stuffing out of him—officially, that is."

"No, sir. But I was tempted." Evan returned the smile.

"Well, you'll be pleased to hear we've got enough proof to crucify the bastard. He won't wriggle out of this one." Vaughan actually chuckled and slapped his hand down on a pile of papers lying on the desk. "Look what just came in, Hopkins. The forensic results have arrived. Just what we hoped. The DNA test came back positive."

"What does that mean, exactly, sir?" Evan asked.

"The DNA we found on her body is his. Hundred percent match."

Chapter 13

Evan ran back to his car, two steps ahead of a meter attendant who was looking satisfied as he tucked a ticket under a windscreen wiper on the next car. He jumped in and drove down to the waterfront. It was only when he was standing at the prison gate that he realized he should probably have gone through the solicitor, but he wasn't prepared to wait any longer or risk being turned down.

"Police," he said to the man at the gate, bringing out a warrant card and hoping that the gate guard didn't check it too thoroughly. "Evans. I spoke with Tony Mancini yesterday. I need to speak with him again."

He was shown straight to an interview room, and a few minutes later Tony was ushered in. He looked at Evan hopefully. "You've found something already?" he asked as the door closed behind him.

"You bloody well bet I have!" Evan struggled to keep himself from yelling. "You lied to me, boy. I let myself be taken in by you and your acting skills, and all the time you lied to me!"

A guarded look returned to Tony's face. "What are you talking about. I never lied to you."

"Don't give me that crap. You know damned well you lied."

Tony made tut-tutting noises. "I thought you didn't approve of bad language," he said.

"You better watch yourself or I'll knock your block off," Evan snapped.

"I don't have to talk to you without my lawyer present." Tony backed away as Evan loomed over him.

Evan grabbed him by the shirt front and almost lifted him from the ground. "Listen to me, you little prick. Your lawyer won't have a hope in hell of getting you off this time. They've found your DNA on the girl's body!"

He realized almost as the words came out that he could find himself in deep trouble for being the first to divulge such evidence, but by the time he'd come to his senses it was too late.

"What have you got to say to that?" Evan demanded.

Tony was staring at him defiantly. "Okay, so we had sex. I never said we didn't."

"You had sex with her? When?"

"That evening. Then. I went up to her house to see her and we started talking and—well—we'd sort of fancied each other from the start. So one thing leads to another, right? We're making out then she gives me this kind of look and she says wouldn't it be a lark to do it right there on the lawn, right outside the window where her mum is having her bridge party? So we went behind this big bush, right close to the house, and we did it. It wasn't half bad either. She's a good little mover."

Evan looked away, feeling repulsed. "And then?"

"We'd just finished and we were lying there, giggling, because we heard someone in the house say, 'One no trump,' when suddenly she says, 'Someone's coming. You'd better beat it quick. You'll be in trouble if the dog gets out and finds you.' So I zipped up my pants and got out through the hedge like I told you."

"And you didn't see who arrived?"

"No, but I heard her talking to someone. I heard her raise her voice, but I didn't hear what she said and I didn't wait around."

"You say this was around nine-thirty?"

"Something like that. I don't know how long we'd been talking and making out in the garden, but it was dark so it must have been at least nine-thirty."

"And you didn't hear anything at all of the other voice, the man she was talking to?"

"I couldn't even tell you if it was a man," Tony said. "I wasn't too keen on her dog taking a bite out of my backside."

"You said she raised her voice. Was she crying out, in alarm, would you say?"

"Well, if she'd yelled 'help, help,' I'd have gone straight back, wouldn't I? I don't think she sounded scared. Just shouting at someone, that's what it sounded like. Having an argument."

"How did she know someone was coming? Did you hear a car pull up? Someone coming down the path?"

"I can't say I heard anything, but I had—like—my mind on other things at the time, didn't I? I didn't hear a car door or nothing."

"We're not likely to come up with any other witnesses," Evan said.

"This is going to look pretty bad for me then, is it?" Tony asked as if this fact had only just sunk in.

"Very bad," Evan said.

"What are you going to do?"

"Me? I don't know that I can do anything. I don't work for the police down here. I'm already risking my job by coming to see you like this. I'll be in a heap of trouble when they find out I told you about the DNA."

"So if you don't want to help me, why did you bother to come?" He stood there, arms folded across his skinny chest, chin jutting out defiantly.

"Exactly why should I want to help you? You tell me that," Evan demanded. "You're not exactly someone I think of as a long lost brother."

"Look, I said I was sorry about your dad."

"You've said a lot of other things that haven't turned out to be true."

"Okay, so I've done some stupid stuff in my life, but I didn't kill Alison. I swear I didn't. You will help me, won't you? That toffy-nosed git of a solicitor—he's no use at all. He thinks I did it. He's not even going to try."

"Is there anything else I should know?" Evan asked coldly. "Anything else you might have lied about, or conveniently forgotten to tell me?"

"Nothing. I swear."

"There better not be."

Evan didn't look back as he left the room.

Evan sat for a long time in his car, watching seagulls wheeling overhead and listening to their screeching cries. His fingers gripped the steering wheel. He was not by nature a violent person, yet every encounter with Tony brought out angry, violent thoughts, leaving him taut as a coiled watch spring. Why was he putting himself through this? Every instinct in his body was telling him to forget about the whole thing. If DCI Vaughan found that he was interfering in the case, taking the side of a man the police all wanted to see convicted, he'd call Evan's superiors in North Wales and Evans would find himself out of a job. What would policemen like Bill Howells, colleagues of his dad, think if they found out he was working secretly to free Tony Mancini? And what would his mum think? Evan drummed his fingers on the steering wheel. The problem was that deep down he felt that his dad wouldn't have backed out. His dad would have wanted him to go on with it.

But I'm bloody well going to make sure of my facts this time, he decided. I'm not sticking my nose out for Tony Mancini only to find he's been lying again. He started the engine, swung the car around the roundabout, and headed out of Swansea, in the direction of Bridgend where the South Wales Police was headquartered.

He found the home-office pathologist working cheerfully in his lab at the county morgue. It had been Evan's experience that pathologists rarely looked like people who spent most of their waking hours delving into body parts. The one in North Wales looked like a prim schoolmaster. The one he faced today looked more like a farmer or pub owner. He was big, red faced, and jolly.

"Hello, young man? What can I do for you?" he asked as Evan came in. "I know you, don't I?"

"Evan Evans." He went to extend his hand, noticed what the

pathologist had been doing, and thought better of it. "You knew my dad, and I think we met a couple of times."

"Robert Evans's son? Of course. And now you're here on this new business."

"They said you did the autopsy on Alison Turnbull?"

The doctor nodded.

"I wondered if you could tell me—was it clear that she was raped and then murdered?"

"You mean was she suffocated at the same time the rape was going on?"

Evan cleared his throat, trying to phrase the question. "No, I meant could it be possible that she had sex before she was killed, but that the two weren't connected?"

The pathologist paused, digesting this new theory, nodding several times. "Well, that's an interesting thought. She'd certainly had intercourse very shortly before she died, so it was always assumed that it was murder following a rape."

"Can you tell that it was rape? I mean, were there signs of violence?"

"Apart from the bruises on her face, no. There weren't. There were no signs of considerable force, if that's what you mean."

Evan found himself flushing and was glad that the light in the room was so focused on the autopsy table, leaving the rest in gloom. He would never be comfortable discussing the subject. "So it could have been consensual sex?"

"With someone who didn't kill her?"

Evan nodded.

"Then he'd probably been watching, because the two events were only minutes apart. You're coming up with an unlikely scenario here. Any reason why?"

"Just a theory of my own I was testing. And how exactly was she killed?"

"Suffocated with a hand over her mouth. That's why we thought he probably did it as he was raping her. Maybe she cried out and he put his hand over her mouth to shut her up. That's happened before. And that way she wouldn't have been in a good position to struggle. It's not that easy to stop a person from breathing for long enough to kill them."

"Are you sure it had to be a man who killed her?"

Again the pathologist seemed intrigued by the thought. "It would have taken a darned strong woman. There were fingermarks on her cheeks where he clamped on to her with considerable force. And if she wasn't being raped at the time, if she was standing up and free, she'd have had a good chance of breaking the hold and getting away."

"Was it definite that she only had sex with one bloke?"

"Unless one of them was wearing a rubber." Again, he seemed intrigued, then gave Evan a knowing grin. "Now that's an interesting thought. She wasn't a virgin, you know. Not exactly the little convent girl that Mummy and Daddy thought she was." He peeled off his gloves and dropped them into a bin, then went over to the sink and began washing his hands. "Two different men involved. I'd like to hear where you came up with this theory. Most interesting. What does the DCI think of it?"

"I haven't told him yet," Evan said. "I haven't told anybody. I'm just gathering facts at the moment, for my own satisfaction, so I'd be grateful if you didn't say anything to the DCI about my being here. I'm sure I shouldn't be poking my nose in. I'm not even with the South Wales Police any longer."

"Perfectly understandable," the pathologist said. "You want to be actively involved in getting the little bugger convicted. Anyone can understand that."

"All the same . . ." Evan began.

The pathologist touched the side of his nose. "Mum's the word." He chuckled. "I'll be interested to hear if you get any further with your theory. Two lurkers, eh? One of them she lets have sex with her, the other finishes her off. Fascinating."

"Thanks a lot, sir. It's been good talking to you."

The doctor gave a cheery wave from the sink as Evan left the lab. He heaved a sigh of relief as he got back into his car. He had found the interview embarrassing although he had managed to conduct himself well enough. A policeman was supposed to ask any question under the sun, to be uninvolved with any kind of crime, no matter how grisly or bizarre. Sometimes he wondered if he had the personality for a detective. Was he really more suited to the quiet life in Llanfair, where Mrs. Powell-Jones's complaints were the biggest drama of the day?

The thought of Llanfair made him wonder what was happening up there. He shouldn't have run out on them. It was cowardly. He saw that now. And he'd probably have been more use up there than here, running in circles trying to prove Tony Mancini's innocence. The problem was whether he could live with himself if Tony was sentenced to life in prison for a crime he didn't commit. And he hated to be defeated by anything. If Tony was indeed innocent, then someone else had to have had a reason for murdering Alison. The Turnbull's house wasn't the kind of place any pervert would have picked at random—stumbling upon Alison to rape and murder her. There was no way of knowing that an attractive young girl lived behind those high hedges. So either it was someone Alison already knew, or someone who had seen her and found out where she lived. And if he could go on Tony's word, she had sounded more angry than alarmed when he had heard her talking to the person who arrived as he ran off. Someone she knew then. The next step should be to visit Mrs. Turnbull again and get a list of Alison's friends.

"Just a couple of days more," he told himself. "I'll give it to the weekend, and then I'll give up and go home."

It was almost five o'clock by the time he drove back to Swansea. He realized, with another pang of guilt, that he hadn't been home for lunch. His mother would have been expecting him, even though he hadn't said anything about his being there. Bronwen had told him that he spent his life as the eternal Boy Scout, trying to do good deeds and please other people. Maybe it was true, but he couldn't change who he was.

He wondered if he had time to visit Mrs. Turnbull again that evening. If Tony had been telling the truth, one of Alison's friends had driven her to the clubs when she slipped out at night. That person might have seen someone hanging around Alison or know if anyone had been pestering her. Then there were the young men Mr. Turnbull had mentioned—those suitable young escorts from the country club set whom Alison hadn't really fancied. Also worth checking out.

But when he slowed outside the Turnbull's house, he saw that there were cars in the driveway. Not police vehicles, but ordinary cars. He wondered if Mrs. Turnbull had already gone back to her card parties or afternoon at homes. In any case, he couldn't very well barge in on her. He'd have to come back first thing in the morning. As he drove into the driveway to reverse out of the cul-de-sac, he looked up and noticed for the first time a house to the left of the Turnbull mansion, visible between the trees. As he stared at the upper windows, he thought he saw a curtain twitch. This might be the break he was looking for—a nosy neighbor who might have a good view of the Turnbull's front garden. He'd also pay a visit there in the morning.

"You've been gone a long time," his mother greeted him. "I hope you've had a successful day."

"Not very," he said. "The police think they've got the evidence they need to convict Tony."

"Well, I'd call that good news." Mrs. Evans beamed. "I bet you were glad to hear that, weren't you?"

He smiled and said nothing. How was he ever going to tell her that he was working to break down that evidence? How would she ever forgive him when he did?

Chapter 14

After a mercifully light supper Evan found it impossible to settle. He attacked the lovespoon again, but soon grew frustrated at his inept attempts. He supposed that young men long ago had nothing better to do that whittle on long winter nights, and thus had more practice. His spoon was taking shape rather like a flying camel doing the splits. Around nine o'clock he decided that at least he could go and inspect the club where Tony claimed he met Alison. Somebody there might have seen them together. Somebody might even have seen Alison's encounter with another man.

"You're never going out again at this time of night?" Mrs. Evans looked horrified.

"It's only nine o'clock, Ma, and I thought of someone I might question about Alison Turnbull's murder. We need all the evidence we can get, you know."

"Are you trying to tell me the police here aren't doing everything they can?"

"No, of course not. This is only because I want to be involved. I *need* to be involved."

"All right, then." She brushed down her apron in a characteristic gesture Evan remembered well from former occasions when she didn't really approve, but couldn't think of a good enough reason to forbid him to do something. "Off you go. But be careful. You're all I've got now. Running around all night isn't safe anymore."

He gave her a kiss on the cheek then grabbed the car keys from the hall table.

Kingsway looked empty and dead, and he found a parking space easily. Fast-food wrappers and old newspapers littered the pavements. Many of the shops had empty windows or the words GOING OUT OF BUSINESS SALE on them. Not the most thriving area of the city. A drunk tottered past, a bottle in a brown bag raised to his lips. A couple of girls loitered in the shadows. And this had been the thriving main street of town when Evan was a boy. All the good stores had now moved to the new shopping centers. Now only the pubs survived.

There were several clubs advertising music and dancing, but most were closed until the weekend. There was music coming from the upstairs room at the Monkey's Uncle as Evan climbed the stairs, but as he entered the large warehouselike space, he saw that it was only coming from a speaker system. Most of the tables around the wall were empty. It was a large, depressing-looking room with black-painted brick walls and no windows. A couple of girls were dancing halfheartedly with each other. Evan went up to the only employee he could find, serving cans of Pepsi at a bar table.

"Police, you say?" The young bloke glanced around nervously. "We don't do nothing illegal here, mate. Everything by the book."

"I just wanted to ask you some questions about the girl who was murdered a couple of weeks ago—Alison Turnbull. You must have read about it in the papers."

"Of course. But the bloke's already behind bars, isn't he?"

"We're just trying to substantiate some of the things he's claiming for his defense," Evan said. "For one thing, he claims that he and the girl used to meet here. Did you ever see her at the club?"

"Do you have a photo?"

"Not with me. I can get one."

"I saw her picture in the paper, but I can't say the face rang a bell. If she came here Friday or Saturday nights, then we're jammed solid. Several hundred kids, and they don't dress like their photos when they're here either. Spray-painted hair, rings through everything. The lot."

"Then what about Tony Mancini? Did that name ring a bell when he was arrested?"

"Yeah, I think it did. But there again, I might have read it somewhere else. We don't go in for names. They pay their money at the door, and they get in. No questions asked. They come for a good time; we give them one. You should come back tomorrow night when the joint is jumping, as they say. You couldn't hear yourself speak then. Very lively. We get kids from as far away as Llanelli and Talbot and all over the place. We pack 'em in, especially when we've got a top band like Defenestration or Raging Speedhorn." He looked to Evan's face for recognition. When he saw none, he continued, "We get all types of bands playing here—garage, goths, metal, the lot. I'm not really into British metal myself—a lot of alcoholic uncles in spray-on trousers, most of them, but it's what the kids like."

Evan felt he should say something, but he hadn't a clue what the man had been talking about. Garage? Goths? Raging Speedhorn? He was definitely feeling his age.

"You don't mind if I talk to the kids who are here tonight, do you? At least we can make ourselves heard."

"Be my guest. Oh, and if you come back tomorrow, don't make it too obvious you're police, will you? We don't want to clear the place out."

But half an hour later, when he left, he was no wiser. None of the young people at the club knew Alison or Tony or remembered seeing them at the club. "You don't really notice who's here on Friday or Saturday nights," one girl said. "Except for sexy blokes, of course. We're always on the lookout for sexy blokes."

Her friends giggled and eyed Evan shyly.

He'd have to go back the next evening, Evan thought grimly. He'd never been a fan of crowded places or loud music. He wasn't looking forward to it at all.

He drove home and phoned Bronwen.

"I'm glad to discover you haven't abandoned me." Bronwen attempted to sound lighthearted, but Evan heard the annoyance in her voice. "I thought it might be like the old days—return her to her parents and make a quick getaway."

"Sorry, *cariad*," Evan said, "but you can't imagine what's been happening here. It's been rather like riding a runaway train." He summed up the progress of the day. "So now I'm completely undecided. I don't know how much I can trust Mancini, and even if he's telling the truth, I don't know how on earth anyone would ever prove him innocent. And I've been thinking about Llanfair. I ran out on them, and I don't feel too wonderful about that either."

"Dear, dear. You are rather awash in guilt tonight. Is that what visiting your mother does to you?" She laughed this time. "Evan, you don't always have to make yourself miserable by trying to do the right thing, you know."

"I know, but . . ."

"But you're going to whether I like it or not?"

"Look, I'm sorry for abandoning you. Just give it another day. I've got some leads I'd like to follow. I'd like to speak to Alison's friends, for one thing. It seems she wasn't the perfect little angel her parents thought she was. Maybe she had other unsuitable friends, apart from Tony, that her parents knew nothing about. And there were a couple of so-called suitable young chaps the parents liked, but Alison didn't. Oh, and another thing, there could be a nosy neighbor. I saw the upstairs curtains twitch when I was reversing the car outside the Turnbull's house this evening. And I'd like to check on Mr. Turnbull's factory too. I gather they had to call the police when one of his former employees showed up at his house, hurling abuse."

"Goodness, Evan, that sounds like enough to keep you busy for another week. Well, don't expect me to stay here any longer. I've had just about as much as I can take of hearing about what a success Gillian has made of her life and how her baby is a child genius and why couldn't I have patched up my differences with Edward and why did I have to be so bloody Welsh."

"Look, I'll come and pick you up on Saturday, I promise," Evan said. "Just give me tomorrow to get as much done as I can, all right? I have to go back to that bloody club when it's in full swing, although I can't see any of the kids there wanting to talk to me. I'll stand out like a blooming—"

"Flamingo in a chicken house?"

"The other way around. Flamingos are bright and elegant. I understand the clubgoers all have blue, pink, or purple spiked hair, rings through everything, and clothing that appears to be spray-painted onto them. You can imagine how I'll stand out. They'll guess I'm a policeman right away and clam up."

"I'd love to see you if one of the girls asks you to dance." Bronwen chuckled.

"Very funny. If it's as packed as the manager says it is, then there won't be any room to dance. That's what I'm hoping for."

"You should go out tomorrow and get yourself some sexy jeans and a T-shirt that says something rude." Bronwen was laughing now.

"It's all right for you," Evan said.

Bronwen grew quiet. "Evan," she said at last, "why are you putting yourself through all this? It sounds to me as if Tony Mancini is adept at lying his way out of anything. Have you thought what it might do to your career if you fight for him and then find out you were wrong?"

"I know, I have thought about it," Evan said. "All I wanted to do was get at the truth enough to satisfy myself, and now it seems I'm digging myself into a deeper and deeper hole."

"Then call it quits, for God's sake. Come and rescue me and let's drive down to Penbrokeshire and spend some time together. We can go on some lovely walks and heal our spirits."

"That does sound very tempting."

"Then let's do it!"

"Just give me tomorrow, all right?"

"All right, I suppose. But if you don't show up at the weekend, I might just run off with one of the very boring men my mother has been introducing me to."

"Oh, it's other men now, is it? Is she trying to find a better substitute for me?"

"I don't know what's going through her mind. She says how delightfully fresh faced you are—whatever that means, but then she starts rambling about Nigel Ponsonby-Smythe or a similar one who has made a fortune as a stockbroker and won Wimbledon in his spare time."

"I'll be there," Evan said. "By the way, how is Mary's Little Lamb doing? In disgrace again?"

"Absolutely the reverse." Bronwen started laughing. "Ever since he frightened Mrs. Todd, Daddy has decided he's a wonderful creature, and he's been following Daddy around like a dog. Daddy can't stand Mrs. Todd, you see. She tidies his drawers and overstarches his shirts. And we've had some good news about Daddy's sheep—it seems he might be eligible to get them vaccinated, because they are so rare."

"That is good news."

"It's a pity the vet can't do it while Prince W. is here, isn't it?"

"It's a pity they can't vaccinate every herd in Britain in time."

"Daddy says they could have done, but most farmers wouldn't do it because then their meat couldn't be sold abroad. Stupid, isn't it?"

"I expect they're regretting it now. I wonder what's happening in Llanfair. I don't like to call."

"There's nothing we can do about it anyway," Bronwen said. "It's just one of those horrible things. Oh, let's get away together, Evan. What with the foot-and-mouth and the possible closing of my school and Tony Mancini and my parents, I just need some quiet time to recuperate."

"We will, *cariad*. In fact it sounds wonderful."

"I'll see you at the weekend, then?" Bronwen sounded wistful.

"I'll be there."

When he hung up, Evan stood staring at the phone, then he stomped outside to the shed to lift weights. He was going to get back in shape if it killed him.

He was out jogging before breakfast and found he could now run a good half mile before becoming winded. A few days hiking with

Bronwen would definitely help him get into condition. Of course, the egg, bacon, sausage, and fried bread his mother insisted on cooking for him wasn't going to help, but he ate it without comment. It was the least he could do to make her think she was taking good care of him.

"Well, this is nice," she said, as she put the plate in front of him. "Takes me back to the old days when Robert was alive and you were off to school in the mornings. I never let either of you leave the house without a decent breakfast, did I?"

"No, Ma, you took great care of both of us."

"And it wasn't enough, was it? I couldn't protect him when he needed it."

"It was his job, Ma. You know as well as I do that being a policeman is a risky business."

"Then why in God's name did you have to follow him into it? Why don't you get yourself a nice, steady job, away from shootings and violence? You've got yourself a lovely girl in that Bronwen. You don't want her to go through what I did, do you?"

"I'm up in North Wales—we're not quite as violent up there, you know. The sheep behave themselves most of the time." He attempted to make a joke of it, but it was a valid point. All the more reason to play professional rugby if he was offered the chance. He was tempted to run down to the shed and pump some more iron before he set out, but he had a full day ahead of him. He had made a list of people to question. By the end of it he might have some idea if anyone else had a motive for killing Alison Turnbull.

Chapter 15

There were no cars in the driveway when Evan stopped his car in the cul-de-sac outside the Turnbull's house around nine-thirty that morning. As always the street was deserted and the only sounds, when he got out of the car, were sparrows twittering, a pair of wood pigeons cooing in a big pine tree, and far off, a cuckoo. Evan stood, in dappled shade, listening, enjoying the peace. Then he took a deep breath and followed the hedge around the property until he came to the gap Tony said he had used. He slipped through and stood among shrubs, his presence successfully blocked from all but the most prying of eyes. He moved from shrub to shrub until he was close to the front of the house. It would have been child's play for anyone to have come and gone unseen, unless someone actually happened to be looking down from the upstairs windows at the time. His gaze moved across to the house to the left of the property where he had seen the movement yesterday. Yes, the area around the front porch might well be visible from that upstairs window. He'd pay a call after he'd talked to Mrs. Turnbull.

As he stood there, Evan noticed that the so-called ground floor of the Turnbull house was not actually at ground level. The windows were about head height, and partially blocked by the tall hydrangea bushes. A line of rhododendrons grew a few feet away, creating a grassy walkway between rows of shrubs. So this was where Tony and Alison's tryst had taken place. Not quite as risky as it had sounded. Unless the window was open and someone had looked down, they would have been invisible. He moved cautiously, trying to find the spot where the encounter might have taken place. There were no clues that he could see—no blossoms on the ground, indicating the bush might have been shaken, or someone might have brushed against it, but then the Turnbulls obviously had a gardener who would have tidied the area. And the police would have gone over it too. Too bad that the grass beneath his feet was well watered and springy. He bent down, hoping against hope to find something—a cigarette stub, a lost earring, but found nothing. As he stood up, he noticed that his hand was damp. Alison's back might have also have been damp if she had lain here. He could ask about that when he next spoke to the police.

"Ow!" The word was out before he remembered to be quiet. He looked at his left hand and saw that it was bleeding. Not all the flowering bushes were rhododendrons—there were a couple of large rosebushes; with a goodly array of thorns, one of which had nicked his hand. So the couple obviously wouldn't have chosen this spot. There, in the gap between the hydrangeas. They must have lain there. Evan squatted and searched, not knowing what he hoped to find. After a minute or so he straightened up again and continued his route along the front of the house.

When he was a few feet away from the front steps, the deep barking began. The dog must have some kind of sixth sense to pick up his presence when he was clearly not making any noisc. Hc rang the bell and waited. A strange woman in a white overall opened the door.

"Sorry I took so long coming," she said, sounding a little out of breath. "I had to shut the dog in the kitchen first. He's such a nuisance with strangers."

As if on cue, more barks echoed from the end of the passageway.

"He'd certainly make intruders think twice about entering," Evan commented.

The housekeeper nodded. "Mr. Turnbull had him trained at the guard dog school. Being on the council he gets all kinds of crack-pots showing up at the house."

"Pity the dog wasn't let out that evening," Evan said.

"That evening?"

"When Alison was killed."

"Yes, well, Mrs. Turnbull had the bridge ladies, didn't she? A couple of them are frightened of Brutus so Mrs. T. keeps him shut up. Now what was it you wanted?"

"Constable Evans again with a couple more questions for Mrs. Turnbull," Evan said.

The housekeeper gave him a look of contempt. "What is it now? Can't they leave the poor woman alone, always badgering her and questioning her? Isn't it enough to lose her precious child, without having to go through all this?"

She spoke with the heavy Welsh singsong of South Wales. Evan took this to mean she was a Welsh speaker and switched to Welsh. She shook her head instantly. "I'm sorry, I don't speak the language. I'm ashamed of myself, but there it is. Never got a chance to learn it when I was growing up. In fact when I was at school we were punished if they heard us speaking Welsh in the playground. That's how it was in those days."

But she looked at Evan more kindly. "Hold on a moment. I'll see how she's doing and whether she wants to speak to you. She wasn't feeling too well this morning. Bad headaches, you know. She always was delicate. And if she has to put up with much more of this, she'll crack, you mark my words."

"I'm sorry. I won't upset her, I promise. You know, maybe you could answer my questions so we don't have to trouble her at all."

"Me?"

"You probably know everything that happens in the family as well as they do."

"Well, I wouldn't say that, but I've been with them for twenty years, before Alison was born, look you." She gave a small, satisfied smile. "So what was it you wanted?"

"All I wanted to know were the names of some of Alison's friends," Evan said.

"Alison's friends?"

"Yes. The young man in custody says he met Alison and was friendly with her. We need to prove whether he's lying or not."

"A no-good, common boy from Penlan know Alison? The cheek of it. I should think not." The housekeeper smoothed down her apron in a gesture that reminded him of his mother. "They were very particular who she mixed with. Only the top drawer was good enough for Alison."

"So who did she mix with?"

"Well, now. She didn't have that many friends here anymore, on account of being sent away to boarding school when she was thirteen. Before that she used to go to Tawe House. Do you know it?"

Evan did. When he was at school it was where the snobby girls went. He remembered them, in their brown uniforms and panama hats, walking past the grammar-school boys, pretending not to notice them but talking a little too loudly in their upper-class accents about parties and riding lessons and country club dances.

"There's a girl called Sarah Wheatley who still calls Alison," she said. "And a Charlotte Williams. They still go to Tawe House. She might still be in touch with other friends from there, but I don't know about her friends from her present school. None of them has been here to stay. All over the country, I expect they are."

Evan lowered his voice. "What about boyfriends?"

"Oh, she wasn't allowed boyfriends. Her parents didn't approve of that kind of thing. Very strict with her, they were."

"So no boys ever came to the house?"

"I didn't say that. Young Simon Richards used to play tennis with her. Mr. and Mrs. Turnbull are very friendly with the Richards. And Charles, of course. He'd show up from time to time."

"Charles?"

"Charles Peterson. You know, Peterson's the builders? Their son. He was rather smitten with her, I think, but she wouldn't give him the time of day. Well, of course he was no oil painting—a little too chubby for her taste, and red hair too. She didn't like the red hair. Always had grand ideas, young Alison. Between you and me"—she leaned closer to Evan—"they brought her up to want only the best.

And that's not always good for a child, especially an only child. She'd try to boss me around sometimes. Of course I didn't let her get away with it. But I tell you, if she'd been my child, she'd have been over my knee with a good hiding. Her mum did try to keep her in line, but her dad was far too soft on her. She could wrap him around her little finger."

"Do you live in?" Another thought had occurred to him.

"No, sir. I go home at five o'clock. I've got my own family to take care of, although sometimes I stay late if Mrs. T. is having guests to dinner."

"But you didn't stay late the night Alison was killed?"

"No, I didn't. I made some little sandwiches for the bridge ladies, and some fairy cakes, and I left them on a tray ready for when she wanted refreshments."

"On a tray?"

"Yes, so that she could carry it through to the drawing room. Sometimes they liked to snack when they were playing."

"I see. And who were these ladies she was playing with?"

"Well, I don't know exactly who was there that particular night, see. But usually it was Mrs. Richards I told you about, Mrs. Haveshans from next door, and the vicar's wife, and . . ."

"Who are you gossiping with, Alice?" An imperious voice came down the stairs and Mrs. Turnbull appeared, holding on to the banister as if walking was an effort. She looked paler and frailer this morning, although it was hard to tell under the makeup. Again she was perfectly attired in a smart dress and high-heeled shoes. A large broach in the shape of a lizard adorned one shoulder. It looked as if the sparkles in it could be real diamonds.

The housekeeper flushed as she turned to see her mistress. "This young man is from the police, ma'am. He had a couple of questions, and I didn't like to disturb you."

Mrs. Turnbull's gaze fastened on Evan. "You again?" she said. "What do you want this time?"

"I only wanted the names of some of Alison's friends, and your housekeeper has been most helpful."

"Alison's friends? Why? What is this about?"

"Just double-checking Tony Mancini's story."

"That he knew Alison? I told you before that was utter nonsense. Now will you stop pestering us. I don't want to see you here again, is that clear? Go away and leave us in peace."

"I'm sorry to have disturbed you." He nodded to the housekeeper. "Thanks for your help."

As the door closed Evan heard Mrs. Turnbull's sharp voice. "Exactly what were you telling him?"

Chapter 16

Evan walked down the driveway and headed for his car. Then he changed his mind and pushed open the gate to the next-door house. It was a high, wrought-iron gate, and difficult to open. Not the kind of place that welcomed visitors. He hoped the garden didn't contain a guard dog and made his way cautiously to the front door. This house was not as grand—just a simple white stucco, two-story building, with black trim around the windows and a red-tiled roof. He rang the bell and, after a long wait, the door was opened by an elderly man with wisps of white hair framing a worried face.

"Yes, may I help you?" The voice was frail and a little guarded.

"I'm sorry to trouble you, but I'm working with the police on the murder case. I noticed that one of your upstairs windows overlooks the Turnbull's garden, so I just wondered whether the police have questioned anyone in the house yet about what they might have seen."

"Yes, they did come here," he said, "but I told them I couldn't help them. My wife and I live here alone, you see. I have become very shortsighted, and my wife is an invalid."

"She wouldn't have that upstairs room, by any chance, would she?"

"As a matter of fact, she does."

"Then could I possibly speak to her? She might just have seen something that could help us."

"I think that's very unlikely," the old man said. "As I told you, she is an invalid."

"But able to get to the window," Evan countered. "I saw the curtains twitch when I was here last. Someone was keeping an eye on me."

The old man sighed. "I don't suppose it can do any harm to talk to her, but I warn you, you won't get much out of her. Come on in then, young man."

"I'm Constable Evan Evans." Evan extended his hand.

"Justin Hartley."

The name rang a bell in the recesses of Evan's mind. "Dr. Hartley? Weren't you the Latin teacher at the old grammar school?"

"That's right. Did you go there?"

"Yes, but I think you retired soon after I arrived, and I never did take Latin."

"Shame on you." The old man smiled. "The most useful subject a young person can study. Know Latin and you know how languages work—the roots of English and most other languages we study are in Latin. And translating Latin prose is a little like unraveling a puzzle. It would have been good for your detective work. Come on, then, you'd better meet my wife while she's awake." He led the way up the stairs. "Her mind isn't what it was," he added, "but she has some days when she's more alert than others."

"So you didn't hear anything that night?" Evan asked the man.

"Nothing before I saw the flashing lights and heard an ambulance outside. But I go to bed early and I sleep in that room at the front of the house."

They reached the upstairs landing. "I've just had an idea," the old man said. "I wonder if you might do me a small favor. Would you mind terribly if I nipped out to buy some supplies while you were talking to my wife? I hate to leave her alone, and it's hard to find someone willing to stay with her while I pop out occasionally."

"I'd be happy to, sir." The men exchanged smiles.

Dr. Hartley turned a key and unlocked a door. "I'm afraid I have to keep it locked in case she becomes confused and falls down the stairs," he said. "She tends to wander at night."

He opened the door and stepped inside. "Hello, my dear. I've a visitor for you."

Evan followed him into a bright, sunny room with a bed in one corner, an armchair facing a TV set, and a chaise near the window. A sweet-faced old woman was sitting at the chaise, and her face lit up when she saw Evan. "I hoped you were coming to see us when I saw you get out of your car," she said, "but you went next door instead."

Evan's hopes rose. "How do you do, Mrs. Hartley," he said, taking her frail hand in his. It felt very cold. "I'm Evan Evans. Your husband invited me to have a chat with you."

"How delightful." She was still beaming at him. "Do take the armchair."

Dr. Hartley nodded to Evan and closed the door on them. Evan sat. Mrs. Hartley's face took on a guarded, cunning look. "Ah good. He's gone. Now I can find out why you're really here." She leaned toward Evan. "Have you been sent to get me out?"

"To get you out?"

"I had hoped they'd send someone to rescue me," she said. "To take me home. I've been kept a prisoner here for years, you know. They treat me well enough, I suppose, but it's not like being at home, is it?"

Evan was confused. "No, I suppose it's not. Where is your home then?"

"Far away. You have to go on a train."

"You and your husband used to live somewhere else?"

"I don't have a husband . . ."

"The man who showed me to your room?"

She leaned closer again. "Is that what he's been telling you? They are very clever, aren't they? He's the jailer. He's in charge of this institution."

Evan got up and walked to the window. It did indeed overlook the front of the Turnbull's house, as well as part of the street.

"You must see a lot going on from up here," he said.

"Oh yes. I just wish there was more to see. Not the busiest of streets, is it?"

"What about the house next door?"

"Not at all what it was when we lived there. When I was a girl there were always parties and croquet—such gaiety."

"*You* lived in the house next door?"

"Oh yes, but of course it was different then."

"How different?"

"It was a ship, wasn't it? We used to sail all over the place when I was young."

Evan appreciated Dr. Hartley's warning that it wasn't going to be easy to get any facts out of his wife.

"What about the people who live there now? Do you see much of them?"

"I don't see much of the little girl anymore. I think they've taken her away. Maybe it's the same people who keep me locked up here. The mother is a very busy woman—always darting in and out and I don't like *him*. Too much shouting."

"Shouting? At whom?"

"Always shouting. Just like my father. My father shouted a lot too. We were four sisters. He expected us to come running as soon as he yelled. And he'd lecture us, too, if we did anything wrong. Once I said to him, 'Daddy you can certainly talk!' and he got very angry with me. I thought he was going to hit me, but he didn't. He was a strict man, my father, but he never hit us. And he was nice sometimes. He'd take us for picnics in the motor car on Sundays. Do you like picnics? I always thought they were magical." She leaned forward again. "The jail doesn't allow picnics very often."

"A couple of weeks ago there was a disturbance at the house next door," Evan said quietly when she paused. "Something happened. Something not very nice. You didn't see or hear anything, did you?"

Mrs. Hartley was still staring past him with a faraway expression on her face. "I was the next to oldest," she said. "Catherine was the oldest, and Daddy got angry with her the most. 'What kind of food is this?' he yelled at her. 'I'm hungry and this is nothing but a little tart.' But then he gave us money for new clothes . . ."

"Mrs. Hartley," Evan repeated patiently. "That night, when the girl next door was killed. Do you remember anything about it? Before the ambulance came? Your husband said that he saw the flashing lights of the ambulance. Do you remember that too?"

He thought he noticed a flicker of remembrance in her eyes. "There was another ambulance there earlier that evening."

"Another ambulance? Are you sure."

"Oh yes," she said, nodding vehemently. "There are always ambulances outside that house—day and night, ambulances parked there. I don't know what they do to each other, but they are always requiring ambulances."

"Dear me," Evan said, with sinking heart. "So you didn't see anyone going up the front path that night?"

"Which night was that?"

"When the ambulance came."

"There are always ambulances at that house. Day and night."

Evan was glad when Dr. Hartley appeared again. "I don't suppose she could help you, could she?" he asked as he led Evan down the stairs.

"Not really, sir. She talked a lot about when she was a little girl. Said she used to live on a boat next door."

Dr. Hartley laughed. "Did she really? I must say it's amusing in a sad way. You never know what's going to come out next. It all has a basis in reality, of course. Her father was in the navy, although stationed on shore for most of her life."

"She talked a lot about her father."

Dr. Hartley nodded. "He was a rather imposing man. I was terrified when I first met him. No wonder he's still clear in her mind. Actually, she remembers the past quite well, but the present is another matter. She doesn't know me most of the time. And she doesn't recognize this house, which I find really distressing. We've lived here for forty years now. It breaks my heart when she begs me to take her home."

"It must be very hard for you."

Dr. Harley pressed his lips together for a moment, then said, "Very hard," in a gruff voice. "She can't really be left, you see. One never knows." He looked at Evan, appealing for understanding. Evan nodded. "I keep her door locked, but she can be surprisingly strong and cunning when she puts her mind to it. So I appreciated the chance to pop out for a few minutes."

He came to a halt at the front door. "We had a daily woman, but she left. I think washing all those sheets was too much for her. And I haven't managed to find another one yet." He hesitated, looking at Evan. "Look, you wouldn't like a cup of tea, would you? I'm about to make one for myself."

Evan was impatient to be off, but he saw the old man's face. "Thanks very much," he said. "I'd love a cup."

It was a good hour later when Evan finally got into his car. He sat for a while, staring at the words he had scribbled in his notebook during his talk with the Turnbull's housekeeper. He should start with Mrs. Turnbull's bridge ladies: Richards, Haversham, and the vicar's wife. It should be easy enough to look up their addresses in the phone book, but the vicar's wife would be the easiest to locate. It was just a question of which parish.

The closest church turned out to be in a less affluent neighborhood, so it would be highly unlikely that the Turnbulls would wish to be seen there. That meant Oystermouth was a better bet and Evan drove out beside the water. He glanced longingly at the sparkling blue of Swansea Bay with the green Gower Peninsula reaching a long finger out into the water on the west side. Hiking with Bronwen did seem infinitely more desirable than this wild goose chase he had set himself. With every interview he came away none the wiser. All he had to go on was Tony's word, which didn't count for much, a father who yelled and made enemies, and a mother who had asked, when she thought he was out of earshot, "Exactly what were you telling him?" Just enough to keep him suspicious and involved.

The woman who opened the front door of the vicarage had dark hair pulled back in a ponytail and was dressed in shorts and a halter top.

"Sorry to trouble you," Evan said, "but I wondered if I could speak to the vicar's wife."

"You're speaking to her." The woman looked amused. "What can I do for you?"

"I wondered if you are a friend of the Turnbulls?"

"Oh dear," she said, her smile fading. "Not another reporter, I hope. Those poor people have been through enough already."

"Not a reporter. Police, actually. I wondered if anyone had asked you about the night Alison was killed. Were you one of the bridge ladies who was in the house at the time?"

"Yes, I was. It was most—distressing. That awful shriek of despair and then finding her lying there."

"But you didn't hear anything earlier?"

"That's the strange thing. We didn't. We were concentrating on the bridge game, of course. It could be that we were in the dining room, having stopped for refreshments when it happened. We were certainly there when Frank found her. Margaret wasn't feeling too well, you know. She gets terrible migraines. She was dummy and she went upstairs to get herself one of her headache tablets. She told us to go ahead and help ourselves to food and wine when we'd finished the rubber. She was going to lie down for a few minutes. Then she was quite agitated when she came into the room. She said she couldn't find her glasses and she'd be right back. Then we heard her awful scream, and we rushed to the front door and there was poor little Alison. Too horrible for words."

"And the dog didn't bark at all?"

She paused to think. "No, I can't say that I heard the dog bark. But he was shut in the kitchen. Mary Richards is afraid of him, you know, so they keep him shut up when we come."

"Mary Richards, and presumably you had a fourth player?"

"Yes. Jane Haversham."

"And where might I find them?"

"The Richards are out in Langland—Brandy Cove Road. Jane Haversham is a neighbor of the Turnbulls, but they are away at their French cottage at the moment."

Evan hesitated, wanting to ask more questions but not sure what to ask. "Did you know Alison well?" he said at last.

"Not well. She's been away at school for the past four years, but I saw her from time to time."

"And how would you have described her?"

She thought for a moment. "Typical teenager, I suppose you'd say. I know that she and Margaret had been clashing a lot lately. Margaret didn't approve of the things Alison wanted to wear, the music she listened to—the sort of thing we've all been through in our time." She smiled. "And of course it wasn't made any easier because her father adored her and let her have her own way all the time. He thought the sun shone out of Alison's head. Well, she was a lovely child, and sweet natured too, basically." She frowned. "It was a horrible, horrible thing to do. It has shattered those people's lives, as well as snuffing out a bright, hopeful little candle."

Chapter 17

As soon as he left the vicarage, Evan drove straight to the Richards—one of the remaining bridge players the vicar's wife had mentioned. She had given him the address willingly enough. "It's worth exploring every avenue, isn't it? No jury is going to be convinced if we can't come up with good solid evidence, although I don't think that Mary Richards's testimony will be all that reliable. A bit of a waffler and prone to flights of fancy, if you know what I mean. So take anything she tells you with a grain of salt."

As it happened, Mary Richards didn't tell him anything. There was nobody home except the daily woman. Mrs. Richards had, apparently, gone to Cardiff shopping, as she usually did on a Friday. Wouldn't be home until evening and then they had theater tickets. So that would have to wait until tomorrow.

The clock on the Guildhall chimed noon and reminded Evan that it would be diplomatic to go home for lunch. He had made the right decision, as his mother had prepared a lovely piece of smoked haddock with mashed potatoes and peas.

"Fish on Friday," she said, as she put the plate in front of him. "I hope that's all right with you."

Evan smiled at the stubbornness of tradition. It had been fish on Friday ever since he could remember. Since the family had never been Catholic, he wondered where this self-imposed rule had come from. Probably from his grandmother and her mother before that, back to the time when everybody was Catholic, before Charles Wesley converted Wales. He didn't find it a hardship to eat the moist, flaky fillet, dotted with melting butter, on his plate.

"Just to warn you," he said, when he had finished eating, "I'm going to fetch Bronwen some time over the weekend, so we might need to make up another bed again for a night or two. That's all right, isn't it?"

"Why wouldn't it be all right? Your intended is always welcome here, as you know. I thought it was a bit funny, myself, going off and leaving her alone in the first place. Your father and I always did everything together. None of this flitting in one direction and then another."

"Except for when he went to watch Swansea Town play football," Evan reminded her.

She smoothed down her apron. "Yes, well you wouldn't want me standing among a lot of hooligans, would you?"

After lunch Evan decided to tackle Penlan—the large council estate that sprawled, row after row of uniformly ugly houses, over one of the hills that flanked the town. He parked outside a row of shops, hoping that this gave his car less chance of being vandalized, then walked through the estate to Tony Mancini's house. He wasn't sure what he hoped to find up here, but he needed to get the feel of Tony's life for himself. The houses were typical of postwar council developments—built in rows of eight, with brown pebble-dash exteriors that were now peeling and in urgent need of repair. The small front gardens were overgrown with weeds, or piled with old car parts, abandoned sofas, or bits of lumber. A place of little beauty and little hope, Evan thought. Occasionally he passed a garden whose owner had made an effort and created a tiny patch of beauty—a flower bed amid neat crazy paving, a birdbath surrounded by petunias, a small, well-mowed lawn, complete with two grumpy-looking garden gnomes.

Tony's mother had made no such effort. The front garden was

concreted over, and a rusting Ford Fiesta with no wheels was propped up on bricks. The front gate almost came off in his hand. A woman came to the front door, cigarette in one hand. She was still wearing a dressing gown and slippers, her eyes bleary and her hair tangled from sleep. She eyed him suspiciously.

"Yes? If you're from the council about the drains, it's about bloody time." As she spoke Evan noticed she had a missing front tooth.

"I'm not from the council, ma'am. I'm from the police," Evan said.

The eyes instantly became wary and hard. "Oh yes? He can't have done anything this time because he's safely behind bars."

"You're Tony's mum?"

"No, I'm the bleeding Queen of England. What do you think?"

"I'm trying to help Tony," Evan said. "I don't think he did it."

"Of course he bloody did it." She spat out the words. "If he told you he didn't, he's lying. He's tried to lie his way out of everything since he used to help himself to sweets from the jar. A born little liar, that's what he is. So don't waste your time, mate. Let him rot, for all I care. I'm done with him."

"But he was living here, until he got arrested?"

"I suppose he was. Off and on. When he bothered to turn up, like. To tell you the truth, Sid was about to kick him out."

"Sid?"

"My bloke. Couldn't stand the sight of Tony. A good-for-nothing, that's what Sid said. Said it made him sick."

Evan nodded. "Mrs. Mancini—you know Tony better than anyone. Did it surprise you to learn that he'd been arrested for rape and murder?"

That made her stop and think for a moment. "Well, yeah, I suppose it did. Not the murder bit. I mean, he'd already shot a copper, hadn't he, so that didn't surprise me at all. But the rape bit—well, I would have said Tony was as crooked as a bent pin, but I wouldn't have called him violent. I took him to see *Bambi* when he was a kid, and he cried all the way through it. Sid used to wonder if he was a fairy 'cos he never seemed to have girlfriends. No, I can see him helping himself to a girl's handbag, but not to anything else she might have to offer."

"When he came home that night," Evan went on, "how did he behave? As usual? Was he upset?"

"He was hopping mad that the police had picked him up. 'I was just minding my own f-ing business,' pardon my language—that's what he said. 'He had no right. I'm going to tell my probation officer that they keep picking on me.' "

"Thank you," Evan said. "You've been very helpful."

"Have I? I don't want to be. The longer they keep him behind bars, the better, if you ask me. They should shut him away for life. Proper criminal mind, that's what he's got. Never did have a sense of right and wrong. It was always, will I get caught or won't I? That's how that type of person thinks, you know."

"So you had problems with him as a little boy, then?"

"All his life. Well, he was too much for me to handle, wasn't he? His dad walked out on us when he was still a toddler. He needed a firm hand. Sid's been trying to take him in hand, but it's too late now. He's already bent."

Evan took a deep breath. "Well, thanks again, Mrs. Mancini."

"Ta ta, then. But I wouldn't waste any more time on him, love. He's not worth it."

She closed the door. Evan walked back down the front path. This time the gate did come away in his hand.

He went back to the car, which was sitting there untouched, then cruised around Penlan. There were children playing in the streets, pushing dolls' prams or kicking soccer balls. They looked up with hard, suspicious little faces as he passed. At last he found a group of boys sitting on the steps of a block of council flats. Evan got out of the car. The boys stared at him suspiciously, tense and ready for flight.

"Can you blokes help me?" Evan called out, in the lilting sing-song of the Swansea accent. "I'm looking for someone."

He approached them. "Any of you know a bloke called Jingo?"

"Jingo? Jingo Roberts?" The boys were still eyeing him with great suspicion.

"That's right. Used to be a friend of Tony Mancini's."

"What's he done?"

"He hasn't done anything. I'm—I'm working with the solicitor who's trying to help Tony, so he's sent me to talk to his friends."

"Tony doesn't belong to the gang anymore," one of the smaller boys blurted out before he was elbowed in the ribs by a bigger boy. "Jingo doesn't want him."

"I know that," Evan said, "but I'd still like to speak to him. Any idea where I can find him?"

"You're trying to help Tony?" another of the boys asked.

Evan nodded. "Maybe."

"Jingo says he did it," the smallest boy said, moving out of the reach of another elbow. "Jingo says he's dead meat if ever he gets out again."

"You think someone set Tony up, mister? Paid him back, like?" a serious boy of Indian descent asked.

Now that was an interesting thought, Evan decided. Out of the mouth of babes! He straightened up. "Something like that. So where can I find Jingo at this time of day, do you think? Does he work?"

For some reason this made them smirk.

"Nah. Jingo don't work. Don't need to, does he?"

"He lives with his mum. Thirty-four Conway Street," the small boy said. Then he added quickly, "Don't go hitting me again. I'm telling Dad. He could easily have found it out for himself, couldn't he?"

"Thanks." Evan gave what he hoped was a friendly smile. Future gang members, he thought as he walked away. Were they destined to follow in Tony's footsteps?

Conway Street was near the top of the hill and afforded a lovely view out over the green valleys beyond. In other parts of the world people paid a high price for views like this. He wondered if anyone here appreciated it.

A tired-looking woman opened the front door only wide enough to peer out.

"Jingo isn't home," she said bluntly in response to Evan's question.

"Any idea where I can find him then?"

She shrugged. "I'm not his secretary. He comes and goes as he pleases."

"I understand he doesn't have a job at the moment."

"That's right. On the dole again. Not much work to be had around here, is there? What did you want him for?"

"I wanted to speak to him about Tony Mancini."

"That little shit? Jingo don't want no more to do with him after what he did to that girl. He doesn't approve of violence against women. I brought him up to respect women, see. You'll not find my Jingo laying a hand on a girl."

"So when do you think I might find him at home?" Evan persisted.

She shrugged again. "Like I said. He comes and goes as he pleases."

"Hey, Ma. Do we have any more of those salty bacon crisps?" a voice shouted from a back room.

"Well, what do you know?" Evan grinned. "He decided to come home, by the sound of it."

"You better get out here, love," the woman called into the house. "There's a man wants to talk to you about Tony."

The door opened wider, and a tall, bony young man with short, spiked red hair stood facing Evan. He had that very white skin that sometimes accompanies red hair, very light eyes, and the ring through his left eyebrow gave him a permanent frown. He was wearing tight black jeans and a muscle shirt, and he looked at Evan with an insolent sneer. "Copper, are you?"

"Maybe."

"Go on. Of course you are. I can tell one a mile off. Got a particular smell to them."

"I haven't come to trade insults," Evan said. "I just wanted to ask you a couple of questions about Tony. You two used to be good mates once, right?"

"Tony was in my gang. That's not exactly the same thing. I told him what to do. He did it."

"Like shooting that policeman?" Evan couldn't help the words from escaping and regretted them instantly.

"He was holding the gun." The insolent smile never faltered. "But the little shit tried to bring me into it in court, didn't he? I've never forgiven him for that. Rangers don't squeal on other Rangers, especially not on me."

"So you haven't seen him recently."

"Not to talk to. No."

"So what do you think about this latest thing. Were you surprised?"

Jingo shrugged. "I didn't think he had it in him. I thought he was actually a timid little prick when it came down to it."

"He says he knew the girl. He met her clubbing. You never saw them together, did you?"

"I wouldn't know her from Adam, would I? And I don't go clubbing. It's for kids. You grow out of it, don't you?" He moved toward Evan in a manner that Evan was supposed to find threatening. "Look, mate, I don't know what you want from me, but I wouldn't help Tony Mancini if he was about to fall off a mountain and I had the only rope." He fixed Evan with a cold stare. "Got it? So bugger off."

Evan was glad when the last houses of the Penlan estate were left behind him and the blue waters of the bay came into view. He stopped beside Cwmdonkin Park, where Bronwen had sat beside the Dylan Thomas memorial, spouting Thomas's poems. The wind in his face was fresh as he strode over the springy grass. That place had left a bad taste in his mouth. He could understand psychologists arguing that Tony hadn't had a fair chance in life. The one interesting fact that had emerged was that the people he had interviewed were all surprised that Tony had committed such a crime.

What he needed was a list of other people with a motive. The only motive so far seemed to hinge around the character of Mr. Turnbull—the man who yelled a lot at home, according to Mrs.

Hartley, and the factory owner who had an angry ex-worker show up at his house. It would be worth finding out if there were any more disgruntled workers with good reasons to pay back their boss. Then the housekeeper had told Evan that the dog had been attack trained because Turnbull's role on the council inspired cranks and hate calls. Had there been one particular case that had made him get a guard dog? He should swing by the council offices before they closed for the weekend.

Having decided on this course of action, Evan took one last look at the city spread at his feet, gave the Dylan Thomas memorial a friendly pat, then sprinted back to his car. His legs were already feeling a little stronger. He pictured himself, rugby ball tucked under one arm, as he crossed the touch line for a try.

There was a vacant parking space outside the new Crown Court building, opposite the Guildhall. Evan looked up at the concrete structure as he parked and got out. "Five years? Five years for my husband's life?" His mother's outburst resonated through his head. He shook the thoughts away and dodged traffic to cross the street.

The art deco building of the Guildhall was a sharp contrast to the stark, gray concrete opposite. It had been built in the thirties, when people needed cheering up and there were enough unemployed craftsmen to create the intricate parts. It was bright and cheerful inside with murals and marble stairways. After being directed a couple of times he found the room that housed the secretary to the city council. She listened to him politely.

"Made threats against Mr. Turnbull, you say?" She wrinkled a little button of a nose. "No, I can't say I ever heard that. Of course, Mr. Turnbull is rather strong in his opinions sometimes. The homeless people on the streets, for example. Mr. Turnbull calls them a blot on society. He said if he had his way he'd give them a good scrubbing and a pick and a shovel and make them work for their food. That didn't go down too well with the do-gooders, of course. And there were protests outside the Guildhall when the council voted to pull down some historic wharf buildings to make way for the new waterfront project."

"Historic wharf buildings?" Evan laughed. "They were awful old places, about to fall down anyway. I used to play there as a kid."

She smiled. "To the conservation league they were historic. There was a big hoo-ha about it, but the project went ahead anyway."

Evan nodded. Enough to make people protest and get annoyed, but nothing that would make a person so angry that he took it out on Turnbull by killing his most prized possession.

"That night Alison was killed," Evan said, "Mr. Turnbull was at a council meeting, I understand. He came home to find the body."

"That's what I read in the papers," the girl said. "I was a little bit surprised, actually."

"Why was that?"

"Well, we had two members away on holiday and one off sick, so we didn't have a quorum. The meeting was cut short. They were out of here before eight."

Chapter 18

So Mr. Turnbull hadn't come straight home from a council meeting. Evan put the car into gear and moved out into the traffic. What did that prove, actually? He wondered if the local police had checked on Turnbull's movements that evening, whether he should mention the discrepancy to them. Then he dismissed the thought. Lots of people run little errands when they find themselves with time to spare. He might even have stopped off at a pub for a quick one. Nothing changed the fact that he arrived home around nine-forty-five to find his daughter lying dead on his doorstep. And it appeared that there was no one with a big enough grudge to kill Alison.

The streets were filling up with cars, and pedestrians darted out into the traffic. He glanced at his watch. Almost five o'clock. Businesses were knocking off for the day. On a whim he drove up to the Unico site. Sure enough, workers were streaming out of the gates—groups of girls and women talking together as they hurried to be first in the queue at the bus stop, and men in dirty work clothes, sauntering past the girls, hurling cheeky comments in their direction. Evan parked and got out of his car. Some of the men were heading for the Queen's Head pub across the street. The pub sign outside depicted the stern profile of an aging Queen Victoria. There must have been times, Evan thought, when the locals would have preferred the queen's head, John the Baptist–style, on a platter. He followed a group of men into the bar and ordered himself a Brains. He didn't actually like the beer, which came from nearby Cardiff, but he thought it diplomatic to blend in. He took a big gulp, wondering how best to approach the men from the factory when one of them stopped him on his way back from the bar.

"I know you, don't I?"

Evan tried to remember the face. "I don't know. You might do. I grew up here. I went to the old grammar school, what's now Bishop Gore comprehensive."

The man shook his head. "No, I didn't go to a brainy school like that. Wait a minute. You played rugby."

Evan beamed. "That's right. Did we play against each other?"

"Not me, boyo. I don't enjoy blokes stepping all over my face. But I had a mate who played, and I remember seeing you down at the St. Helen's ground, right?"

"Yes, I played there quite often."

"You still playing?"

"No. Don't have time anymore, although I am thinking of getting back to it. I live up in North Wales now and they're starting a pro team up there, so I hear."

"Professional rugby? You're good enough for that, are you?"

"We'll have to see, won't we. I've been out of it for almost five years. But it would be brilliant if I could make the team."

"I'll say. Getting paid to play a sport—that's every bloke's dream, isn't it? You say you moved up to North Wales?"

Evan nodded.

"What the bloody hell for? A lot of rabid nationalists up there, going around singing songs in Welsh from what you see on the telly."

Evan smiled. "Oh, it's not such a bad life, especially if you love the outdoors, like me."

"What do you do up there? I always thought there were no jobs anymore."

"That's true enough. The slate mines have all closed. Farming and tourism—that's about it, really. And farming's taking a big knock this year with the foot-and-mouth epidemic."

"It's bad up there, is it?"

"The local farmers were about to slaughter their flocks when I came away. I was glad to get away, I can tell you. I'm the local policeman, and I was going to have to keep the peace between the farmers and the army."

"Smart of you to get away."

"So what do you do?" Evan asked innocently.

"Me? I work for Unico, just across the street. We make computer housing."

"Doing all right, are they?"

"Doing all right? Can't keep up with demand, boyo. Old Turnbull's always trying to get us to put in more overtime, but my Sharon put her foot down. 'If he wants you to live at the bloody factory, tell him to build you a house at the bloody factory then.' That's what she said." He clapped Evan on the shoulder. "There's a group of my mates over there. Why don't you come and join us?"

"Thanks a lot." Evan held out his hand. "The name's Evan."

"Neil Jenkins—I know, same name as the rugby star. I get people asking me for my autograph all the time. Over here then." He led the way through the now-crowded bar to a group of men who had found themselves a table in the corner. "I've met a bloke I used to watch playing rugby," Neil Jenkins announced. "Evan, this is Tom, Dave, Rhodri, Martin, and Patch."

The men grinned and nodded. One of them grabbed a chair from a neighboring table. Evan sat.

"He lives up in the North now. Can you imagine that? He says it's terrible with all the foot-and-mouth disease up there."

"I reckon it's terrible without the disease," one of the men said. "I reckon I'd die of boredom. Only got one cinema up there, haven't they? And nobody speaks bloody English?"

"Don't they say the local social club is a sheep tied to a telephone pole?" a large man in spattered overalls asked, his bulky body shaking at his own joke.

Evan ignored it. "Do you all work for Unico?" he asked.

The men nodded. "That's us. Turnbull's slaves."

"Is that the same Mr. Turnbull whose daughter was killed?"

"That's right, poor bloke," the older, skinny man in the corner said. "I can't say I'm too fond of Turnbull as a boss, but I wouldn't wish that on my worst enemy."

"Bit of a tartar is he then, Turnbull?" Evan asked.

The men glanced at each other then nodded agreement. "If he doesn't like what you do, he sacks you on the spot. No questions asked," one of them said. "For example, if he came in here and overheard us talking about him, we'd be out."

"You always have to watch what you're saying," the skinny man agreed. "You never know when one of his spies is lurking. No one's safe."

"Well, except for one person." The big man in the overalls gave Evan a nudge and a knowing wink. "But then I wouldn't be willing to do what she does to butter up to the boss."

"He wouldn't fancy you, boyo. You don't wear your skirts short enough," Neil Jenkins said, setting off a chain of ribald comments. Evan sat quietly, observing. The boss's secretary, obviously. He had wondered about the look that had passed between them. It wouldn't be the first time that a secretary had provided more than coffee and typing for her boss. He noticed that glasses were empty and offered to buy the next round.

The first time it was refused. "No, no, you're the visitor. Isn't he, boys? Can't make him pay for the privilege of being in Swansea."

But Evan knew Swansea manners too well. It was polite to refuse the first time. He repeated the offer. This time it was accepted. "Oh well, if you insist, I suppose another pint might not be such a bad idea."

He went up to the bar and came back with a full tray.

"You were talking about Turnbull dismissing his employees if he overheard them talking about him," he said when they had all taken a preliminary swig. "Didn't I read something in the local paper a little while ago about a man going berserk at Turnbull's house?"

"Oh, you mean Kelly," several of the men said in unison. "He was mouthing off about safety conditions when he came off shift and Turnbull overheard him. 'Go and get your cards, you're fired,' Turnbull told him. Kelly nearly blew a gasket. 'You can't fire me for saying what I like on my own time,' he tells him. 'It's a free bloody country, you know. I'm entitled to my own opinions.' 'Of course you are,' Turnbull says, 'but I'm also free to sack any disloyal employees.' "

"So he came after Turnbull, did he?" Evan asked.

"Got himself roaring drunk then went down to his house and called him out to fight," the skinny man said with a grin. "That was typical Kelly. Bit of a troublemaker. Irish, you know. They're a bunch of hotheaded bastards, aren't they?"

"So what happened?"

"Nothing. Kelly spent the night in jail, and Turnbull didn't press charges."

Evan shifted on his seat. "Has that kind of thing happened to anyone else recently?"

Several heads shook. "No other hotheaded Irishmen around, as far as I know," one of them said at last.

"There was that Mancini kid. The one who they say killed Turnbull's daughter," a freckle-faced boy chimed in for the first time. "Turnbull sacked him on the spot, didn't he?"

"Of course he did," Neil Jenkins said. "I would too if I'd caught a bloke with his hand in the petty cash. He's lucky Turnbull didn't press charges. Always was a slippery little bastard, if you ask me. Jeff Pritchard swears the kid nicked his Crunchie Bar from his lunch box."

The men laughed as if this was a good joke.

"Jeff and his Crunchie Bars. Yes, that would be a matter of life or death to him."

Evan sat quietly among them as conversation moved on. He could do some further checks on Kelly, of course, but it seemed as if Tony Mancini was the only one with a recent grudge against his former boss. He finished his pint and made an excuse to leave before another round was bought.

• • •

As Evan let himself into his mother's house he was surprised to hear voices coming from the kitchen. His first thought was that Bronwen had returned. A big smile crossed his face as he hurried down the hall.

"Now how did you get here?" he asked, pushing open the door. "Too impatient to wait until tomorrow?"

"Always impatient to see you again, love." The dark-haired woman at the table gave him a sultry look.

"Maggie. What are you doing here?" Evan asked.

His former girlfriend was sitting at the table, wearing short white shorts and a black tank top that revealed an expanse of midriff. One shapely leg was crossed over the other one. A cigarette dangled between her fingers.

"Is this a nice surprise?" Evan's mother was looking pleased with herself. "She stopped by and I invited her to have supper with us. Nothing fancy. I just made a lamb *cawl*." She dipped a ladle into the thick lamb stew on the stove and began spooning into a bowl. "So how was your day?"

"Productive."

"I was just telling Maggie that you're helping out the local police, making sure they've got enough evidence to send that boy to jail for good this time."

"And where is Blodwyn? Upstairs weaving or spinning?"

"Her name is Bronwen and she's at her parents' house. I'm going to fetch her tomorrow."

"She seems a little on the boring side," Maggie said. "What exactly do you two do for fun up there among the sheep?"

"Oh, we find enough to amuse ourselves." He gave her a challenging smile and was glad to see it had the right effect. "Bronwen isn't exactly the village girl, you know. She went to Cambridge University. Her parents own a huge house and half a bloody county."

"Then what in God's name is she doing stuck in a dreary spot like Llanfair?"

"She likes it, as I do. Not everybody likes noise and music and hype all the time."

"Rather you than me." She accepted the bowl of stew that Mrs. Evans put in front of her. "So your mother tells me that you're thinking of getting married."

"That's right."

"Had any more thoughts about my proposition the other night? The rugby team, I mean?"

"I've been thinking about it."

"And?"

"I'm still thinking about it."

"Stew will want to know soon. If the team gets the go ahead, they'll be working out in a couple of weeks."

Evan nodded and busied himself eating the soup. Maggie chatted away brightly to Mrs. Evans about local scandals and people Evan didn't know. He was glad he wasn't expected to join in. After the plates had been cleared away, Maggie got to her feet. "Well, I suppose I'd better be going then. I've got to meet the boys down the pub at nine. Stew will wonder where I've got to."

"See Maggie to the door then, Evan," Mrs. Evans said. "And do stop by again, dear, won't you? It really brightens up the place when you're around."

They walked in silence to the front door.

"I get the feeling your mum isn't too hot on Bronwen then. She welcomed me like a long-lost daughter. When I was around all the time, she couldn't stand the sight of me."

"That's the way my mum is. She'd prefer you right now because that would mean I'd have to stay here in Swansea."

"Would that be such a bad idea? You could always go back to your old job, couldn't you? They must be grateful for all the work you're doing for them right now. And we had a lot of fun in those days, didn't we?"

"Yes, we had a good time," Evan agreed.

"We should never have broken up. We were good for each other."

"I wasn't the one who broke up," Evan said. "As I remember, your last words to me were that you didn't want to 'wait around for a loony.' "

Maggie winced. "Yes, well, I was younger then. You don't always stop and think what you say when you're young, do you? And you were acting like a mental case, weren't you—lying there, not bothering to get up and not wanting to talk to anyone."

"Shock and depression don't exactly equal loony," Evan said. "Still, it was all for the best. It was one of the things that made me get away, and I'm happy with the life I've chosen and the woman I've chosen too."

Maggie shrugged. "Each to his own, as they say. See you around then. Let Stew know about the job."

"Do you need a lift somewhere?"

"Me? Don't worry. I can walk. It's not far to the pub." She tossed back her mane of dark hair and set off up the street, leaving Evan feeling slightly guilty, although he didn't know why. He went out to the shed, thought about lifting some weights, then thought again. Did he really want anything to do with an organization that would be somehow linked to Maggie? He stood there in the half darkness, trying to imagine the fans screaming as his team scored the winning try. There was certainly nothing like the adrenaline rush of playing on a winning team, scoring the winning try. Nothing in his present life came close. It was certainly tempting.

There was no point in arriving at the Monkey's Uncle before nine-thirty or ten o'clock. Evan remembered from the time he was on the beat in Swansea that the clubs only livened up after that hour. He dressed in the most casual clothes he owned—a pair of jeans and a black T-shirt. Even so, he looked too old and too clean cut. He tried restyling his hair, but it didn't seem to want to adapt to a more trendy style. He certainly wasn't about to go out and buy styling gel. Eventually he drove off, not too hopeful about getting much out of the kids at the club and certainly not looking forward to the evening ahead. This time he had pictures of both Tony and Alison, cut from the newspapers, in his wallet.

Sound was spilling out onto Kingsway, the deep throb of the bass beat coming up through the soles of his feet as he waited in line. Rather than flash his warrant card this time, he paid admission and moved up the stairs as part of a throng of kids. Some of them looked at him strangely. He gave what he hoped was an encouraging smile. A couple of the girls smiled back. The sound grew louder as they moved up the stairs until it hit him with an almost physical blow as he entered the room. The joint certainly was jumping tonight. The room was in darkness, except for a laser light show that flashed random red patterns across walls and ceiling and a twirling glass ball that peppered the dancers with squares of spotlight. Up on the stage at the far end, five shadows in black leather moved in grotesque exaggeration to the music—if that is what it could be called. They were all tall, skinny, and had long untidy hair; it was hard to tell if they were male or female until one of them grabbed the mike. "I wan-choo!" he roared into it in a gravelly voice. "I wan-choo. I wan-choo." Each time he shouted the words, he struck a provocative pose, hips thrust forward, lower lip pouting open. "I wan-choo." Those seemed to be the only words, but the kids loved it. They stood, packed onto the floor so tightly that real dancing was impossible, jerking to the rhythm, hands swaying above their heads, girls squealing from time to time.

Evan eased in against a wall. He saw no chance of questioning anybody with this row going on. He looked around for a bar and found only soft drinks being served. Of course, the place catered to a very young crowd. In spite of the lack of alcohol, some of the kids already looked high or spaced out, making Evan wonder what kind of drugs were being passed around in the darker corners. He had heard about ecstasy but hadn't come across it in his own experience. A girl in the center of the floor had both eyes closed and was swaying like a young tree, arms above her head. The expression on her face was close to ecstasy. Evan watched with interest.

The number ended. Evan pulled out the photos, although the light was too poor to see much. He showed them to one group after another but got no response.

"I come with my mates. I don't notice who else is here," one girl said.

"My boyfriend would kill me if I checked out other blokes," another added.

At last, in desperation, he went downstairs again to the kiosk at the front entrance, where money was taken and the kids were vetted before entering. He showed the pictures to the two young men at the desk. One was large enough to be an official bouncer if needed.

"You don't remember either of these kids coming to the club recently, do you?" Evan asked.

The two boys peered at the pictures. "What's this in aid of?" one of them asked. "Are you police?"

"Yeah," Evan admitted. "We're checking out this bloke's alibi. He claims he used to come here on Friday nights. I thought you might have seen him or the bird."

"I don't think I've seen her," the other boy said, "but I'm pretty sure I've seen him."

"Can you remember when and who he was with?"

"It wasn't long ago. Two or three weeks, I'd say. I went out for a smoke and I noticed him hanging around outside, talking to a tall bloke with red hair. Then the redheaded bloke left, and this one came into the club. I'm pretty sure it's him."

"Brilliant," Evan said. "Thanks. Cheers. You've been very helpful. Now I suppose I'd better go up there again and see if anyone remembers seeing her."

Reluctantly he climbed the stairs. A slow number was now being played, the bodies on the floor twitching to the deep thud-thud of the drum beat. Evan leaned against the wall, and let his gaze sweep the room. He knew the logical thing to do would be ask some girl to dance and then start chatting. But he wasn't very good at chatting and even worse at dancing. The girls all seemed to be in tight little cliques. At a far table he noticed a group with their heads together, talking away as if the sound didn't bother them at all. They were dressed in what he supposed was the current fashion—skimpy halter tops, skin-tight jeans, hair all the colors of the rainbow and spiked too, rings through eyebrows, lips, and, he suspected, navels. One of the girls looked up, and he saw her start as she noticed him across the room. Not a bad-looking kid if it wasn't for the blue spiked hair. He started to inch around the wall, dodging flailing arms and legs, toward her. It was only when he was a few feet away that she turned around again and he recognized her.

Chapter 19

Evan sauntered over to the table and stood looking down at the expectant group of girls. "You want to dance?" he asked the girl with the blue spiked hair.

"All right." She got to her feet, giving her friends an embarrassed smile. "See you later then." She followed him out into the middle of the dance floor. Evan went to put an arm around her waist, thought better of it, and began to gyrate in time to the music. She started to move with him.

"I thought you said you were a hopeless dancer."

"What are you doing here?" Evan hissed into her ear.

"I've gone undercover." Bronwen gave him a challenging smile. "I knew you'd be useless in a club."

"Too bloody right." He was still gazing down at her in stunned admiration. She even had a small stud through her left nostril. "You look amazing."

"Flatterer. I bet you say that to all the teenage girls. And now that I know you go around picking up strange chicks in clubs, I'm keeping closer tabs on you."

The music changed to a slower beat. He put his arms around her waist and pulled her closer, taking care not to hold her too comfortably. "So how did you get here?"

"I got fed up with sitting at home, waiting to be rescued from a fate worse than death. So when I found that the Fearnalls were coming into Swansea today, I hitched a ride. Then I had fun shopping at all the trendy boutiques and here I am."

"You look amazing."

"You already said that. Do you think I should keep the look?"

"That is only a wig, isn't it?" A worried frown crossed his face.

"And the stud is only screwed into my nose, but I'm obviously convincing so far. I've found out a whole lot of good stuff from my new mates over there." She turned back to them and waved. "They think you're cute, by the way. Too old, but cute."

The number ended.

"Taking a quick break, everyone," the lead singer announced.

Evan let his hands slide from her waist. "I should let you get back to your table to carry on the good work then."

She nodded. "Yes, I don't want them to think I'm a pushover. Why don't you wait for me outside? It's over at midnight."

"All right. I'm parked a little way down the street."

He started to walk her back to her table. She put out a hand to stop him. "See you later, then."

As she reached the girls at her table Evan heard her say, "I thought I'd never get rid of him. Did you see the way he danced?"

He could still hear the giggles as he reached the door. He let himself into the car and sat in the cold darkness, waiting. He knew he should be grateful that she had come to help him. He knew he shouldn't feel annoyed, but he did. He was supposed to be the one who investigated and solved crimes. Now it seemed that Bronwen might even be better at his job than he was. The possibility of the rugby team seemed all the more promising but getting back in shape all the harder with Bronwen back again. He didn't want to tell her what he was doing, in case he tried out for the team and didn't make it. He was, after all, a little old for boyish dreams.

The waiting seemed to go on and on. He was only wearing a T-shirt and wished he had brought a jacket. At last a great tide of young people spilled out onto Kingway, passing him in noisy groups, girls flirting with boys, boys flirting with girls, in final pick-up attempts of the night. At last he caught sight of her in the rear-view mirror, still with her giggly friends.

"See you tomorrow maybe," he heard her call, then she ran to the car, a little unsteady on her high platform shoes. She opened the passenger door and got in. "Let's get out of here before they see it's you," she said.

"Who do they think it is?" He started the car and pulled away from the curb.

"My dad. I told them he always insists on coming to get me. That way I didn't have to hang around picking up boys with them."

Evan looked at her and laughed. "I'd love to see their faces if they found out you were really a twenty-nine-year-old school-teacher."

"Benefits of good genes and a pure life," Bronwen said, removing the blue spiked wig and shaking out her hair. "I've always looked young for my age. I used to ride for half fare on the buses when I was a sixth-former. Oh, it feels wonderful to have that thing off my head."

"Where on earth did you find it?"

"At a costume shop. Cool, isn't it? My new mates thought I was majorly cool."

"You said you'd found out good stuff." He put the car into low gear to climb the hill. "Have you really found out anything useful? Did any of them know Alison?"

"Oh yes." She looked smug. "Well, they didn't exactly know her, but they knew who she was. One of them, Tiffany, told me something very interesting. She said that Alison was using cocaine."

"What?" Evan almost missed the bend in the road. "How would she know that?"

"Well, she didn't exactly know, but she overheard Alison talking to a friend back in the spring. Alison must have been home for the Easter holidays. Tiffany was in the loo at the club, and she says she heard this girl mention coke. Then she went on talking about how hard it had been to get her hands on the money and how Tony had better show up with the goods. They obviously didn't know that anyone was in the end stall, Tiffany said, and she was curious because they both had posh accents. So she peeked out and saw them, and then later that night she kept her eye on Alison and she saw her go off with Tony Mancini."

"She knew who he was, did she?"

"Oh yes. They all knew who he was because he was Penlan rubbish and he'd just got out of prison, so they knew enough to stay away. Besides, he wasn't exactly sexy, so it wasn't as if they were missing anything, according to them."

"Well, I'll be—" Evan muttered. "Now I'm beginning to put two and two together, Bron. The only piece of useful information I gathered this evening was that someone had seen Tony outside the club talking to a tall, red-haired boy. That had to be Jingo Roberts, leader of Tony's old gang, who claimed that he hadn't seen anything of Tony since he got out of jail. And Tony lied to me again, claiming that Jingo didn't want anything to do with him. But obviously he's back at his old job—running errands for Jingo. When you think about it, it makes sense. Why else would an attractive, posh girl like Alison Turnbull want to hang around with a skinny nobody like Tony Mancini?" He slapped his hand excitedly against the steering wheel. "And that was why he went to her house that night, Bron. Now I come to think of it, he said he was bringing her something. That something must have been cocaine."

The excitement drained from his voice as he took this one stage further. "Oh my God, Bronwen. There's no way he'll talk his way out of this one. They'll crucify him."

"And you don't think he should be crucified? Isn't it time to face facts, Evan? He was her drug dealer. Maybe she hadn't paid up. Maybe she had talked too much. Drug dealers are always bumping off dangerous clients. He had sex with her, and then he killed her."

Evan sighed. "I don't know anymore, Bron. I just don't know what to think. I was so sure he was innocent and now, every time I turn around, we've come up with more proof that he's guilty as hell. Maybe you're right about me. You always said I'm too gullible. He's probably just a good liar, and he knows a sucker when he sees one."

The car came to a halt outside Evan's house. "So what will you do now?" Bronwen asked.

"Go and talk to him first thing tomorrow morning. Get the truth out of him this time, even if I have to beat it out of him."

He came around to open her car door, but she was already halfway out. "I hope your mother won't mind my reappearing like this."

Evan took in the tight tank top with the red lips across it. A worried frown crossed his face. "Where are your real clothes?"

Bronwen bent to retrieve the carrier bag at her feet. "I've got jeans and a shirt in here. I changed in a lady's loo. Do you think it matters how I look at this time of night? At least I've taken off the blue hair."

"My mother will have gone to bed anyway," Evan said. "Of course, that doesn't mean she won't wake up the moment she hears my key in the door. She always used to."

"All right. I'll put on my own shirt, just in case." Bronwen slipped it over her head.

"So where did you leave the rest of your stuff?"

"At home. I slipped out with the minimum of baggage. Nightdress, toothbrush. That's about it. I thought we could go back and collect my suitcase on our way home."

"And Prince William. I hope you haven't forgotten about him."

"He'll be fine until we pick him up. Of course, he might have doubled in size. Daddy is spoiling him with all kinds of tidbits."

He put his key into the front door. "You take my room, and I'll sleep on the sofa," Evan whispered as he shut the door behind them.

"I can take the sofa."

"Not if you want to avoid giving my mother a heart attack when she comes down in the morning." He grinned at her. "I'm glad you're here." He took her into his arms. "I really missed you."

"I thought you were having too much fun without me and didn't miss me at all. I thought that maybe the sultry Maggie was keeping you entertained."

"Don't be daft." He thought it wise not to mention the visitor earlier that evening. Women were apt to take things the wrong way. Instead he bent to kiss her.

"Evan? Is that you? You've not brought Maggie back with you at this time of night, have you?" his mother's voice came down the stairs.

Evan sighed. "No, Mum. It's Bronwen. She missed me and she's come back. She's taking my room and I'll have the sofa tonight, so go back to bed."

In the morning the atmosphere around the breakfast table was decidedly strained.

"I was sure Evan told me he was going to fetch you today." Mrs. Evans put a cup of tea in front of Bronwen.

"He was, but I got impatient and hitched a ride with friends."

"If you'd only let me know you were coming, I could have got the room ready." Mrs. Evans flashed a reprimanding glare. "I got the fright of my life, waking up and seeing the two of you down there. It's not like you, Evan, to come sneaking in and out in the middle of the night."

"Mum, I am thirty years old. I didn't think I had a curfew any longer." He tried a smile but she was clearly not amused.

As soon as breakfast was cleared away they made an escape.

"I'm clearly not in her good books now," Bronwen said.

"She doesn't like surprises. Never did." Evan squeezed her shoulder. "And it has nothing to do with you. She's only worrying that the house wasn't perfect. She'll get over it."

"So are you going to confront Tony now? I presume you don't want me with you."

"I don't think they'd let you in. And you're right. I wouldn't want you there." His face lit up. "But I do have a good idea. You were so successful last night. How about a repeat performance today?"

"The blue wig?"

"No, let's not go that far. I wondered if you could speak to some of Alison's former schoolfriends for me. They might tell you things they wouldn't tell me."

"How should I present myself? I'd need an excuse to go barging in."

"You could say you were at boarding school with Alison. You were in the sixth form when she was a new girl. You'd just heard what happened to her. If you leave your hair loose and wear those sexy jeans from last night, you can get away with looking young enough."

"I'm glad you found the jeans sexy." She smiled at him. "Betsy better watch out. She'll have a fashion rival when I get home."

"So you'll do it?"

"Of course. Give me the names and addresses."

Half an hour later Evan was parked outside the prison. The guard at the gate recognized him. "Another grilling for Mancini?" he asked. "Give him hell. Cocky little bastard."

"Don't worry about that." Evan nodded grimly. He tried to collect his thoughts and calm his racing pulse as he followed the guard down the tiled hallway to the interview room. It seemed to take a long time for Tony to appear. When he came in and saw Evan, his eyes were hopeful.

"You got something for me? You getting me out of this dump?" he asked as the guard locked them into the room together.

"I've got something for you, all right," Evan said, trying to keep his voice even. "But not quite the same sort of thing that you were bringing to Alison Turnbull the night she died."

The expectant look faltered. "What d'you mean?"

"You know damned well what I mean, you lying little prick. Did you think I was completely stupid? You've done nothing but lie to me since the first time I saw you. I should have put my hands around your throat then and finished you off."

Tony backed away from him. "You can't touch me. I'll push the button for the guard, and they'll get me out of here."

"Not a moment too soon," Evan said. "This is it, Mancini. You can go to hell and rot there, which is what you will do when they hear what I'm going to tell them."

"You found out about the coke then?"

"Half the sodding world knows about the coke, Tony. If they'd taken the trouble to ask questions, any little old lady doing her shopping could have told them!"

"Okay, so that's how I met her." His arms were crossed defensively. "She'd got hooked on the stuff when her parents sent her to some posh place in Switzerland last summer. When she came back here, she looked for a local supplier."

"And she latched on to your friend Jingo."

"I told you, Jingo kicked me out of the gang. He's got nothing to do with it."

"Of course he has. You don't want me to believe that you were the dealer, do you? You don't have the class, Tony. You're just the runner, the delivery boy. Lying's not going to help you anymore, and neither am I. I've had enough of sticking my neck out for you." He took a step toward Tony, towering over him, threatening. "You were seen, outside the club, talking to Jingo a couple of weeks ago."

Tony had backed away until he was against the brick wall. Evan gave him a look of disgust and turned away. "I've had enough, Tony. You deserve everything you're going to get. All you've told me so far is a pack of lies. Let's see if you can lie your way past the jury this time."

He strode to the door and rapped on it to be let out.

"No, wait," Tony called after him. "Okay, so I lied to you about Jingo, but I had to, didn't I? I had no f—" He broke off before uttering the swear word. "No choice."

The guard opened the door. "Sorry, mate. A few more minutes," Evan said, and the door was closed again.

"What do you mean, you had no choice?" Evan eyed Tony coldly from beside the door. "Everyone has a choice."

"I told you Jingo kicked me out of the gang after I ratted on him. That was true. But then he came round to see me one night after I got out of the YOI. He said the police were tailing his best boys. He said I'd be the last person they'd suspect, because they knew how he felt about me. He said it was my one chance to get back into the gang, if I kept my mouth shut and did what I was told. He said"—he broke off, licking his lips nervously—"he said if

I let on we were working together, I'd wind up stuffed down a sewer."

Evan nodded. "So he dealt, you delivered. He gave the orders, and you did what you were told. Did he tell you to get rid of her? Hadn't she paid her bills on time?"

Tony's eyes were darting furiously around the room. Evan watched his Adam's apple dance up and down his skinny neck. "I didn't kill her. I swear to God I didn't kill her. How many more times do I have to say it? I might have started off bringing her the goods, but we had sex because she liked me. And I liked her."

"You went to the house to bring her the cocaine she had ordered, right?"

Tony nodded. "So what happened to it?"

"What do you mean?"

"Presumably you gave it to her before you left."

"Yeah." Tony's face was screwed up in concentration. "Yeah. I gave it to her right away. She promised me she'd have the money in the morning. I told her that I'd be in big trouble if I didn't hand over the money by midday. She swore she'd have it." He stared down at his foot in its worn trainer. "There was always a problem with money. Her parents kept her short. They paid for everything, but she had no cash of her own."

"So where did she get it?"

"Here and there. Sometimes she lied to her dad about needing stuff for school or entry money for a horse show. Sometimes she got her mum to buy her expensive clothes then she took them back and got the cash, but it was always a hassle. Remember when I got sacked?" He looked up sharply at Evan. "They found me at the petty cash. She wanted me to do that. She said her dad always had so many twenties in the petty cash box that he'd never miss a few."

"She used you, then."

He nodded. "I suppose she was good at using people."

"And you got fed up with being used, so you killed her."

"No! I'd have done anything for her. She was special. She was the only girl who ever liked me for myself. Can't you get that into your head!"

"And can't you get into your head that there's nothing I can do to save you once the drug angle comes out? I still want to know what happened to the package. How big was it?"

"The usual size. About this big." His fingers made a rectangle about the size of a cigarette packet.

"Did she put it in a pocket right away?"

Tony shook his head. "I don't remember."

"According to you, you had sex in the bushes. Did she keep it in her hand? Did she put it down somewhere safely?"

Tony shook his head again.

"You ran off in a hurry. You heard her talking to someone, and she was found dead shortly afterward. And yet there was no mention of finding a packet of cocaine in her pocket. I don't think she'd have had time to go into the house, hide the coke, and then come back out again to be killed. And why would she have come back out again?"

"Search me." Tony shrugged.

"Presumably the officer who picked you up did search you," Evan said. "You're lucky he didn't find any drugs on you, or a large sum of cash."

Tony slumped onto the hard chair. "You're going to tell them, aren't you?"

"It will come out anyway. Bound to. Besides, I'm a policeman. I can't withhold evidence."

"Yeah. Another fucking copper. You're all the same in the end."

This time Evan ignored the language. "At least I don't lie to people."

"There's nothing you could have done anyway. You're as useless as that little ponce they've got to represent me in court. No bloody good any of you." He went to the door and hammered on it. "Get me out of here right now," he demanded.

Chapter 20

Evan had arranged to meet Bronwen at noon. It was still before ten. He felt angry and restless, not looking forward to his encounter with the police, unable to shake the feeling that he was betraying Tony. Of course he had to share the information he had found. He had no choice. And yet he knew the DCI would see this as the icing on the cake—the reason Tony was visiting Alison that night—and come up with a whole slew of perfect motives for killing her. Her father kept her short of money, so she didn't always pay up on time. Maybe she had blabbed to her parents. Drug dealers didn't think twice about getting rid of a difficult client.

Evan took this thought one stage further. If Tony really didn't kill her, then maybe Jingo, or the boss above him, had sent someone else out to get rid of Alison Turnbull. And what perfect timing to be able to pin the killing on Tony. Perfect revenge for squealing on Jingo the last time he was in court. That, of course, would be up to the police to pursue if they wished. He was going to meet Bronwen so they could take off for a long walk along the cliffs and get the bad taste out of his mouth.

He thought of going for a cup of coffee, but he was too keyed up to sit alone in a café. He wanted to be out there, doing something useful, and he didn't feel ready to hand over the investigation yet. He remembered he hadn't yet spoken to Mrs. Richards, the bridge player, who was not conveniently in France. Even if he owed nothing to Tony, at least he should follow through his own investigation and get the testimony of the other women who had been in the house when Alison was murdered. One of them might have seen or heard something they hadn't considered significant until now.

There were two cars parked in the Richards's circular driveway this morning, a black BMW and a Porsche. No lack of money there either. Mrs. Richards herself opened the front door.

"Oh," she said, her face registering disappointment, "I thought you were the dry cleaners. I need my dress for the party tonight."

"Sorry to disappoint you." Evan smiled. "I wondered if I could take a minute of your time to ask you a couple of questions about Alison Turnbull."

"Alison?"

"Yes. I understand you were playing bridge at the house the night she was murdered."

"You're not another policeman, are you? I am so very tired of talking to policemen. I have told them, over and over, that I heard or saw nothing unusual. We had a pleasant bridge game, apart from poor Margaret's headache, which made her bidding not very reliable. It was all a normal evening until that awful scream from outside the front door, and Frank standing there over Alison's body." She shuddered. "I'll never get that scene out of my mind for as long as I live. She looked so unreal, you know. Like a scene in a play. Lying there quite peacefully, like Snow White. In fact we all thought it was a poor joke until we saw that he was really crying." She shuddered. "So I'm sorry. There's really nothing else I can say."

She went to shut the door.

"One more thing. About your son, Mrs. Richards." Evan put his hand against the door and held it open.

"Simon? What on earth has he got to do with it?"

"May I speak to him, please? I'm talking to all of Alison's friends, and I understand he was one of her escorts to dances and things."

"Maybe once or twice a year, at our insistence. And they played in a tennis tournament together once, but I wouldn't exactly call him one of Alison's friends. In fact I think they found each other mutually boring."

"Might I have a word with him?"

"I'm afraid he's not here." She eyed him coldly. "He's up in Scotland, on an Outward Bound course. He left last week."

So one of the suitable young men was now conveniently out of the way. This could be coincidental, of course, and have nothing at all to do with Alison, but his curiosity was now piqued enough to decide he should also seek out the other young man the housekeeper had mentioned: Charles Peterson, son of Peterson's the builders.

Peterson's Builders had a big yard down by the docks on the other side of the river Tawe. Evan feared it might be closed on a Saturday, but the tall gates were open and two men were standing talking beside a pile of bricks.

"Any idea where I might be able to find Charles Peterson, the owner's son?" Evan asked.

"He should be back soon, shouldn't he, Dai?" The man looked at his colleague for affirmation.

"He actually works here?" Evan couldn't believe his luck.

"I don't know if I'd call it work," the other man said, smiling. "But his dad has him help out during his summer holidays. Wants him to learn the business. I don't think young Charles is all that keen if you ask me."

"And he's working today?"

"His father asked him to run a load of rebar over to the site of the new shopping center we're building. That was some time ago. He should be back, if he hasn't gone gallivanting around with the van again."

"It's all right if I wait?" Evan asked.

"Fine with us, mate. We don't own the place."

Evan went to sit on a stack of pallets, and the men went back to their discussion. It was pleasant sitting in warm sunshine. Through the wire mesh of the fence he watched the boats in Swansea Bay.

After a while the sun became distinctly hot, and he shifted to a position in the shade. If Charles Peterson had gone off gallivanting, as the man had suggested, then maybe he wouldn't even bother to bring the van back today and Evan was wasting his time. He'd have to see if the men would give him the Petersons' home address. He got up and was crossing the yard when a square white van came in through the gates at high speed. Evan jumped aside as it stopped within inches of the pile of bricks. He heard a muttered, "Bloody young fool," from the man who had emerged from the office.

The van door opened and a young man jumped down. He was large and chubby, round faced, and wearing round glasses that gave him an owlish appearance. The copper-colored hair that flopped across his forehead made him look like an overgrown schoolboy. He was wearing jeans and a red Wales sweatshirt that looked too hot for the weather.

"Did my dad phone yet, Dai?" he called and began to cross the yard.

"Your mum did. She said to remind you that they've got people coming at six, so make sure you're home in good time."

Charles Peterson made the sort of face a schoolboy might make. "The Richards for dinner. I'd forgotten. I think I'll be conveniently delayed."

"Someone's here to see you, Charlieboy," the other man said, indicating Evan. "Been waiting quite awhile."

Charles turned to look at Evan and gave him a bright smile as they walked toward each other. "You've been waiting for me? Sorry. They probably told you I was out running errands again. I'm the general dogsbody around here. My father claims its learning the business, but actually it's just slave labor. So what did you need to see me about?"

"I'm working on the Alison Turnbull case," Evan said. "I understand you were one of her friends."

Charles flushed. "I wouldn't say I was her friend. We grew up together. Our mothers are friends."

"But you've been called upon to escort her to dances, that type of thing?"

"Occasionally."

"You've heard they have a young man in custody for her murder."

Charles nodded. "Yes, I heard. Thank God for that. It proves the police aren't completely useless, doesn't it?"

Evan ignored the temptation to produce a warrant card. "Look, the reason I'm here is that we're trying to find out where Alison might have met the person they have in custody. He's claiming that he knew Alison, so we're trying to establish whether any of Alison's friends ever saw them together."

"He knew Alison?" Charles sounded exactly like the Turnbulls and the other members of their set. "I thought he was an ex-jailbird from one of the council estates. I'm sure he couldn't have met Alison. Her parents were very strict about where she went."

"It seems she might have gone clubbing a few times. Do you know anything about that?"

"I can't believe her mother would have let her. Are you sure?"

"She might have sneaked out. She never mentioned any of this to you?"

"My dear chap, I wasn't exactly her bosom pal, you know. My father plays golf with Mr. Turnbull. Our mothers play bridge. My parents volunteered me to take Alison to a couple of dances because I was a suitable, safe escort for her. She made it very clear that I wasn't her choice of escort."

"And what did you think of her?"

"She was a nice enough girl."

Evan noticed that he had looked away. "The housekeeper thinks you were rather keen on her."

Charles flushed almost as red as his sweater. "Maybe I was. But that has nothing to do with anything. She made it very clear that she had no interest in me."

"When was the last time you saw her?"

"Oh, ages ago. Not since the Easter holidays, I think. We had a do at the country club and she was there, but she wouldn't even dance with me. I've been working for my father all summer, so I haven't had a chance to spend time at the country club or see friends. The old man likes to crack the whip, you know."

As Charles was talking, Evan's gaze drifted to the van beside them. It was an old-fashioned delivery van, tall, square, and white. An idea started to form in his head as he remembered Mrs. Hartley's words, "Ambulances, always ambulances outside that house." From her position at the side window, she wouldn't have been able to see the writing on the side of the van and it might well have looked like an ambulance, especially since her perception of reality was already distorted.

"So you're telling me that you hadn't seen Alison at all this summer?" he asked.

"No, I don't think I did." Charles's gaze was focused on the pile of bricks at his feet.

"Not even in her garden?"

This produced the wanted reaction. Charles looked up, startled.

"What on earth are you talking about?"

"Did you go to spy on her often, Charles?"

"You're out of your mind. Why would I want to spy on her?"

"Because you were obsessed with her. You had a crush on her, and she wouldn't give you the time of day."

"Absolute rubbish. Please leave or I'll call the police."

"Actually I'm a policeman. What if I told you that you'd been seen in the Turnbull's front garden?"

"What? By whom? When?"

"On the evening she was killed, Charles. You went there on the evening she was killed, didn't you?" Even as he said it, he knew he was bluffing and it could backfire on him. But it was a risk worth taking, especially as Charles Peterson was starting to sweat.

Charles looked at Evan defiantly. "And you claim somebody saw me? Absurd. Just what are you trying to suggest?"

"You were driving the firm's van, weren't you, and it wasn't the first time you had driven the van to spy on Alison. You came in through the hedge and then you stood among the bushes. Were you just waiting to catch a glimpse of her or hoping to make her change her mind about you?"

"All right. What if I was there? I didn't do any harm."

"Didn't you, Charles? You didn't see her with another boy and were so overcome with jealousy that you killed her?"

Charles was really sweating now. Beads of sweat were running down his round, red face. "She wasn't with anybody." His voice had risen. "She was lying on the hammock on the other side of the garden, listening to her CD player. She often liked to do that in the summer. I watched her for a while, then I went."

"What time was this?"

"I had the van back in the yard by eight-thirty, so it was before that. The sun hadn't set because it was shining directly into my eyes as I turned into the Oystermouth Road." He stared defiantly at Evan. "You can check with my father. He was still in the office when I brought the van back. He would have given me hell if I'd been any later."

"You could have returned later in your own car, I presume," Evan suggested.

Charles snorted. "My own car? I don't own a car. I own sod all. My father is a self-made man, you see. He started with nothing, and he wants me to get the feel of starting with nothing too. I have less to live on than any of my friends at uni. The only time I can go anywhere is when I can sneak out the van."

Evan watched him steadily. "I suppose I have to believe you then. If you really cared about Alison as much as you say you did, you'd definitely want her killer caught and convicted, wouldn't you? So I'm asking you once again—is there anything you know or suspect that could help us?"

"But they've already got the bloke behind bars."

"They might not be able to make it stick without more evidence, so anything you can remember or tell us about her friends might help. Do you know anything that we should know, Charles?"

"Nothing. I told you she couldn't stand the sight of me. She told me I was too fat and boring." He bit his lip.

"When you were there, watching her that evening—did you see anyone or anything unusual? Did you pass anyone in the street? Were there any cars parked nearby?"

Charles screwed up his face in concentration then shook his head.

"There were cars parked in the driveway. One of the women got up and came across to the window. I had to dodge back into the bushes pretty quickly. I didn't stay long because the bloody dog started barking."

"So they didn't have the curtains drawn then?"

"No, I told you. It was still daylight."

"Right. Thanks for your help then." Evan couldn't think of anything else to say. Charles had the same kind of open face as his own. He thought he'd be able to detect if Charles was lying.

"One more thing." He turned back as Charles was about to walk away. "What about drugs?"

"Drugs?" He looked genuinely surprised.

"Do you ever use them? Do you know anything about Alison using them?"

"I shouldn't think Alison did. They didn't ever let her out alone. I smoked a marijuana cigarette once. Frankly it didn't do much for me. Everyone else was giggling and I just sat there. But that was it—the sum total of my drug experience. I told you—my father doesn't give me an allowance. I have no money for any kind of expensive habit."

Evan left him going into the office. "If you want me home, you'd better come and get me," Evan heard him saying into the phone. He got in his car and drove away. Charles Peterson had seemed like an open book, and everything he said indicated that he had nothing to do with Alison's death. But Evan had been taken in by good liars before, and Charles had the best motive of all—he had been madly in love with a girl who didn't love him.

Bronwen was waiting in the coffee shop in the small pedestrian mall behind the bus station, a half-empty cappucino in front of her. Her hair was still loose and flowing over her shoulders, and she wore no makeup. She looked ridiculously young.

"Hello," she said as he sat down opposite her. "I hope you have behaved yourself. Did Tony Mancini confess?"

"To the drugs, yes," he said, looking around to see who was in earshot. "He admitted he was making a delivery that night. But he still insists she was alive and well when he left her. Which leaves us with another question—what happened to the packet of cocaine? Surely the police must have done a thorough search of the grounds."

"Unless the person who killed her took it with him."

Evan nodded. "Which is all the more reason to suspect a drug connection."

"So what are you going to do now?"

"Tell the police, of course. There's nothing else I can do."

She nodded and took a sip of her coffee. "So you're off the hook."

"And we can have the days off I promised you. The trouble is that I really want to see this through."

"Don't tell me you're feeling bad for Tony Mancini, Evan. You tried bloody hard for him, and all he did was lie to you. Even if he didn't kill her, he's a drug runner. He'll go to jail whatever happens."

"I know." He beckoned to the waitress and ordered them both more coffee. "I had a couple of other encounters this morning." He described his interviews with Mrs. Richards and with Charles. "One son conveniently off in Scotland and the other admits to spying on Alison in her garden."

Bronwen took a sip of coffee and digested this. "You should suggest the police check out their alibis, shouldn't you? And their fingerprints or whatever else policemen do. My, aren't they going to be impressed with what you've turned up so far?"

Evan smiled. "I haven't asked you how you got on with Alison's friends. Anything interesting turn up?"

"Not much. Only that she hated her mother."

"She did?"

"Yes, couldn't stand her, according to both friends. She said her mother ruined her entire life. She was too strict. She never let her do anything or go anywhere. And she never forgave her for sending her away to school."

"Interesting. So she didn't want to change schools."

"She loved her old school, apparently. She was doing well there and had loads of friends."

"Any idea why they did send her to boarding school? Do you think it was snobbery—wanting their daughter to go to an expensive boarding school?"

"Could be, although her friend Charlotte came up with an interesting statement. She said Alison thought her mother was jealous of her. As soon as she started to grow up and look pretty, her mother didn't want her around the house any longer. She saw Alison as a threat."

"That doesn't jibe with always wanting to go shopping with her and driving her everywhere, does it? It's probably all talk—the way teenagers always gripe about their parents. And anyway, it has nothing to do with her being killed, does it? Did either of the girls know about the drugs, by the way?"

"If they did, they weren't going to tell me. They both claimed they weren't that close to Alison any longer and had no idea whom she went around with—although Charlotte did admit to knowing that Alison sometimes managed to sneak out through her bedroom window at night."

"One of her friends must have had the car that picked her up," Evan said. "Tony said she got a friend to drive her when she went clubbing. We need to find out whom she was seen with at the club."

"I thought you were bowing out and handing over to the police." Bronwen gave him a quizzical look.

"I am, but I can't help being curious, can I? And I'd love to be able to pin something on that cocky bastard Jingo."

"Because he gave the order to kill your father and got away scot-free?"

"And because he looked at me as if he knew I couldn't touch him. At least I can tell the police what I know about Tony's drug connection and make things damned unpleasant for Jingo."

The waitress came with two coffees and then delivered two glasses of wine to a couple of gray-haired ladies at the next table. A murmur of surprised whispers went around the café. "Would you look at that," the woman sitting on the other side of Evan muttered to her friend. "Wine. And it's not even midday yet. And in a respectable coffee shop too. What is the world coming to?"

"I've probably been condemned for ordering cappucino," Bronwen whispered. "Nasty Continental habit." They exchanged a smile. Evan looked at her, with her ash blond hair lying over her shoulders and her blue eyes smiling at him and thought he'd never seen anything more lovely in his life. His first impressions of her had been of someone unreal, belonging to another place, another time. This had been enhanced by the clothes she wore, ethnic vests, long skirts, swirling capes. Now she looked like a fresh-faced teenager, and equally miraculous.

"What?" she asked, sensing his gaze. "Do I have a milky mustache?"

"No. You look perfect." He finished his coffee and got to his feet. "Let's get my talk with the police over, and then we'll take a long walk over the cliffs and blow all those unpleasant memories away."

The police station had a deserted air about it. Evan wondered whether fewer crimes were committed at weekends or if it was just fewer staff on duty. He had left Bronwen at a bookstore, where she claimed she would be happy all afternoon if it came to that. The woman at the reception desk knew him by now and merely nodded when he said he had to speak to the Major Crimes Unit. He found only Dave, the junior member of the team, reading the newspaper.

"Hello, mate," Dave said cheerfully. "If you're looking for the DCI, he's out, as usual."

"Any idea when he'll be back?"

Dave grinned. "He doesn't share privileged info like that with me."

"I'd better wait," Evan said. "I've picked up some information he might need."

"Oh yeah?" Dave looked interested.

Evan pulled out a chair and sat at the table. "Tell me, Dave," he said, "do you know if a full autopsy was done on the girl? Were any drugs found in her system?"

Dave looked up with surprise. "Drugs? I never heard any mention of drugs. What makes you ask that?"

"I've been doing a little checking of my own," Evan said. "It seems she might have liked a little cocaine now and then, and someone was supplying her."

"Bloody 'ell," Dave said. "You're sure about this, are you? The DCI won't be too pleased. He thinks he's got the case all sewn up."

"He probably has," Evan said. "Tony Mancini was delivering the goods that night. I just wondered whether the cocaine he brought her was ever found."

Dave shook his head. "If it was, it went into someone's pocket. I was the one who typed up the crime-scene description and inventory of her clothing." He pulled his chair closer to Evan's. "So you really found out that she was a druggie and Mancini was her supplier? How did you do that?"

"Asking around," Evan said. "It would have come out sooner or later."

"So why do you reckon he killed her? Most dealers like to keep the customers alive. Bad for business to bump them off."

Evan leaned toward him and lowered his voice. "Between ourselves, I'm not at all sure he did kill her. I'm hoping if you boys take up this drug angle, we might find out that someone else had a reason to—" He broke off as the door burst open. DCI Vaughan swept in, followed by two other plainclothes officers. The DCI's face was flushed, as if he had been running. Evan got to his feet, as did Dave.

"Evans has come to . . ." Dave began, but the DCI ignored him.

"What the devil do you think you're doing?" he yelled at Evan. "Who gave you permission to tread on my turf?"

"I just thought maybe I could help, sir—" Evan started to say, but the DCI cut him off.

"I gave you permission to go and talk to Mancini—once, because of your father. I said you could ride along if you wanted to, because your father was a good bloke. But that didn't give you permission to go running around behind my back like some Hercule Bloody Poirot."

"Sorry, sir," Evan tried to say. "I was about to turn over the information, which is why I'm here, and I think—"

"I've had complaints, boy." DCI Vaughan continued to yell at full volume. "I've had Mrs. Turnbull on the phone, bleating at me. You've been harassing her friends and upsetting her. Now get the hell out of here and stay out. Try and interfere again and I'll be on the phone to your superior in North Wales. You'll be out of the force so quickly your feet won't touch ground. Do I make myself perfectly clear?"

"Yes, sir," Evan muttered. He had no choice but to make an exit through the door that the officer was holding open for him.

Chapter 21

Evan located Bronwen in the cookbook section.

"You're back quickly," she said, looking up from the stool where she sat, an open book on her knee. "Wasn't anyone there? Look, I've found a Moroccan recipe book. I've always wanted to try couscous." She was smiling, then she saw his face. "Evan, what happened?"

Evan grabbed her hand. "Let's get out of here," he said. "We've got to talk."

He said nothing as they made their way to the front entrance of the store and out onto the street.

"What is it?" she asked again.

"Something's not right, Bron." His voice was shaking. "I'm beginning to think there might be a cover-up."

"A cover-up? What do you mean? Who's covering up?" Bronwen stood looking up at him while the tide of Saturday shoppers parted and swept around them.

He was gripping her shoulders. "If you wanted the truth about who killed your daughter, you'd welcome any help you could get, wouldn't you? Any possible lead. Anything that might provide proof. The DCI has had Mrs. Turnbull on the phone, complaining that I've been harassing her and her friends. I've been ordered to stay away."

Bronwen was silent, digesting this information. "You think they really know who did it, and they'd rather let Tony Mancini take the blame?"

"What other explanation could there be? I couldn't have been more polite to Mrs. Turnbull or her friends. I asked no prying questions. Nobody could have accused me of harassing, except maybe I was a little heavy with Charles." He took her arm as a large pram bore down on them. "Come on, let's get out of here. Let's walk." He strode out, down through the shopping center and out to the waterfront, walking so fast that Bronwen had to break into a trot to keep up with him. At last, as they crossed the street and were met by the salty wind from the Bristol Channel, he slowed his pace. "Okay, Bron, why would they want me off the case?"

"Two reasons I can think of—apart from making a bloody nuisance of yourself." She paused to smile up at him. "One would be because they suspect who really killed Alison and, for some reason, want to protect him. Or would rather that Tony was jailed in his place. The other could be that they know about Alison's drug problem and don't want it to come out. That would all tie in with the parents' behavior, wouldn't it? They sent her far away to school. When she was home they overprotected her, drove her everywhere, wouldn't let her out of their sight. Now they are scared that it might become common knowledge—"

"And it would hurt his standing in the community and chances of becoming lord mayor," Evan finished for her. "So maybe one of them discovered the packet of cocaine and whipped it away before the police arrived. But that still doesn't get us any closer to who killed her—someone they know or someone they suspect was connected to Alison's drug habit."

"Evan, you've been ordered off the case, remember," Bronwen started, but he ignored her and went on talking.

"That Richards woman—I hardly spoke to her, so why did she call Mrs. Turnbull and say I was harassing her? And her son went on an Outward Bound course in Scotland last week. Very conveniently out of the way, wouldn't you say? Now how do we check on someone who is in Scotland?"

"I'd say that Charles Peterson sounds like the most likely suspect so far," Bronwen said. "You say he had a crush on Alison. He admitted loitering in her garden watching her."

"You're right." Evan nodded. "Maybe he was there later than he claimed. He spied on Alison and Tony. And watching the girl he fancied having sex with another boy might well have pushed him over the edge."

Bronwen looked up at his face. "So do you think that the Turnbulls found some kind of evidence to show that Charles killed Alison, but when Tony Mancini was brought in instead, they decided they'd rather let him go to prison than one of their own set?"

"It's not how my mind would work," Evan said, "but I can't answer for their social set. Obviously status means a lot to them—and being elected bloody lord mayor."

"It would be easy enough to check on Charles's alibi. If they lock the builder's van in the yard each night, then he would have had to bring it back on time. His parents would know if he'd kept the van out for the night."

"They may not want to tell if he did."

Bronwen sighed. "Either way it's none of our business anymore," she said. "You've been ordered off the case."

"I know." Evan stopped walking and stood, staring out to sea. Seagulls wheeled and mewed above their heads. From farther down on the beach came the shrieks of children, playing at the water's edge. A perfect summer's afternoon at the seaside, reminding him of his own youth.

Bronwen slipped her arm through his. "There's nothing more you can do, Evan. Come on. Let's go on that walk we've been talking about. Let's walk all the way to Oystermouth again, and we can look at love spoons in that funny little shop."

They started to walk along the seafront, but as they drew level with the Guildhall, Evan stopped. "I'm sorry, Bron. I can't let it go like this. It would haunt me for the rest of my life."

"Don't be an idiot. The DCI has ordered you off the case. You'll get yourself thrown out of the force."

"I've just thought what I can do," he said. He took her hand and half dragged her across the street to the Crown Court building.

"Evan, wait," Bronwen protested. "It's Saturday. Nothing will be open."

"Something will." Evan charged ahead. Inside he located an office that was open and a list of area solicitors. From that it wasn't hard to get the home address of Richard Brooks, Tony's solicitor. He found a public phone and dialed Brooks's home number. It rang several times before it was picked up.

"Sorry I was so long getting to the phone," the voice at the other end said, panting slightly, "I was down at the other end of the garden."

"Mr. Brooks. It's Evan Evans. You took me to see Tony Mancini."

"Yes?" The voice sounded guarded now.

"Could we meet somewhere? I've come up with important information I'd like to share with you."

"On a Saturday? Can't it wait?"

"No, I don't think it can."

There was a pause, then he answered, "All right. You can come out to the house, if you like. It's in the new estate on the Llanelli Road."

"I get the feeling I'm being dumped again," Bronwen said as Evan put down the phone.

"It probably would be better if I went alone," Evan admitted. "He's not going to want to discuss his client with a third person present."

"So it's back to the bookstore." She looked crestfallen. "At least I'll be an expert in cooking couscous by the end of the day."

He put an arm around her. "You can come along, only maybe you should wait in the car while I talk to him. Then we'd better go home because you know my mother will have lunch waiting, whether we want it or not."

"I have to admit," Bronwen said, "that the prospect of facing your mother is overcome by the desire for a good meal. I am getting seriously hungry."

Richard Brooks's house was in a small enclave of new detached homes at the outskirts of the city. There was a tricycle on the front path and a line of nappies flapped in the breeze behind the fence. Evan made a mental note that this man, who looked so much younger than him, was already established with a family. It was about time he moved on to the next stage of his own life.

As Evan went up the front path, Brooks called to him and came through a side gate, still in his gardening clothes, the knees of his trousers plastered with soil.

"Sorry. You caught me digging out the pea plants," he said. "My, but they've been prolific this year. It's wonderfully therapeutic having a vegetable garden, don't you think?"

"I haven't had a chance to try it yet, but I hope to soon," Evan answered. "And I'm really sorry to disturb you on a Saturday. I won't keep you long."

"Do you mind if we sit on the patio? My wife won't be at all pleased if I come into the house in muddy clothes." He led the way through a side gate and pulled out two wrought-iron chairs. "Can I offer you a beer?"

"Better not, thanks. I've got my girlfriend waiting in the car." He realized as he said it that the word fiancée still didn't come naturally to him. "Look, I'm here because I want you to do me a favor."

"Yes?"

Evan took a deep breath. "I want you to take me on, officially, as your assistant. You don't need to pay me, but I want to be put on the books."

"What on earth for?" Brooks couldn't have looked more surprised.

"Because the police have forbidden me to have anything to do with the Mancini case, and I don't want to stop."

Richard Brooks laughed uneasily. "Why would you want to do this?"

"That should be obvious. I don't think he's guilty."

"But, my dear chap," Brooks exclaimed, "you, of all people. Why would you want to go out of your way to help a repulsive little twerp like Tony Mancini? I have to tell you that there's a lot you probably don't know about him. Drugs. Gangs. The works. Not a nice character, I can assure you. I got landed with him because I'm the junior in the firm and nobody else wanted anything to do with it. I'll go through the motions. Hire him a competent barrister, make sure he gets a fair trial. But I won't weep when they send him off to jail. It's where he belongs."

"Maybe, but not for a crime he didn't commit." He stared past Brooks at the nappies, flapping noisily in the stiff breeze that had sprung up. "Do you know how hard this is for me? I've been struggling with my own conscience ever since I met him. And when I found out about the drugs, I was all set to hand him over to the police. But the Turnbull family and friends are going out of their way to have me taken off the case. So now I have to find out why, and who. If not Tony, then who did kill Alison?"

"They won't thank you for it if you do prove him innocent," Brooks said. "Everyone in the South Wales Police would love to find him guilty."

"I know that. It's something I've got to live with. Easier than knowing I let an innocent man be locked away for life. So will you do it? Will you let me tell you what I know so far?"

Brooks sighed. "I wish I had never been a bloody Boy Scout," he said. "All right. Tell me what you know."

Chapter 22

A few minutes later Evan jumped back into the car. "Right, Bron. Home for lunch and then we've got work to do."

"What sort of work? He agreed to your crazy request then, did he?"

"Reluctantly. But he did have to admit that I'd put forward a good case in Tony's defense.

"So what are you going to do now?"

"Check out Charles Peterson's alibi, to start with."

"You'll have his family phoning the DCI again if you pester them."

"I thought I might just slip into the builder's yard and see if Charles has to log that van in and out. And I've a job for you too, if you feel up to it?"

"After last night's triumph and then this morning's successful sessions, I think I've got the hang of this sleuthing business rather well. What do you want me to do?"

"This probably has nothing to do with the case at all, but Turnbull lied about where he was that night. He said he came from a council meeting. I checked at the council offices and found the meeting had been cut short that night because too many members were out of town and there wasn't a quorum. So I just wondered where Turnbull went on his way home. And I have an idea."

"Yes?"

"I think there's hanky-panky going on with Miss Jones, his secretary. I picked up vibes between then when I was in his office, and then some of his workers hinted at much the same thing."

"So you want me to check if he visited her that night?"

Evan nodded. "It might fill in another piece of the puzzle."

"Although, as you say, I can't see what it might have to do with Alison being killed. He still arrived home at the same time and found his daughter dead."

"But he lied. Always useful to check out a lie."

"Of course he lied." Bronwen laughed. "You'd lie if you'd spent the evening with your bit of stuff. Although in your case," she paused, "it wouldn't do much good. You'd go bright red and look as guilty as hell. In fact I'll have no problem keeping tabs on you, my sweet."

"Well, that's nice to know, isn't it." He pulled out into the main stream of traffic heading into the town. "But Turnbull's lying is important. It's just another thing that proves this wasn't the perfectly happy model family they want people to think they were. I wonder what else they might be trying to hide?"

"Ma, we're home," Evan called as he opened the front door. There was no smell of cooking. That was a bad sign. He went through to the kitchen, ahead of Bronwen. "Weren't you expecting us for lunch?" he asked. The table wasn't laid. Mrs. Evans sat reading the newspaper.

"I thought you'd be out, doing your detective work." She didn't look up. "I had Bill Howells on the phone awhile ago. Very upset, he was. He said the detective inspector was furious with you and that you might have spoiled their whole case with your interfering." She raised her eyes to confront him. "What on earth's got into you, Evan? You know better than that. I can understand how you feel about getting Tony Mancini convicted good and proper this time, but that doesn't give you the right to interfere with what the police are doing. Your dad would never have done that. He wouldn't want you to either."

"Sorry, Ma," Evan muttered, feeling about five-years-old again. He half expected to be sent to his room.

"You think you know better than senior officers, do you? You think they don't know their job, is it?"

"Of course not. Look, I said I'm sorry. Let's drop it. Bronwen and I haven't had any lunch yet, but we can get a bite to eat at a café."

"Sit down, the pair of you. I can make you some ham sandwiches, I suppose." She got up and was instantly bustling around the kitchen. "Put the kettle on then. I expect you could both do with a cup of tea."

Evan let out a sigh of relief as they left again after lunch. "That was tricky, wasn't it?" he muttered as he opened the car door for Bronwen.

She nodded. "Definite frost in the air."

"I don't know what she's going to say if she finds out I've been trying to prove Tony Mancini innocent. I have a feeling if I get him off, I won't have a friend in the entire city of Swansea."

"You'll have me," Bronwen said. "I admire what you're doing, Evan. I know how hard it must be for you. I think you're completely crazy, by the way, but I still admire you."

They drove up to the Unico factory, where only a guard was on duty in the main building. Bronwen managed to convince him that she was the long-time friend of Miss Jones and she was visiting Swansea, trying to track her down. She came out triumphant with a home phone number and then set up an appointment to meet.

"How did you persuade her to see you?" Evan asked in admiration.

"I'm a schoolteacher, I can sound authoritative if I have to." Bronwen looked smug.

Evan dropped her off at the row of houses where Turnbull's secretary lived, then drove to Peterson's builder's yard. He was annoyed to find the tall gates locked and the van parked in the yard beside a large flatbed lorry.

Before going home Evan decided to pay another visit to Mrs. Hartley, the elderly neighbor who had first spotted Charles's van parked outside the Turnbull's house. Now that he had a description of Charles, she might remember seeing him in the Turnbull's front garden. And a recollection of him might just jog her memory of other things she had seen and heard that night.

There were cars parked in the Turnbulls' driveway as he drove past their house. He was careful to park behind the hedge out of sight. He didn't want Mrs. Turnbull on the phone to the DCI again. Dr. Hartley took awhile to open the door.

"I'm sorry, but she's had a bad day today," he said, indicating up the stairs with a nod of his head. "She does, from time to time. She's been crying and begging me to take her home. It's—very hard to take. I gave her a sedative. She's sleeping peacefully now."

"Right. Sorry to have troubled you then." Evan turned to go.

"Come back tomorrow, if you like." Mr. Hartley managed a smile. "She may be right as rain then. You can never tell."

Evan wanted to say something, but he couldn't think of anything.

Bronwen was already seated in his mother's kitchen by the time Evan arrived home. The two women were having a cup of tea, and Evan thought he heard animated conversation and laughter as he opened the front door. At least that was one good sign. They broke off as he came into the room, and he had the impression they were annoyed at being disturbed.

"Well, here you are, at last then." Mrs. Evans got to her feet and lifted the tea cozy from the pot. "We wondered where you'd got to."

"Oh, just talking with a bloke who used to be a teacher at my school." Evan looked across and caught Bronwen's eye.

"A teacher from your old school, is it? That's nice." She poured the tea and put a large slab of *bara brith* in front of Evan. "I expect you'll be needing something to keep you going before your supper.

I got some kippers for tonight, if that's all right with you. Bronwen tells me she likes kippers just fine." She smiled at Bronwen. Evan sensed that somehow during his absence, Bronwen had become the favored one. Maybe because his mother was still angry at him and hoped Bronwen would be able to make him see sense.

"I thought Bronwen and I might go for a little walk before supper, if you don't mind," he said to his mother. "I've hardly seen her all day."

"So I've been hearing. And you just ran off and left her at her parents' house with nothing to do and nowhere to go, so I've heard. That's not the way to win a young girl's affection, Evan. My Robert always devoted his spare time to me. If he wasn't working, he was at my side."

Evan thought this was a slight rose-tinting of history. His father, he remembered, had been a keen lawn bowler, a keen supporter of the Swansea football club, and not against a swift half at the pub. Bronwen got to her feet. "A walk would be nice. It's turned into a lovely evening, hasn't it?"

Once outside, she slipped her arm through his. "I was worried about you," she said, "but I couldn't let your mother know."

"What was there to worry about?"

"Evan!" She looked shocked. "If you really believe that Tony Mancini is innocent, then obviously the person who killed Alison is still out there. You have to watch yourself."

"I'm fine, *cariad*. You don't have to worry about me." He squeezed her hand.

"Of course I worry about you. If there is some kind of drug connection, we know how those people behave. One of them killed your father, remember?"

Evan nodded. "I'm hardly likely to forget that, but I still think that the cover-up is more likely. I didn't have much luck checking out Charles Peterson's alibi, but I'll try again in the morning."

"So you're ruling out the drug connection, are you?" she asked.

They paused at a railing, overlooking the downs. The wind blew Bronwen's hair into her eyes. "Not entirely," Evan said. "The one thing I don't quite understand is leaving the body on the doorstep.

That doesn't fit Charles Peterson's character at all. If he'd killed Alison in a fit of rage and jealousy, his entire instinct would be to hide the body where it wouldn't be found for a long while. He'd probably have stuffed her into the van and dumped her into the ocean."

"It does smack of revenge killing, I agree. Whoever left her there wanted to send a message—"

"Or to punish her parents somehow. What about your interview with Turnbull's secretary?"

She grinned. "Oh, I'm turning into a supersleuth. You'd be so proud of me. We chatted away. I told her I'd worked for Turnbull long before her time, and he had made a pass at me and I wondered if he'd been like that with all the girls.

"She was worried for a moment. She thought I might be planning to bring a sexual harassment suit. I told her no, just curiosity. I had handled him just fine. Bit of a pussy cat really. And she'd agreed. He was very sweet when you got to know him. All he wanted was affection really. That cold wife of his had shut him out of her bedroom long ago. Was it any wonder that he turned to someone young and warm and pretty?"

"She told you all that, did she?"

"And more. She'd have gone into vivid bedroom details, if I'd let her. Actually I think she's rather proud of being Turnbull's mistress. She sees it as a status symbol."

"So was he with her that evening?"

"Of course he was. That and most nights when he was supposed to be working late, or playing golf, or going for drinks at the country club. He left her place about nine-fifteen, she thinks."

Evan digested this. "That's about right. He would have driven home slowly so that he'd arrive at the usual time a council meeting would be over."

"So we know a little more about Mr. Turnbull, but it doesn't help us much, does it? It doesn't give us anyone else with a motive." She turned her head so that the wind came full into her face, sweeping her hair back like a ship's figurehead. "Look, do you want me to go back to the club tonight? I told my new friends I'd see them again. I might be able to get some more information out of them. Now I know what two of Alison's girlfriends look like, I can ask if they might have been seen at the club. One of them might even show up."

"And you could ask about Charles Peterson too, although I can't see him as the clubbing type. I'm sure he'd be an even worse dancer than me. Unfortunately, I don't know what Simon Richards looks like, but you could drop his name and see if you get any reaction."

"Right oh, then. It's back undercover. I must say it is rather fun. And there's something about the blue spiked hair too. Blokes don't mess with girls with blue spiked hair."

They walked back in companionable silence.

Chapter 23

Evan's mother clearly disapproved of their going out again after supper that night.

"It's like Paddington Station around here with all the coming and going," she said. "Why on earth do you need to be out at this time of night?"

"It's only nine o'clock, Ma, and we are on holiday. How often do Bronwen and I have the chance to go out in the evenings? There's nothing to do up in Llanfair." Evan patted her shoulder. "Don't wait up. We may be late."

Mrs. Evans sniffed and folded her arms. Evan thought he caught the muttered word "gallivanting."

Bronwen changed clothes and put on the wig in the ladies' room at the bus station. "Off to work then," she said, as he pulled up across from the Monkey's Uncle. "Don't wait for me outside this time. I don't want to blow my cover." She grinned. "How about that—I'm even learning the jargon. Why don't you park up that side street so that nobody sees me getting into your car, just in case."

"All right."

She climbed out, adjusted her wig, and then ran across the road. Suddenly Evan got the feeling that she had taken over. This was a new, confident Bronwen he hadn't seen before. He gave her one last look as he drove off. She had joined the line of young people making their way into the club. He parked where she suggested and then went to a nearby pub. There was a loud American gangster film on the telly and he didn't enjoy drinking alone, so he walked around a bit; then it started to rain and he went to sit in the car. He must have dozed off, because he was suddenly conscious of the sound. He sat up and saw the crowd of young people spilling out onto the street. A couple of uniformed police stood at the end of the side street where he was parked, watching the crowd. They were certainly loud enough. Shouts, snatches of song, wild laughter, echoed back from the tall buildings along Kingsway. Evan watched and waited. At last the crowd thinned, then dwindled to stragglers. The policeman officers moved on, leaving an empty Kingsway before him. Still he waited, but Bronwen didn't come. She had told him where to park, so she couldn't have forgotten.

Finally he could stand it no longer and got out of the car. A band member with wild hair was maneuvering a large instrument case down the stairs of the club. "Is anyone still up there?" Evan asked.

"Only Joe, packing up his drums," the boy replied in a heavy South Wales accent.

Evan waited until he came down then went up the stairs. The ball and the laser light had been turned off and a single naked light bulb showed the peeling black paint on the walls and the litter-piled floor. He looked around then went downstairs again. A couple of girls were talking to the boy from the band as he opened up the back of a van.

"I'm looking for a girl," Evan said. "I was supposed to meet her here. She's got blue spiked hair, and she was wearing a white halter top. You didn't see her, did you?"

"I saw her earlier," one of the girls said. "She was sitting with Tiffany and her friends, wasn't she?"

"Tiffany. That's right. Did she leave with them?"

"No. I saw them going down the street quite awhile ago."

"Girl with blue spiked hair?" the band member asked, looking up from the back of the van he had been loading. "I saw her when

I was taking the first load of stuff down to the van. She was talking to a bloke with red hair. Tall, skinny bloke with a ring through his eyebrow. I think you're out of luck, mate. She went off with him."

Evan fought to remain calm.

"Did you happen to see which direction they went in?"

The band player shook his head. "I just saw them walking toward the stairs while I was unplugging my amps. I only noticed because I thought it was a good color combination, him with red hair, her with blue. I'm in art school during the day. I notice stuff like that."

"And how long ago was this?"

The boy shrugged. "Fifteen minutes maybe. I can't really say."

"You girls didn't see them walking past you, did you?"

The girls looked at each other before shaking their heads. "We were talking to some boys," one of them said. "They wanted us to go to a coffee bar with them, but they were a bit boring so we had to ditch them."

"Right. Thanks." Evan left them and ran back to his car. Stay calm, he told himself. There has to be a good reason for this, but he couldn't come up with one. Surely Bronwen would never have left the club willingly with Jingo. She must have realized who he was. Had he described Jingo well enough so that she knew who she was dealing with? He tried to go through their various conversations, worried that he might have failed to mention Jingo and that Bronwen might have left with him quite innocently. He felt cold sweat trickling down the back of his neck. He started the car and took off too quickly, almost clipping the bumper of the car in front of him. It was all his fault. He should never have encouraged Bronwen to get involved. Now she thought she was some kind of hot detective. She must have come up with a good lead to go off without telling him or leaving him some kind of message. She probably didn't even consider the risk she was taking.

Kingsway was deserted. The pavements glistened with moisture in the light of the street lamps. A couple of streetwalkers still stood in doorways, but apart from them there was no sign of life. Where would they have gone? Think, dammit, he commanded himself. He started to drive around aimlessly, circling the block, then widening the circle, past the Quadrant shopping center, past the bus station, along the waterfront. They could be anywhere by now. He started to drive toward Penlan, but then turned around again. Why would Jingo want to take Bronwen up there? Evan wished he knew what vehicle Jingo drove. Had any kind of car been parked outside Jingo's house that day he had visited? He didn't think so. The street had been empty. Those council houses often had prefab garages coming off an alley at the back. If you lived in a council estate you weren't stupid enough to leave your car outside.

At last he found himself driving down to the dockland, to the spot where his father had been killed. It had changed a lot in the past five years, part of the waterfront gentrification process, and there was now a new marina and condo development in place of the old quayside. Not the kind of place now you'd be involved in gang business.

Maybe he should go back to the side street and wait. She'd come looking for him when she got rid of Jingo. If she got rid of Jingo. If Jingo didn't get rid of her. A clock on some church tower chimed one. He drove along Kingsway again. Slowly. The Monkey's Uncle was now closed for the night like everything else. Should he go home, just in case she had gone there or phoned? He drove up the hill like a mad thing, ran into the house, and found the place in peaceful darkness. For once his mother had not waited up. There was no message by the phone in the front hall.

Back to the car again and then he headed for Penlan. He knew it was a waste of time to go up there, but he had to do it anyway. If Jingo was carrying out some kind of gang meeting or drug transaction, it wouldn't be where he could be spotted from the street, and if he wanted to get rid of Bronwen—"Don't say that. Don't even think it!" Bronwen was smart, she wouldn't put herself in danger. She knew what she was doing. She'd be okay. She had to be okay.

Even the council estate rested in silent darkness. No lights showed behind closed curtains. No music came out of pubs. No late lovers lingered at front gates. Evan drove past Jingo's house. No car was parked outside, and it was in darkness. Should he wake them up and ask Jingo's mother if she knew where her son was? As if she would tell him if she did know. And he had no warrant to search the house. Waste of time again. He knew what he had to do—go to the police, that was obvious. They might know where someone like Jingo could be found. They would come with the power to question and to search and to bully if necessary. But going to the police would be admitting that he had not obeyed DCI Vaughan's command. They'd have little sympathy for him or Bronwen. Anything bad that happened would be his own fault for meddling. And he'd be out of a job in the morning.

Not that that mattered if Bronwen was found safe. Nothing mattered except finding her safe. He drove back down the hill into the town center and slowed outside the main police station. Would they do anything to help? He knew the rules as well as they did: Bronwen wasn't a relative, and it wasn't easy to report a sane adult as a missing person. It wouldn't be easy to convince them that she had left against her own will, from a noisy club, with hundreds of people watching.

If only Bill Howells was on duty—even though he was not exactly in Bill Howells's good books at the moment. But Bill was a decent bloke, an old friend of his dad's. He'd help.

The night sergeant wasn't Bill, but he did remember Evan's father and he was persuaded to hand over Bill's home address. It was two-thirty by the time Evan knocked at his door. As he had expected, Bill wasn't at all pleased to see him or particularly sympathetic.

"Why, in God's name, have you got yourself involved in this?" he demanded as Evan started to explain.

"Because I couldn't get your blokes to listen to me," Evan answered. "I left information about Alison's involvement with drugs. Has it been followed up on, do you know?"

"I told you, boyo, I'm not on the case. I'm not part of the drug squad. Just an ordinary copper on the beat, that's all."

"Is there nothing you can do to help? She's my fiancée, Bill. The same bloke who gave the order to shoot my father has gone off with my fiancée. I have to find her."

Bill Howells gave a sigh and ran his hands through untidy hair.

"All right. Hold on a second while I put my clothes on."

A few minutes later they were speeding back into the center of town. "I'll just pop into the station," Bill said, "and have a word with old Trevor at the desk. He can get in touch with the squad cars, but it won't be easy. You say she may or may not be wearing a blue wig."

"He should be easier to spot. Jingo Roberts. Tall, thin bloke with bright red hair. You couldn't miss him."

"Jingo Roberts, eh? I've come across him a few times. Nasty piece of work. All right. As soon as I've talked to Trevor, we'll go out looking ourselves."

They spent a fruitless night covering the whole city, from Port Talbot to the Gower. Bill checked in several times on his mobile, but there was no news, either good or bad. The night had taken on an unreal quality, like one of those nightmares in which time stands still, all motion is slowed down, and a sense of dread becomes overpowering. She had to be somewhere. Would Jingo have driven her out of town, out of Wales? Why?

"You know where this Roberts boy lives?" Bill Howells said.

"Yes, I've been there. It's in Penlan." Evan was so cold and scared that he was shaking.

"Then let's pay him a visit, see if he's home."

The first streaks of cold daylight were appearing on the eastern horizon as they drove up the hill to the Penlan estate. Bill Howells knocked on the door of Jingo's house while Evan stood in the shadows behind him. "Open up. Police," he shouted through the letter box.

After a long pause there was the sound of a bolt being drawn back, and Jingo's mother glared at them. "What the bleedin' hell do you want? It's Sunday morning, for God's sakes. I'm a respectable citizen, I am. I'm calling your superior, mate."

"It's not you I want to see, missus. It's your son. Do you know where he is?"

"Of course I bloody know where he is. He's asleep in his bed, where any sensible person is on a Sunday morning."

"Mind if I go up and see for myself?"

"You got a search warrant?"

"No, but I can easily go down to the station and get one, while my partner here watches the house, if that's what you want."

"I'll go and wake him," she said, still glaring at him defiantly. "He won't be pleased."

Evan heard angry voices then Jingo came down the stairs, dressed in pajama bottoms, his narrow white chest naked.

"What the hell do you want?" he demanded.

Evan fought the desire to grab him, to slam him against the wall.

Bill Howells must have sensed this, because he planted himself full in the doorway. "We're looking for a young woman," he said. "You met her at the club last night. You were seen leaving with her. She hasn't come home."

"You got the wrong bloke, mate," Jingo said. "I didn't have any luck with the birds last night. I caught the night bus home around twelve-thirty, and I was here, in bed, by one. You can ask my mum. She was still up watching the telly when I got home."

"You caught the bus?" Bill Howells asked.

"Yeah. You can check with the driver. He'd remember me."

"What's wrong with your car?"

"What car? I'm a poor, unemployed lad, mate. I don't have no car at the moment." Again that insolent grin.

There was no other choice but to leave. Evan thought he detected a smirk on Jingo's face as he watched them go. He couldn't shake off the horrifying picture of Bronwen, tied up or even dead, somewhere in that house.

"Could we come back with a search warrant, do you think?" he asked.

Bill shook his head. "Wouldn't be any point. By the time we got back here, they'd have hidden anything they didn't want us to find."

It wasn't a comforting thought. Evan drove past his house again and crept inside. Nothing moved. He tiptoed upstairs to check Bronwen's room and sighed as he looked at the empty bed.

"Is that you up and around, Evan *bach?*" His mother's sleepy voice called from her bedroom. "It's still the middle of the night."

"It's okay, Ma. Go back to sleep," he said gently. "I'm going out for a walk. I can't sleep." He had no wish to do any explaining to his mother at this point. He certainly couldn't tell her that he'd lost Bronwen.

"I can't think what to do," he said as he climbed back into the car beside Bill Howells. He imagined calling her parents. He imagined identifying her body when it washed up on some beach. The sky was glowing with early morning light now but the nightmare wasn't ending.

"Not much else we can do right now," Bill said. "I'm on duty at nine. I'll have a word with the Major Crime Unit boys and the drug squad. See if they've got any ideas." Evan dropped him off at his house, then started another round of aimless circling. He tried to give himself a comforting scenario—she had been asleep somewhere or hiding somewhere and now she was making her way home.

Kingsway was still deserted, the Monkey's Uncle firmly locked. He wished he had checked the place out more thoroughly last night. Bronwen thought on her feet. Maybe she had left some small message or clue for him that he had overlooked. The problem was how to get into the building. If he went back to the police station, presumably he could find the name of the owner or some kind of contact phone number. But he might also find himself facing DCI Vaughan and be arrested for interfering. Bill Howells would come on duty at nine. He'd have to wait until then, unless he found a way in.

He parked the car and stood looking up at the building. There was no way into the club from the empty shop on the ground floor. He could see that by peering in through the grimy window. There were no windows in the front of the second story, in fact he didn't remember any windows in the club at all. But there had been a small hallway at the back with toilets and maybe a storage room. One of them might have a window. He walked around until he found an alley at the back of the row of buildings. It was piled with bags of refuse, and it was impossible to tell which building might be the club. When he came to what he thought was the right place, he saw a fire escape that ended just above his head. A little to the right there was a Dumpster. If he climbed on that, then traversed the window ledge, he could reach the bottom of the fire escape and haul himself up. He scrambled up onto the Dumpster, then inched his way across the grimy window. It was lucky he'd done a bit of climbing in his life, he decided. It was even luckier that he had started training again. It was hard work to hold onto the metal grid of the fire escape and then swing his legs up so that he got a foothold and was able to heave himself up and over onto the stairs. He made his way up and stood staring into the window of a strange office. He was climbing the wrong building.

He looked up. It would be easy enough to get onto the roof. Maybe he could find out which building housed the Monkey's Uncle from up there. He scrambled over the tiles of the attic and stood panting on the flat rooftop. He saw at once that he'd wasted his effort coming up here. The building to his left had a steeply pitched roof with slick slates on it and a very rickety-looking gutter at its edge. He wasn't about to try to traverse that one. And he was pretty sure that the Monkey's Uncle had to be in that direction.

"Bugger," he said out loud. So much for James Bond–style heroics. They never worked in real life. He had just lowered himself successfully onto the fire escape and was about to climb down again when there was a scrabbling sound and pigeons fluttered out from a rooftop to his right. He looked up and saw a face staring down at him.

"Evan?" a voice called. "Is it really you?"

Relief flooded through him. "What are you doing up there?"

"Watching the sunrise, how about you?"

Anger spilled over with the flood of relief. "I've been out looking for you all night. I've been worried out of my mind."

"Well, it hasn't exactly been pleasant sitting up here getting wetter and colder and very scared. It was very clever of you to find me."

"How do we get you down?"

"Good question. I've been asking myself the same thing."

"How did you get up there in the first place?"

"I climbed out of the ladies' loo window and up the drainpipe. Then some idiot closed the window. So I'm pretty much trapped up here. I was worried sick that that creepy man would find me."

"Jingo?"

"You know him?"

"Red hair. Tall bloke."

"That's right. That was him. He was hanging about at the top of the stairs when I was about to leave the club. He stepped out in front of me and asked me if I was the one who had been asking about Alison and Tony. He said he could probably help me because he knew some people who hung around with Alison. They were at a party he was going to, he said. Did I want to come along and meet them?"

"Thank God you didn't go. I'm glad I'd warned you about him."

"But you didn't. Or if you did, I didn't take it in. I was all set to go with him. I told him I needed to go to the loo, and I'd meet him outside. As I came down the stairs, he was on his mobile. I heard him say, 'You were right. She's coming with me. Peterson's then.' And he laughed. Suddenly I got a bad feeling. I mean you'd just been to Peterson's builder's yard down on the docks, hadn't you? That was too much of a coincidence. Either way, I got cold feet. I looked around but my friends had left. Almost everyone had left, and I could see him waiting for me at the bottom of the stairs. He looked at his watch, then he started to come up the stairs again. I didn't wait. I rushed into the ladies' loo and locked the door. I heard him saying to someone else, 'So where did she go? She can't have got out past me.' And the other chap said, 'Maybe she's still in the toilet,' and I knew they were going to come looking, so I didn't know what to do. Then I realized the window was open. I unlocked the door and climbed out of the window. Luckily the ledge was quite wide and there was a drainpipe to hang onto. Then I didn't feel safe there, because anyone could look out and see me, so I managed to scramble up onto this bit of roof that sticks out. That's when I found it doesn't lead anywhere. I was stuck here.

Nowhere to hide. I was sure they'd find me. I kept picturing that face coming up the drainpipe toward me, so I crouched down and didn't move for hours."

"You poor thing. It must have been terrible for you."

"It was stupid of me, really. I don't know why I panicked. I could have just gone down and told him I'd changed my mind. What could he have done on the street?"

"Bundled you into a car and driven off with you. Poked a gun into your side."

She laughed. "A gun, Evan? Aren't you being overdramatic?"

"He had a gun when my father was shot. He didn't do the actual shooting, but it was his gun."

"Oh," she said. Then, "Evan, do you think you could get me down now, please?"

"I'll go for help."

"Take care," she called as he went down the fire escape, "and please hurry back."

"Well, here you are then, thank goodness for that," Mrs. Evans said as they came in through the front door. "I was worried something might have happened to you. You've never been out partying all night, surely? At least you're back just in time for chapel."

Chapter 24

Evan left Bronwen tucked in bed with a glass of warm Ovaltine, and hastily changed his clothes to escort his mother to chapel. Trying to get out of going would take more effort than accompanying her, besides he could sleep through the sermon. It was pleasantly cool inside the chapel building, with the comforting smell of generations of furniture polish. Jingo and Peterson, he thought. How were the two connected? If Jingo had been going to take Bronwen to Peterson's, did that somehow mean that Peterson was in charge, or was a builder's yard beside the docks a convenient place to dispose of somebody? The pleasant coolness suddenly made him shiver. Bronwen had joked about it and made light of her night stuck on the rooftop as they drove home. He wondered if she knew how close she had come to dying.

Did the Turnbulls suspect Charles Peterson? Was he worth protecting, or did he have some hold over them? He was certainly the type nobody would suspect—large, awkward, bumbling. Evan resolved to go back to the Hartley's immediately after he had taken his mother home to see if Mrs. Hartley was alert enough to answer questions today. He felt sleep overcoming him and closed his eyes. Through the open window he could hear outdoor sounds—a cricket match being broadcast on somebody's TV. Children playing in a back garden. A dog barking.

Evan opened his eyes again. The Turnbulls' dog—Peterson had said it started barking so he decided to leave. But the dog had not barked when Tony Mancini was told to go, and he overheard Alison arguing with someone. Why was that? Wouldn't the dog have been shut in the kitchen all evening if one of the women was afraid of it? In which case how did it hear one person and not another? Yet one more question to try and ask Mrs. Hartley.

Evan felt a dig in his side and found the congregation had risen to its feet for the singing of "Calon Lan," one of the good old Welsh hymns he usually loved to belt out with everyone else. Now he couldn't wait for it to be over. His mother dawdled her way out of chapel, stopping to talk to everybody and proudly introducing her son. He gritted his teeth with impatience. Then at last he got her into the car.

"There's no need to rush, it's Sunday," she admonished him.

When he deposited her outside the front door and claimed he had to run a quick errand before lunch, she started to protest. "You're never going shopping on a Sunday."

"Not shopping, Ma. Just someone I have to talk to."

"And you're not still trying to meddle in that police case, are you?"

"I'll be right back, Ma." He got into the car and drove away, watching her staring after him in the rearview mirror. The Sunday morning streets were deserted and steaming as the sun evaporated last night's rain. As he drove into the cul-de-sac, he saw an ambulance in the Hartley's drive. He jumped out and ran up to the front door. It was open and he went in. Through the open French doors, he could see people out in the back garden. A blanket covered something on the patio. Two ambulance men were setting up a stretcher while Dr. Hartley watched, one hand over his mouth. Dr. Hartley heard Evan's footsteps and looked up. The pain on his face was transparent.

"She did it," he said in a choked voice. "She managed to get the window open, and she fell out. Well, I suppose it's for the best, really. Her suffering is finally over."

"I am so sorry," Evan said. "What an awful shock for you."

Dr. Hartley nodded. "I told you she was strong and cunning, didn't I? But I didn't think she'd find a way to unlock those windows. Some days she couldn't even remember how to open a drawer. It's my fault. I should never have left her."

"I'm sure it wasn't your fault," Evan said.

"I only popped out to get milk. The milkman didn't leave our usual pint, and she does like her milky coffee in the mornings. I checked the neighbors but nobody was home, so I thought it would be all right if I just drove to the nearest shop that's open on Sundays. I hadn't realized it would be all the way in Oystermouth. I came back to find the window open and her—lying there."

"You didn't pass any cars on your street, did you?" Evan asked. "A large white van, for instance?"

"No. Nobody. Why?"

"Just a thought," Evan said.

Dr. Hartley face clouded. "What are suggesting?"

"Could anyone have got into the house while you were away, do you think?"

Dr. Hartley looked puzzled. "I locked the front door after me. All the other doors and windows are kept locked because of her."

"And nobody else has a key?"

"Well, the neighbors on both sides know where I keep my spare key. Just in case, you know."

"But the neighbors were out, you say?"

"Yes. The Havershams on the left are away on holiday in France. The Turnbulls were out. He always golfs on Sundays. She goes to church. Why are you asking these questions? Do you think it might not have been an accident?"

He looked at Dr. Hartley's worried face. Poor man, he was suffering enough without any extra guilt and worry. "It's my policeman's mentality, always being too suspicious. I'm sure it happened exactly as you said. She managed to open the window and was trying to escape again." He put his hand on Dr. Hartley's shoulder. "Look, I'm very sorry about your wife. I'll be back if there's anything you'd like me to do for you."

"Thank you. You're most kind, but there's nothing anyone can do now."

He felt a twinge of conscience as he left Dr. Hartley and made his way back to his car. Was it too much of a coincidence that the Turnbulls knew where the spare key was? And even more of a coincidence that the milk wasn't delivered and Mrs. Hartley fell to her death the very day after Evan had started digging deeper into the Turnbull set?

The least he could do was to check on alibis—the Turnbulls first, since they knew where the spare key was. He put his foot down along the Oystermouth Road until he came to the Langland Bay Golf Club. The girl at the reception desk told him that Mr. Turnbull was part of a foursome that started at nine-thirty. "They'll still be out on the course," she told him. "They always walk. Not into carts, these older players."

He took her word for it and drove back to the church. The service had ended and the church was deserted, so Evan rang the bell at the vicarage. This time it was the vicar himself who answered, a thin, worried-looking man with a bald head that made him look older than he really was. No, Mrs. Turnbull wasn't at the service this morning. He was surprised she wasn't there and hoped nothing was wrong. She never missed matins. In fact she usually came early to do the flowers.

"Poor woman," he said. "I'm afraid this has been too much for her. I had hoped that she would find comfort in her faith. But sometimes faith isn't enough, is it? She must be suffering. I suspect she has suffered a lot over the years, one way and another."

"What do you mean by that?"

"One hears things. Not the easiest of husbands. A very demanding social calendar. And now this—her child, the most precious thing in the world to her. I tried to find comforting words, but I'm sure they were inadequate." He sighed. "And I have always suspected that she was rather fragile, emotionally, even though she concealed it well."

Evan walked back to the street along the little flagstone path. Flowers were blooming in herbaceous borders. Bees were buzzing among the lavendar. Rooks were cawing in the churchyard on the other side of the wall. The peaceful scene contrasted with the turmoil of thoughts racing around inside his head.

There were just too many coincidences for Evan's liking. Mrs. Hartley had chosen that very morning to fall from a locked window. Mrs. Turnbull had not gone to church. Why hadn't she gone? Where was she now? Why wasn't the milk delivered to Dr. Hartley's house?

He jumped into his car and drove back along the waterfront. Traffic in the other direction was bumper to bumper as everyone left the city for the beaches. A church bell was ringing somewhere in the distance. Boats were bobbing on blue water. Evan's pulse was racing, still on high alert after the terror of his sleepless night. Deep down he was sure that Mrs. Hartley's death was connected to Alison's. Did the murderer believe that Mrs. Hartley was more lucid than she really was and had seen him that night? Evan remembered mentioning to Charles Peterson that he had been seen in the garden. Had he signed Mrs. Hartley's death warrant by telling him? He pushed the accelerator pedal toward the floor so that the old car groaned in protest. He wasn't even sure where he was going, but the sense of danger that had accompanied him last night was still hovering.

Obviously the logical thing to do would be to go to the police station. Bill Howells was on duty. Evan could tell him his suspicions. This would probably bring down the wrath of the DCI and the rest of the station on him again, but surely they would have to see that Mrs. Hartley's untimely fall meant that a killer was still on the loose. He'd suggest to the police that they dust the Hartleys' house for fingerprints and see if they matched Charles Peterson's. He could also tell them that the name Peterson had come up in Jingo Roberts's overheard conversation. What was the connection there?

He was passing the road that led to the Turnbulls' house, and it occurred to him that he should at least warn Dr. Hartley not to touch anything before the police had had a chance to dust surfaces. He pulled up outside the Hartleys' house. As he started up the driveway, he became aware of a dog's insistent barking. It seemed to be coming from inside the Turnbulls' house. It wasn't the deep, threatening bark that had greeted him each time he had approached the house before. It was a high, strangled yelp of a dog in obvious distress, and it went on and on.

Why hadn't Mrs. Turnbull gone to church? Evan's heart was racing as he ran down the Turnbulls' driveway. The front door was unlocked. He opened it, fearing an attack from the dog, but the barking was coming from upstairs. He went up the stairs, following the sound through a large bedroom with a four-poster bed and rich brocade drapes then into the bathroom beyond. The dog looked up at him and growled.

"Good boy," he said uncertainly. "Good boy."

Then he saw what the dog had been barking at. Mrs. Turnbull lay in the bathtub. The water was pink, and blood was oozing from her wrists.

He forgot to worry about the dog. He pushed past it and lent forward to feel a faint pulse at her neck. He was still in time. The dog must have sensed he was trying to help and had dropped to the floor, whining now. Evan snatched a couple of towels from the towel rail and grabbed Mrs. Turnbull's wrists, lifting her arms up and pressing the fabric hard against the slashes. It looked as though he might be in luck. She hadn't succeeded in severing the arteries properly. When he had kept the wounds clamped shut for long enough to risk letting go for a few seconds, he dragged her from the bathtub and wrapped her in the biggest towels. He bound smaller towels around her wrists, then dashed through into the bedroom to find a phone.

As he hurried back to her, he wondered how he could have been so stupid and so blind. All the signs had been there. She was the one who had complained to the police that he was harassing her and her friends. The vicar had said she was fragile emotionally. A woman on the edge, living a stressful life in the spotlight, hearing the gossip about her husband's infidelities. Alison was growing up beautiful just as she was losing her looks. Alison's friends had said that her mother was jealous of her and sent her away to school. And Alison hated her mother. It seemed significant that there wasn't a single picture of Alison in the Turnbulls' living room and yet there was that big, beautiful picture on Mr. Turnbull's desk. Evan wondered what had made Mrs. Turnbull snap that evening. Had she seen Alison and Tony together when she went to get her headache pills?

The bigger question was—how could she have killed her?

She was a tall woman and Alison might have just taken some of the cocaine Tony had brought. Evan wasn't quite sure of the effects of cocaine, but surely any drug would make reality and danger seem less real until too late.

He checked the wrists and noted they had almost stopped oozing blood, so her apparent unconsciousness was strange. From the color of the bath water, she hadn't yet lost enough blood to kill her.

"Mrs. Turnbull," he shouted. "Can you hear me?"

Eyelids fluttered open.

"Did you take something?"

The eyelids closed again. "Sleeping pills."

"You're going to be okay," he said. "Stay awake. Don't close your eyes. The ambulance is on its way."

Tired eyes opened again. "I couldn't even get this right," she said. Tears started to well up in her eyes. "A hopeless failure, all my life. I couldn't do anything properly. I tried to protect her, but it wasn't enough. I messed that up too."

"To protect her?" Evan demanded. "Protect her from whom?"

"From him."

The eyes fluttered closed again. Evan shook her awake. "Him?"

"My husband, of course." She barely mouthed the words. "I heard them, you see, when I went up to get my headache pills. The bathroom window was open." She closed her eyes as if the memory was too painful to think about.

Evan could hardly get the words out. "Your husband killed Alison—why?"

"He didn't mean to. He swore he didn't mean to. She said she was going to tell everyone the truth about him, starting with those ladies who were playing bridge with me."

"What truth?"

The words were scarcely more than a whisper. "Why do you think I packed her off to school in a hurry? Why do you think I never left her alone?" she asked. Another long pause, then she raised her head painfully. "I caught him, in her bedroom, when she was just a little girl. He promised me it would never happen again, but I saw the way he looked at her."

She drifted into silence. Evan shook her awake again. "So your husband came home and found her with a boy. Is that what happened?" He shook her. "Mrs. Turnbull—is that what happened?"

"I heard them arguing. I heard him saying, 'You're nothing but a cheap little tart!' And she said, 'You can talk, after what you did to me. You think I've forgotten, don't you, but I'll never forget. I'll tell the whole world how you used to creep into my bedroom and then see who will elect you as lord mayor. I'll tell Mummy's bridge ladies right now . . .' "

Evan stared at her for a moment in shocked silence. He collected himself. "Why didn't you stop him?" he asked.

"Because of my stupid pride, of course. I didn't want them to know, did I? I ran down the stairs and told them refreshments were ready. I had to wait until I'd pushed them into the dining room. I didn't think . . . I never, ever thought that he . . ." A tear trickled down her pale cheek. "When I went outside, it was too late. She was lying in a huddle at his feet. He said, 'I think I've killed her, Margaret. I didn't mean to.' " A great sob convulsed her body.

"Why didn't you tell anyone? How could you go on living with him as if nothing had happened?"

"Because I'd lose everything if I lost him. I'd have nothing left at all." She glared at Evan fiercely. "Why did you have to come here? Why couldn't you have left everything as it was? Once you'd opened the can of worms, it was too late. So I decided it would be better if they thought it was me. Frank is valuable to society, you see. I'm not worth anything to anybody. Please don't tell them the truth. Let them think that I did it. Better for everyone, don't you think?"

"I don't think your husband deserves you," Evan said. "Neither he nor your daughter appreciated what a remarkable woman you are."

An ambulance siren cut through his words. Doors slammed. Feet rushed up the stairs. Evan stood to one side as the paramedics ministered to Mrs. Turnbull then carried her downstairs and away. Evan followed them down, shut the front door, and went back to his car. He didn't feel that he could honor Mrs. Turnbull's request to remain silent. Somebody ought to know the truth.

He drove straight back to the golf club. As he played over the conversation again in his mind, he realized that Mrs. Hartley had witnessed that final confrontation after all. She'd heard the whole thing, only in her diseased mind she had garbled the words into something that happened long ago and far away. If only the Turnbulls had realized that she could be no threat to them.

Mr. Turnbull was just walking off the final green when Evan spotted him.

"Sorry to interrupt you, sir, but could I have a word?" he asked quietly.

Turnbull stared at him. "Good God, man, it's Sunday. I'm about to go the nineteenth hole. Your questions will have to wait."

"What I have to say to you can't wait," Evan insisted. "You can hear it from me or from the police. It's about your wife."

Turnbull moved aside from his fellow golfers and grabbed Evan's arm. "Has something happened to Margaret?"

"She just tried to kill herself. I found her with slashed wrists, lying in the bath. She'd also taken sleeping pills."

"Oh, my God. Is she going to be all right?"

"I think I got there in time. She's just been taken away in an ambulance."

"I must go to her. Which hospital?"

"I don't know. I came straight here."

"This has all been too much for her. I knew it would be." He opened the trunk of a blue Mercedes and threw the golf bag inside.

"You know why she did it, don't you, Mr. Turnbull?" Evan asked.

Turnbull looked at him suspiciously. "Distress, obviously."

"Not obviously. She thought that if someone was going to take the blame, it should be her. As she put it, she was less use to society."

Evan held Turnbull's stare for a long moment. Then Turnbull sighed. "What does it matter now? Nothing matters anymore anyway. I lost the only thing I have ever loved. I worshipped that child. I made one mistake. One stupid mistake and Margaret never let me forget it. She kept Alison away from me—"

"She was trying to protect her."

Turnbull looked around the car park. "Are the police on their way here?"

"I imagine you'll meet them at the hospital," Evan said. "And I imagine you'll set them straight on what happened."

Turnbull got into the Mercedes. "Yes," he said. "I'll set them straight."

Chapter 25

"Oh, so there you are at last. I was wondering where you'd got to," Mrs. Evans called as Evan opened the front door. "Sunday lunch was all ready over an hour ago. It's been spoiling in the oven, waiting for you."

"Sorry, Ma. I had some things to do." He gave her a peck on the cheek. "Is Bronwen still asleep?"

"She hasn't come down yet. I looked in on her once, but I didn't like to wake her. The poor girl, you kept her out far too late last night. You can have too much of a good time, you know. Why don't you go and tell her lunch is ready?"

Evan opened the bedroom door softly and stood watching Bronwen sleep. Her hair was spread across the pillow, and she looked young and vulnerable. She must have sensed his presence because her eyes opened and focused on him. "Hello," she said. "Have I been sleeping long?"

"It's almost two o'clock," Evan said. "I was sent up to tell you lunch is ready."

"I hope you had a nice chapel without me?"

"It was the high point of the day, believe me."

She studied his face. "What's happened?"

He sat on the bed beside her and went through the whole morning, detail by detail.

"It's all rather horrid, isn't it?" she said when he had finished. "Nobody ends up happily. I feel rather sorry for all of them."

"Except for Mancini. I imagine he'll be released from prison later today, unless they decide to hold him on the drug charges. I suspect if he's let out this time, he'll be back soon enough. Small-fry like him always get caught."

Bronwen sat up. "Some holiday this turned out to be."

"Evan, if she is awake, leave her in peace to get dressed," Mrs. Evans called up the stairs. "You get down here and carve this leg of lamb for me."

Evan gave Bronwen a kiss on the forehead and went downstairs. They had just finished lunch when there was a knock at the front door.

"I'll go." Evan got up from the table. He was half expecting to see Bill Howells. Instead DCI Vaughan himself was standing on the doorstep.

"I suppose you think you've been bloody clever," he said, not waiting for Evan to invite him in, but pushing past him into the front hall. "I suppose you think now somebody's going to give you a bloody great medal and pat you on the back."

"No sir, I didn't think that at all—" Evan started to say.

"I could have you arrested on the spot, boy. I could call your boss in North Wales and tell him you're an insubordinate, disloyal little git who deserves to spend the rest of his life writing traffic tickets."

He turned to face Evan in the narrow front hall.

"You do what you have to, sir. I did what I had to."

"He's a no good, little son of a bitch. He shot your father, for God's sake. Do you have no feelings, man?"

"Oh yes, sir. Very strong feelings. And the strongest feeling I've got is that my father would have wanted me to do this. So go ahead. Call my boss, if you have to. I may resign anyway, because I'm not sure I want to be a member of a force that cares more about revenge than whether a person is innocent or guilty."

Evan hadn't realized that he had raised his voice until he noticed that the DCI was looking surprised. He checked himself. "I'm sorry, sir, if I went against your orders, but, as you said, I wasn't on your payroll."

"Instead of that we've got a woman lying in hospital with slashed wrists, a prominent member of the community turning himself in, and the unpleasant task of letting that little shit Mancini out of prison." Vaughn sighed.

"They do have a couple of deaths on their hands, between them, you know."

"A couple?"

"Somebody pushed an old lady from an upstairs window this morning," Evan said. "My guess is that Mrs. Turnbull did it. She was willing to do a lot for him. I don't know why, after the way he treated her."

"I should have thought that was obvious," the DCI said. "She liked the lifestyle. She didn't fancy going back to being poor again. I suppose you realize what his arrest will mean, don't you? They may have to close the factory. There will be jobs lost. And all his charity work too—he won't be doing any more of that. You think that's justice, do you?"

"My father was killed, and Tony Mancini was out on the streets again in four years. That wasn't what I call justice either. It seems to me we can't pick and choose justice in this life. We just do our bit, and sometimes we get it right and sometimes we get it wrong."

DCI Vaughan glared at him, two big men, of similar height and build, staring each other down, eye to eye. "You know what you are, don't you?" Vaughan said at last in a quieter voice. "You're just like your bloody father. I never could talk sense into him either. That night he was killed—he should have waited until backup arrived. He should never have gone in there alone. He thought he could reason with a bunch of punks. It was a bloody stupid thing to do."

"I expect he thought he was doing the right thing," Evan said. "I don't think my dad took unnecessary risks."

"Of course he thought he was doing the bloody right thing."

DCI Vaughan snapped, then gave an apologetic half smile. "He was a good bloke, your dad. I'm still angry about losing him. I expect you are too."

Evan nodded. "Being angry won't bring him back, will it?"

DCI Vaughan turned toward the front door. "I'll need you down at the station to make a statement, seeing that you were the one who found Mrs. Turnbull. And I'll need you to talk to the drug-squad boys, although I don't think you'll be telling them anything they don't already know."

"Very good, sir. I'll come down right away if you like."

"Maybe I'd better arrange for an armed escort for you. You won't find yourself too popular at the moment."

Evan thought he detected the barest hint of a smile before the DCI went to his car.

He stood in the hall, collecting his thoughts, before he went back into the kitchen.

"What on earth was all that about?" Mrs. Evans demanded. "And fancy you shouting like that. Who were you shouting at?"

"DCI Vaughan."

"You were shouting at a DCI? *Escob Annwyl!*" She put her hand over her heart. "What on earth came over you?"

"I don't know. I'll probably find I'm out of a job when I get home." Evan looked across at Bronwen. Her eyes were smiling up at him.

"And may I ask why you two were shouting at each other?"

"Tony Mancini didn't kill Alison Turnbull, Ma. I found the real culprit. They'd have rather I'd left it alone."

Her eyes narrowed in disgust. "You were working to prove that monster was innocent? The man who killed your father, and you've just set him free again?"

"I'm sorry, Ma. I'm not all that happy about it either. But he didn't kill Alison, and I couldn't let him be sent to prison for something he didn't do, could I?"

"You should have left it to the South Wales Police. It was none of your business. I'm very disappointed in you, Evan Evans. You've let me down. You've let your father down."

She pressed her lips together and made a hasty exit from the kitchen.

Evan sighed and turned away. "Now you can tell me that I've let you down and that should make it a hundred percent," he said to Bronwen.

Bronwen got up and slipped her arms around his waist. "If you really want to know, I'm proud of you. You did what you thought was the right thing, and you stood up to a DCI as well. If you knew the number of times I have wanted you to stand up for yourself when that awful Inspector Hughes was rude to you, and you never did. So I think this is a good sign." She stretched up and gave him a kiss, then nestled herself against the crook of his neck. His arms wrapped around her and they stood there, silent, at peace together.

Evan made sure that he went to the police station while Bill Howells was still on duty. At least that would mean one semifriendly face in the sea of hostility. Bill was sitting at his desk, and the look he gave Evan was anything but friendly. "Oh, it's you, is it? Come in to tell us you've solved another couple of major crimes for us since lunch or have you come to collect your citations?"

"Give over, Bill," Evan said. "You don't think I've enjoyed doing this, do you? I've just had the DCI bawling me out, and my mother."

"Well, I expect you thought you were doing the right thing." Bill Howells went back to his paperwork. "And a lot of the bad feeling around here is that you showed up superior officers."

"You know I had no intention of doing that," Evan said. "I just wanted to be part of the investigation, that's all. Finding Mrs. Turnbull this morning was pure luck." He paused, watching Bill fill in a column of figures. "The DCI told me to come and make a report, and to talk to the drug-squad blokes too."

Howells nodded. "Right oh. I'll give you the form if you wait until I can get this column to balance. And I think Melcher is in his office. He's on the drug task force. Second door on the right."

Evan started to move away, then turned back. "Look, Bill, I really appreciate what you did for me last night."

Bill Howells gave a grunt and didn't look up. Evan went into Detective Inspector Melcher's office and laid out what he knew about Tony Mancini and Jingo Roberts. As he suspected, he wasn't telling the DI anything he didn't know.

"One more thing, sir," Evan said. "When Jingo Roberts tried to kidnap my girlfriend, he talked about taking her to Peterson's. Any idea what he meant by that? The name Charles Peterson hasn't come up in your work at all, has it?"

"Charles Peterson?" He shook his head. "Name doesn't ring a bell. He probably meant Peterson's builder's yard."

"Are they involved in the drug racket?"

"Not that I know of, but it's a good place to find cement, isn't it? And it's right beside the docks." He grinned as if he'd said something witty. Evan felt sick.

He was relieved when he finally completed the incident form and was able to step out of the police station into the bright, breezy afternoon. He hadn't asked permission to visit Tony Mancini, but he decided that this whole thing might make sense if he had one last chance to talk sense into the boy. He parked outside the prison and rang the bell for admittance.

"You're too late, mate," the gate guard said. "He was let out of here an hour ago. We weren't any more thrilled about it than you."

"Any idea where he went?"

"There was no one here to pick him up, I can tell you that much. He was heading for the bus station."

Evan thanked the gate guard and went back to his car. Tony must have gone home then. There was nowhere else for him to go. All the way up the hill to Penlan, he wondered what he'd say if he found Tony. If Tony was jubilant and gloating, there was always the danger that he might finally lose it and clock him one. He didn't even know why it was important to see Tony again. It would probably only be putting himself through more grief.

He parked next to a rusty old Ford Fiesta and knocked on Tony's front door. Tony himself answered.

"Yeah. What do you want now?" he demanded.

Evan took a deep breath. "The least you could do is to thank me, ungrateful little bastard. I've just got you off a life sentence."

"Yeah, well I suppose . . . ," Tony said and let the rest of the sentence hang.

"Not that it will do you much good," Evan said. "You'll probably find yourself up on drug charges anyway."

"Me? Drug charges?" Tony grinned, that same cocky grin Evan had seen during the trial five years ago. "Now what could they possibly have against me?"

"You were delivering cocaine to Alison Turnbull."

"Who says so?"

"You admitted it to me. And you were caught near her house."

"Didn't have none on me though, did I? All circumstantial evidence, mate. They won't be able to pin nothing on me this time."

Evan realized this was probably true. "Look, Tony, you've had a lucky escape. Why don't you make the most of it? Get away from here. Get away from that scum Jingo."

"What nasty language, Mr. Policeman." Jingo Roberts stepped out into Tony's front hall and stood behind Tony. "If you don't beat it right now, I might have to call the cops and say Tony's being harassed by you."

"Listen to me, Tony," Evan said, ignoring the insolent smile behind Tony's back. "If you get busted, it's you who'll go to jail. He won't. His sort never do. So why don't you get right away from here and find yourself a real job, while you've still got the chance."

"A real job?" Jingo said. "What sort of real job did you have in mind, Mr. Policeman?" He put his hand into his pocket and produced a thick wad of twenty-pound notes. "Does your job pay this well? Tony's got a bright future with me if he does what he's told."

"My job won't wind me up behind bars one day," Evan said.

"It might wind you up dead, though," Jingo said, still grinning.

The desire to hit him was becoming overwhelming. Evan dug

his clenched fist into his side. "Just think about what I said, Tony. Make up your own mind, okay?"

Then he turned and strode back to his car. He thought he heard them laughing behind him.

That evening Evan paid a visit to the pub. It had been a stressful day, the atmosphere at home was still frosty in the extreme, and he felt in need of a pint. He also wanted to see Maggie. He might find himself out of a job when he got home, so there was no harm in letting her know he was still interested in trying out for the rugby team. Luckily Bronwen refused his invitation to accompany him. "No thanks. You go and see your old friends. I've still got to catch up on sleep."

Maggie was standing at the bar with a group of men, but she came across to Evan when she saw him.

"Looking for me, are you? That's a good sign. So you finally got bored with Blodwyn. I knew you would."

"About the rugby team," Evan said. "You know, I think I might be interested after all. I might find myself looking for a job when I get home."

Maggie gave him a beaming smile. "That's wonderful," she said. "Stew will be pleased. He needs someone reliable like you, and your police work would be a help too, dealing with the crowds and things."

"Dealing with the crowds?"

"Well, the assistant manager is really a bit of a general dogsbody, you know. Everything from handling the ticket money to evicting hooligans. I'm afraid the pay won't be brilliant, but it could get better once the club is on its feet."

"You want me to be the assistant manager?" Evan felt his face flushing bright red.

"Yes, didn't I say? What did you think we wanted you for? I told Stew, you can't trust those shifty types up in North Wales. You need someone like Evan who's steady and reliable."

"You know, I'm afraid I'll have to say no after all," Evan managed with great dignity. "If the pay won't be brilliant, that is. I'm getting married, you see. I'll need to earn enough to support a family. But thanks for the offer anyway."

He made his way out through the evening crowd at the bar.

The next morning as Evan was packing his bag, ready to leave, he went into Bronwen's room.

"You said you wanted one of these," he said, and held out an object wrapped in tissue paper.

"What is it?" She gave him an excited smile. "A little large for an engagement ring. Oh."

"It's a love spoon," Evan said, noting the reaction wasn't the one he had expected. "I went to that little shop. You said you wanted one."

"One that you had carved yourself, I meant. Like boys did in the old days."

"I tried that," Evan said. "In fact I started on one while you were away."

"So why don't you finish it?"

Evan went back into his room. "Maybe because it looks like this? Don't laugh."

"I'm not laughing," Bronwen said.

"It looks like a camel doing the splits. I never was any good at woodwork."

"I think it's lovely just," Bronwen said, using one of Betsy the barmaid's favorite expressions. "Bring it home with you, and when you finish it, we'll hang it up in our house."

There was no understanding women, Evan decided. He would never learn what pleased them.

Then finally, they were heading home.

"I hope Eirlys won't mind that I've left Prince William with my parents," Bronwen said. They were driving home by the quicker route, up the motorway on the English side of the border after a couple of days with Bronwen's parents.

"She'll be delighted that he's safe."

"She won't recognize him when she sees him again. He'll be a big fat sheep."

"A big, fat healthy sheep."

"That's true. I think I'm going to miss him. When we finally move into a house of our own, can I have a pet lamb, do you think?"

"I thought most women wanted children."

"I want both." She smiled at him. "Children, dogs, lambs, chickens . . ."

"Hold on a minute, you'll be turning the place into a bloody Noah's ark."

"And why not?" Then her smile faltered. "Evan, look," she said.

"What?"

"The fields."

"What about them?"

"They're empty. No animals in them."

"So they are. That's not a good sign, is it?"

After they left the motorway at Shrewsbury and drove west, the silence became oppressive. Empty field after empty field. Hardly any traffic on the roads. And then they saw the brown pall ahead of them.

"What do you think that is?" Bronwen asked. "A forest fire? I thought we'd had plenty of rain this summer."

They had been driving with the windows down. Soon the acrid smell was borne on the breeze toward them, not the pleasant odor of roasting meat but rather of singed hair and burning bone. Bronwen coughed and rolled up the window. Evan followed suit.

"This is terrible," she said. "There seems to be burning going on everywhere you look."

"I dread to think what we will find when we get home." Evan slowed to negotiate a mound of disinfected straw across the road, then another. "I wonder if I could have done anything if I had stayed here?"

"Of course you couldn't. These things are best left to strangers."

By the time they reached Betys-y-Coed, there were no more burning pyres in the fields and Evan's spirits began to rise. Maybe the disease had bypassed Llanfair after all. They drove past Capel

Curig and up to where the road branched and dropped down to the Llanberis pass.

"I still don't see any sheep," Bronwen said.

There was an ominous silence as they got out of the car. Llanfair was basking in pink twilight, but the place appeared empty and abandoned. On a normal August day there would have been a stream of cars heading back to the hotels on the coast. The little general store and the petrol station would have been doing a roaring trade, but both were closed. As they watched, a lone figure came out of one of the cottages and made his way slowly down the street. Evan recognized Charlie Hopkins. He called out and Charlie came over to the car.

"Hello, Evan *bach*. I'd say welcome home, but it's not much of a welcome, is it?"

"It looks pretty grim, Charlie," Evan said. "What happened to all the sheep?"

"Slaughtered, every single one of them. They didn't wait to check which ones were healthy and which were not. They all went. Poor Mr. Owens, he was shouting and cursing and pleading, but it didn't do any good, did it? They threatened to arrest him if he got in their way. I'm glad you weren't here to see it. And then they made a great big bonfire and everywhere you looked you could see other bonfires burning. The stench of it was something terrible. I said to Mair, I don't think I'll ever fancy lamb again." He gave a resigned sigh.

"Poor Mr. Owens," Bronwen said. "What will he do now, do you think? Are they going to compensate farmers for the animals they've lost?"

"Oh yes, they'll do that," Charlie Hopkins said. "But what good is compensation when he's worked for years building up good breeding stock."

"Like those two prize rams of his," Evan said. "That must have been the most bitter blow."

"I wouldn't exactly say that." Charlie looked around, up and down the deserted street. "If you happen to be ever taking a hike up and over Glydr Fach, you come down to a little stand of evergreen trees in a corrie, and right behind it is a disused sheep byre. Not very visible unless you happen to know about it, which, of course, those soldiers from the outside didn't."

Evan gave Bronwen an incredulous grin. "You don't mean that Mr. Owens has put his two prize rams in it?"

"Well, I wouldn't know, because I'm not sprightly enough to climb up there anymore, but I have seen him heading that way with a bag of fodder from time to time."

"I know I shouldn't really approve of breaking the law," Evan said, "but I'm really glad for him. And glad I wasn't here when he did it."

"Well, anyway, I hope you two have had a nice holiday," Charlie said. "You didn't do anything stupid like run off and get married, did you?"

"Nothing stupid like that," Evan said, smiling at the old man. Bronwen glanced down at the new sapphire ring on her finger and smiled too.

"Oh, and talking of getting married, you'll never guess what's been going on while you were away?" Charlie's old, weathered face lit up. "Betsy's gone and got herself a bloke."

"Really?" Evan asked. "Who?"

"Who do you think? The last person in the world you'd expect. Barry-the-Bucket." He was nodding delightedly. "He took her to the dance last week, and it seems they really hit it off just fine. And now he's showing up at the Dragon every evening with flowers, and they're both acting all daft."

"Barry-the-Bucket. Who would have thought it. Now you're off the hook." Bronwen slipped her hand into Evan's.

"I've lived long enough to know that little miracles are happening every day," Charlie Hopkins said. "That's what we need in times like this—a few little miracles. I'll see you down at the Dragon later then, maybe?"

"Maybe," Evan said. Charlie shuffled on down the street and into the pub. Evan put his arm around Bronwen's shoulders and they stood together, watching the twilight fade behind the black silhouette of the mountains.